W9-AAR-616

A Royal Pain

Berkley Prime Crime Mysteries by Rhys Bowen

Royal Spyness Mysteries

HER ROYAL SPYNESS
A ROYAL PAIN

Constable Evans Mysteries

EVANS ABOVE
EVAN HELP US
EVANLY CHOIRS
EVAN AND ELLE
EVAN CAN WAIT
EVANS TO BETSY
EVAN ONLY KNOWS
EVAN'S GATE
EVAN BLESSED

A Royal Pain

Rhys Bowen

**Doubleday Large Print
Home Library Edition**

BERKLEY PRIME CRIME, NEW YORK

This Large Print Edition, prepared especially for Doubleday Large Print Home Library, contains the complete, unabridged text of the original Publisher's Edition.

THE BERKLEY PUBLISHING GROUP
Published by the Penguin Group
Penguin Group (USA) Inc.
375 Hudson Street, New York, New York 10014, USA
Penguin Group (Canada), 90 Eglinton Avenue East, Suite 700, Toronto, Ontario M4P 2Y3, Canada (a division of Pearson Penguin Canada Inc.)
Penguin Books Ltd., 80 Strand, London WC2R 0RL, England
Penguin Group Ireland, 25 St. Stephen's Green, Dublin 2, Ireland (a division of Penguin Books Ltd.)
Penguin Group (Australia), 250 Camberwell Road, Camberwell, Victoria 3124, Australia (a division of Pearson Australia Group Pty. Ltd.)
Penguin Books India Pvt. Ltd., 11 Community Centre, Panchsheel Park, New Delhi—110 017, India
Penguin Group (NZ), 67 Apollo Drive, Rosedale, North Shore 0632, New Zealand (a division of Pearson New Zealand Ltd.)
Penguin Books (South Africa) (Pty.) Ltd., 24 Sturdee Avenue, Rosebank, Johannesburg 2196, South Africa

Penguin Books Ltd., Registered Offices: 80 Strand, London WC2R 0RL, England

This book is an original publication of The Berkley Publishing Group.

Copyright © 2008 by Janet Quin-Harkin.
Text design by Tiffany Estreicher.

ISBN-13: 978-0-7394-9684-0

PRINTED IN THE UNITED STATES OF AMERICA

**This Large Print Book carries the
Seal of Approval of N.A.V.H.**

This book is dedicated to my
three princesses:
Elizabeth, Meghan and Mary;
and to my princes: Sam and T. J.

Notes and Acknowledgments

This is a work of fiction. While several members of the British royal family appear as themselves in the book, there was no Princess Hannelore of Bavaria and no Lady Georgiana.

On a historical note: Europe at that time was in turmoil with communists and fascists vying for control of Germany, left bankrupt and dispirited after the first great war. In England communism was making strides among the working classes and left-wing intellectuals. At the other extreme Oswald Mosley was leading a group of extreme fascists called the Blackshirts. Skirmishes and bloody battles between the two were frequent in London.

A special acknowledgment to the Misses Hedley, Jensen, Reagan and Danika, of Sonoma, California, who make cameo appearances in this book.

And thanks, as always, to my splendid support group at home: Clare, Jane and John; as well as my equally splendid support group in New York: Meg, Kelly, Jackie and Catherine.

Chapter 1

Rannoch House
Belgrave Square
London W.1.
Monday, June 6, 1932

The alarm clock woke me this morning at the ungodly hour of eight. One of my nanny's favorite sayings was "Early to bed, early to rise, makes a man healthy, wealthy and wise." My father did both and look what happened to him. He died, penniless, at forty-nine.

In my experience there are only two good reasons to rise with the dawn: one is to go hunting and the other to catch the Flying Scotsman from Edinburgh to London. I was about to do neither. It wasn't the hunting season and I was already in London.

I fumbled for the alarm on the bedside table and battered it into silence.

"Court circular, June 6," I announced to a nonexistent audience as I stood up and pulled back the heavy velvet curtains. "Lady Georgiana Rannoch embarks on another hectic day of social whirl. Luncheon at the Savoy, tea at the Ritz, a visit to Scapparelli for a fitting of her latest ball gown, then dinner and dancing at the Dorchester—or none of the above," I added. To be honest it had been a long time since I had any events on my social calendar and my life had never been a mad social whirl. Almost twenty-two years old and not a single invitation sitting on my mantelpiece. The awful thought struck me that I should accept that I was over the hill and destined to be a spinster for life. Maybe all I had to look forward to was the queen's suggestion that I become lady-in-waiting to Queen Victoria's one surviving daughter—who is also my great-aunt and lives out in deepest Gloucestershire. Years ahead of walking the Pekinese and holding knitting wool danced before my eyes.

I suppose I should introduce myself

before I go any further: I am Victoria Georgiana Charlotte Eugenie of Glen Garry and Rannoch, known to my friends as Georgie. I am of the house of Windsor, second cousin to King George V, thirty-fourth in line to the throne, and at this moment I was stony broke.

Oh, wait. There was another option for me. It was to marry Prince Siegfried of Romania, in the Hohenzollen-Sigmaringen line—for whom my private nickname was Fishface. That subject hadn't come up recently, thank God. Maybe other people had also found out that he has a predilection for boys.

It was clearly going to be one of those English summer days that makes one think of rides along leafy country lanes, picnics in the meadow with strawberries and cream, croquet and tea on the lawn. Even in central London birds were chirping madly. The sun was sparkling from the windows across the square. A gentle breeze was stirring the net curtains. The postman was whistling as he walked around the square. And what did I have before me?

"Oh, golly," I exclaimed as I suddenly

remembered the reason for the alarm clock and leaped into action. I was expected at a residence on Park Lane. I washed, dressed smartly and went downstairs to make some tea and toast. You can see how wonderfully domesticated I'd become in two short months. When I bolted from our castle in Scotland back in April, I didn't even know how to boil water. Now I can manage baked beans and an egg. For the first time in my life I was living with no servants, having no money to pay them. My brother, the Duke of Glen Garry and Rannoch, usually known as Binky, had promised to send me a maid from our Scottish estate, but so far none had materialized. I suspect that no God-fearing, Presbyterian Scottish mother would let her daughter loose in the den of iniquity that London is perceived to be. As for paying for me to hire a maid locally—well, Binky is as broke as I. You see, when our father shot himself after the crash of '29, Binky inherited the estate and was saddled with the most horrendous death duties.

So I have managed thus far servantless, and frankly, I'm jolly proud of myself.

The kettle boiled. I made my tea, slathered Cooper's Oxford marmalade on my toast (yes, I know I was supposed to be economizing but there are standards below which one just can't sink) and brushed away the crumbs hastily as I put on my coat. It was going to be too warm for any kind of jacket, but I couldn't risk anyone seeing what I was wearing as I walked through Belgravia—the frightfully upper-crust part of London just south of Hyde Park where our town house is situated.

A chauffeur waiting beside a Rolls saluted smartly to me as I passed. I held my coat tightly around me. I crossed Belgrave Square, walked up Grosvenor Crescent and paused to look longingly at the leafy expanse of Hyde Park before I braved the traffic across Hyde Park Corner. I heard the clip-clop of hooves and a pair of riders came out of Rotten Row. The girl was riding a splendid gray and was smartly turned out in a black bowler and well-cut hacking jacket. Her boots were positively gleaming with polish. I looked at her enviously. Had I stayed home in Scotland that could have been me. I used to ride every morning with my brother. I wondered if my sister-in-law, Fig, was riding my horse and ruining its mouth. She was inclined to be heavy-handed with the reins, and she weighed a good deal more than I. Then I noticed other people loitering on the corner. Not so well turned out, these men. They carried signs or sandwich boards: *I need a job. Will work for food. Not afraid of hard work.*

I had grown up sheltered from the harsh realities of the world. Now I was coming face-to-face with them on a daily basis. There was a depression going on and people were lining up for bread and soup. One man who stood beneath Wellington's Arch had a distinguished look to him, well-polished shoes, coat and tie. In fact he was wearing medals. *Wounded on Somme. Any kind of employment considered.* I could read in his face his desperation and his repugnance at having to do this and wished that I had the funds to hire him on the spot. But essentially I was in the same boat as most of them.

Then a policeman blew his whistle, traffic stopped and I sprinted across the street to Park Avenue. Number 59 was fairly modest by Park Lane standards—a typical Georgian house of the smart set, redbrick with white trim, with steps leading up to the front door and railings around the well that housed the servants' quarters below stairs. Not dissimilar to Rannoch House although our London place is a good deal larger and more imposing. Instead of going up to the front door, I went gingerly down the dark steps to the servants' area and located the key under a flowerpot. I let myself in to a dreadful dingy hallway in which the smell of cabbage lingered.

All right, so now you know my dreadful secret. I've been earning money by cleaning people's houses. My advertisement in the *Times* lists me as Coronet Domestics, as recommended by Lady Georgiana of Glen Garry and Rannoch. I don't do any proper heavy cleaning. No scrubbing of floors or, heaven forbid, lavatory bowls. I wouldn't have a clue where to begin. I undertake to open up the London houses for those who have been away at their country estates and don't want to go to the added expense and nuisance of sending their servants ahead of them to do this task. It involves whisking off dust sheets, making beds, sweeping and dusting. That much I can do without breaking anything too often—since another thing you should know about me is that I am prone to the occasional episode of clumsiness.

It is a job sometimes fraught with danger. The houses I work in are owned by people of my social set. I'd die of mortification if I bumped into a fellow debutante or, even worse, a dance partner, while on my hands and knees in a little white cap. So far only my best friend, Belinda Warburton-Stoke, and an unreliable rogue called Darcy O'Mara know about my secret. And the least said about him, the better.

Until I started this job, I had never given much thought to how the other half lives. My own recollections of going below stairs to visit the servants all centered around big warm kitchens with the scent of baking and being allowed to help roll out the dough and lick the spoon. I found the cleaning cupboard and helped myself to a bucket and cloths, feather duster, and a carpet sweeper. Thank heavens it was summer and no fires would be required in the bedrooms. Carrying coal up three flights of stairs was not my favorite occupation, nor was venturing into what my grandfather called the coal'ole to fill the scuttles. My grandfather? Oh, sorry. I suppose I hadn't mentioned him. My father was first cousin to King George, and Queen Victoria's grandson, but my mother was an actress from Essex. Her father still lives in Essex, in a little house with gnomes in the front garden. He's a genuine Cockney and a retired policeman. I absolutely adore him. He's the one person to whom I can say absolutely anything.

At the last second I remembered to retrieve my maid's cap from my coat pocket and jammed it over my unruly hair. Maids are never seen without their caps. I pushed open the baize door that led to the main part of the house and barreled into a great pile of luggage, which promptly fell over with a crash. Who on earth thought of piling luggage against the door to the servants' quarters? Before I could pick up the strewn suitcases there was a shout and an elderly woman dressed head to toe in black appeared from the nearest doorway, waving a stick at me. She was still wearing an old-fashioned bonnet tied under her chin and a traveling cloak. An awful thought struck me that I had mistaken the number, or written it down wrongly, and I was in the wrong house.

"What is happening?" she demanded in French. She glanced at my outfit. *"Vous êtes la bonne?"* Asking "Are you the maid?" in French was rather a strange way to greet a servant in London, where most servants have trouble with proper English. Fortunately I was educated in Switzerland and my French is quite good. I replied that I was indeed the maid, sent to open up the house by the domestic service, and I had been told that the occupants would not arrive until the next day.

"We came early," she said, still in French. "Jean-Claude drove us from Biarritz to Paris in the motorcar and we caught the overnight train."

"Jean-Claude is the chauffeur?" I asked.

"Jean-Claude is the Marquis de Chambourie," she said. "He is also a racing driver. We made the trip to Paris in six hours." Then she realized she was talking to a housemaid. "How is it that you speak

passable French for an English person?"
she asked.

I was tempted to say that I spoke jolly
good French, but instead I mumbled something about traveling abroad with the family on the Côte D'Azur.

"Fraternizing with French sailors, I
shouldn't be surprised," she muttered.

"And you, you are Madame's housekeeper?" I asked.

"I, my dear young woman, am the Dowager Countess Sophia of Liechtenstein,"
she said, and in case you're wondering
why a countess of a German-speaking
country was talking to me in French, I
should point out that high-born ladies of
her generation usually spoke French, no
matter what their native tongue was. "My
maid is attempting to make a bedroom
ready for me," she continued with a wave
of her hand up the stairs. "My housekeeper and the rest of my staff will arrive
tomorrow by train as planned. Jean-
Claude drives a two-seater motorcar. My
maid had to perch on the luggage. I
understand it was most disagreeable for
her." She paused to scowl at me. "And it is

most disagreeable for me to have nowhere to sit."

I wasn't quite sure of the protocol of the court of Liechtenstein and how one addressed a dowager countess of that land, but I've discovered that when in doubt, guess upward. "I'm sorry, Your Highness, but I was told to come today. Had I known that you had a relative who was a racing driver, I would have prepared the house yesterday." I tried not to grin as I said this.

She frowned at me, trying to ascertain whether I was being cheeky or not, I suspect. "Hmmph," was all she could manage.

"I will remove the covers from a comfortable chair for Your Highness," I said, going through into a large dark drawing room and whisking the cover off an armchair, sending a cloud of dust into the air. "Then I will make ready your bedroom first. I am sure the crossing was tiring and you need a rest."

"What I want is a good hot bath," she said.

Ah, that might be a slight problem, I thought. I had seen my grandfather lighting the boiler at Rannoch House but I had no personal experience of doing anything connected to boilers. Maybe the countess's maid was more familiar with such things.

Someone would have to be. I wondered how to say "boilers are not in my contract" in French.

"I will see what can be done," I said, bowed and backed out of the room. Then I grabbed my cleaning supplies and climbed the stairs. The maid looked about as old and bad-tempered as the countess, which was understandable if she'd had to ride all the way from Biarritz perched on top of the luggage. She had chosen the best bedroom, at the front of the house overlooking Hyde Park, and had already opened the windows and taken the dust covers off the furniture. I tried speaking to her in French, then English, but it seemed that she only spoke German. My German was not up to more than "I'd like a glass of mulled wine," and "Where is the ski lift?" So I pantomimed that I would make the bed. She looked dubious. We found sheets and made it between us. This was fortunate as she was most particular about folding the corners just so. She also rounded up about a dozen more blankets and eiderdowns from bedrooms on the same floor, as apparently the countess felt the cold in England. That much I could understand.

When finished the bed looked suitable for the Princess and the Pea.

After I had dusted and swept the floor under the maid's critical eye, I took her to the bathroom and turned on the taps. "*Heiss Bad für* . . . Countess," I said, stretching my German to its limit. Miraculously there was a loud whooomph and hot water came forth from one of those little geyser contraptions above the bath. I felt like a magician and marched downstairs triumphantly to tell the countess that her room was ready for her and she could have a bath anytime she wished.

As I came down the final flight of stairs, I could hear voices coming from the drawing room. I hadn't realized that yet another person was in the house. I hesitated at the top of the flight of stairs. At that moment I heard a man's voice saying, in heavily accented English, "Don't worry, Aunt. Allow me to assist you. I shall personally aid in the transportation of your luggage to your room if you feel it is too much for your maid. Although why you bring a maid who is not capable of the most basic chores, I simply cannot understand. If you choose to make life uncomfortable for yourself, it is your own fault." And a young man came out of the room. He was slim, pale, with ultra-upright carriage. His hair was almost white blond and slicked straight back, giving him a ghostly, skull-like appearance—Hamlet come to life. The expression on his face was utterly supercilious—as if he had detected a nasty smell under his nose, and he pursed his large codlike lips as he talked. I had recognized him instantly, of course. It was none other than Prince Siegfried, better known as Fishface—the man everyone expected me to marry.

Chapter 2

It took me a moment to react. I was rooted to the spot with horror and couldn't seem to make my body obey me when my brain was commanding me to run. Siegfried bent and picked up a hatbox and a ridiculously small train case and started up the stairs with them. I suppose if I had been capable of rational thought I could merely have dropped to my hands and knees and pretended to be sweeping. Aristocrats pay no attention to working domestics. But the sight of him had completely unnerved me, so I did what my mother had done so successfully, so many times and with so many men—I turned and bolted.

I raced up the second flight of stairs as Siegfried came up the first with remarkable agility. Not the countess's bedroom. At least I managed that degree of coherence. I opened a door at the rear of the landing and ran inside, shutting the door after me as quietly as possible. It was a back bedroom, one from which we had taken the extra quilts.

I heard Siegfried's footfalls on the landing. "This is the bedroom she has chosen?" I heard him saying. "No, no. This will not do at all. Too noisy. The traffic will keep her awake all night."

And to my horror I heard the footsteps coming in my direction. I looked around the room. It contained no real wardrobe, just a high gentleman's chest. We had taken the dust sheets off the chest and the bed. There was literally nowhere to hide.

I heard a door open close by. "No, no. Too impossibly ugly," I heard him say.

I rushed to the window and opened it. It was a long drop to the small garden below, but there was a drainpipe beside the window and a small tree that could be reached about ten feet down. I didn't wait a second longer. I hoisted myself out of the window and grabbed onto the drainpipe. It felt sturdy enough and I started to climb down. Thank heavens for my education at finishing school in Switzerland. The one thing I had learned to do, apart from speaking French and knowing where to seat a bishop at a dinner table, was to climb down drainpipes in order to meet ski instructors at the local tavern.

The maid's uniform was tight and cumbersome. The heavy skirts wrapped around my legs as I tried to shin down the drainpipe. I thought I heard something rip as I felt for a foothold. I heard Siegfried's voice, loud and clear in the room above. "*Mein Gott,* no, no, no. This place is a disaster. An utter disaster. Aunt! You have rented a disaster— and not even a garden to speak of."

I heard the voice come across to the window. I think I have mentioned that I am also inclined to be clumsy in moments of stress. My hands somehow slipped from the drainpipe and I fell. I felt branches scratching my face as I tumbled into the tree, uttering a loud squeak. I clutched the nearest branch and held on for dear life. The whole thing swayed alarmingly but I was safely among the leaves. I waited until the voice died away then lowered myself down to the ground, sprinted through the side gate, grabbed my coat from the servants' hallway and fled. I would have to telephone the countess and tell her that unfortunately the young maid I sent to the house had suddenly been taken ill. It seemed she had developed a violent reaction to dust.

I had only gone a few yards down Park Lane when somebody called my name. For an awful moment I thought Siegfried might have been looking out of a window and recognized me, but then I realized that he wouldn't be calling me Georgie. Only my friends called me that.

I turned around and there was my best friend, Belinda Warburton-Stoke, rushing toward me, arms open wide. She was an absolute vision in turquoise silk, trimmed with shocking pink and topped with cape sleeves that fluttered out in the breeze as she ran, making her seem to be flying. The whole ensemble was completed with a little pink feathered hat, perched wickedly over one eye.

"Darling, it *is* you," she said, embracing me in a cloud of expensive French perfume. "It's been simply ages. I've missed you terribly."

Belinda is completely different from me in every way. I'm tall, reddish-blondish with freckles. She's petite, dark haired with big brown eyes, sophisticated, elegant and very naughty. I shouldn't have been glad to see her, but I was.

"I wasn't the one who went jaunting off to the Med."

"My dear, if you were invited for two weeks on a yacht and the yacht was owned by a divine Frenchman, would you have refused?"

"Probably not," I said. "Was it as divine as you expected?"

"Divine but strange," she said. "I thought he had invited me because, you know, he fancied me. And since he's fabulously rich and a duke to boot, I thought I might be on to something. And you have to admit that Frenchmen do make divine lovers—so naughty and yet so romantic. Well, it turned out that he'd also invited not only his wife but his mistress and he dutifully visited alternate cabins on alternate nights.

I was left to play gin rummy with his twelve-year-old daughter."

I chuckled. "And flirt with the sailors?"

"Darling, the sailors were all over forty and had paunches. Not a handsome brute among them. I came back positively sex starved, only to find all the desirable males had fled London for the country or the Continent. So seeing you is a positive ray of sunshine in my otherwise gloomy life. But darling Georgie"—she was now staring at me—"what have you been doing to yourself?"

"What does it look as if I've been doing?"

"Wrestling with a lion in the jungle?" She eyed me doubtfully. "Darling, you have a wicked scratch down one cheek, a smudge down the other, and you have leaves in your hair. Or was it a wild roll in the hay in the park? Do tell, I'm mad with curiosity and I'll be even madder with jealousy if it was the latter."

"I had to make a speedy exit because of a man," I said.

"The brute tried to attack you? In broad daylight?"

I started to laugh. "Nothing of the kind. I was earning my daily crust in the usual way, opening up a house for people arriving from the Continent, only the new occupants turned up a day early and one of them was none other than the dreaded Prince Siegfried."

"Fishface in person? How utterly frightful. What did he say when he saw you garbed as a maid? And more to the point, what did you say to him?"

"He didn't see me," I said. "I fled and had to climb down from an upstairs window. It's a good thing we became so adept at drainpipes at Les Oiseaux. Hence the scratches and the leaves in my hair. I fell into a tree. All in all a very trying morning."

"My poor sweet Georgie—what an ordeal. Come here." She removed the leaves from my hair, then took out a lace handkerchief from her handbag and dabbed at my cheek. A wave of Chanel floated over me. "That's a little better but you need cheering up. I know, let's go and have lunch somewhere. You choose."

I desperately wanted to have lunch with Belinda, but funds were horribly low at that moment. "There are some little cafés along Oxford Street, or one of the department stores?" I suggested. "They do ladies' lunches, don't they?"

Belinda looked as if I'd suggested eating jellied eels on the Old Kent Road. "A department store? Darling, such things are for old women who smell of mothballs and suburban housewives from Coulsden whose hubbies let the little woman come up to town for a day's shopping. People like you and I would cause too much of a stir if we appeared there—rather like letting in a peacock among a lot of hens. It would quite put them off their grilled sole. Now where should we go? The Dorchester would do at a pinch, I suppose. The Ritz is within walking distance, but I rather feel that all it does well is tea. The same goes for Brown's—nothing but old ladies in tweeds. There is no point in going to eat where one can't be seen by the right people. I suppose it will have to be the Savoy. At least one can be sure of getting decent food there—"

"Just a moment, Belinda." I cut her off in mid sentence. "I am still cleaning houses for a pittance. I simply couldn't afford the kind of place you're thinking of."

"My treat, darling," she said, waving a turquoise-gloved hand expansively. "That yacht did put into Monte Carlo for a night or two and you know how good I am at the tables. What's more, I've made a sale—someone has actually bought one of my creations, for cash."

"Belinda, that's wonderful. Do tell."

She linked arms with me and we started to walk back up Park Lane. "Well, you remember the purple dress—the one I tried to sell to that awful Mrs. Simpson because I thought it looked like an American's idea of royalty?"

"Of course," I said, blushing at the fiasco of my brief modeling career. I had been called upon to model that dress and . . . well, never mind.

"Well, darling, I met another American lady at Crockford's—yes, I admit it, gambling again, I'm afraid—and I told her I was an up-and-coming couturiere and I designed for royalty, and she came to my studio and bought the dress, just like that. She even paid for it on the spot and—" She broke off as a front door opened and a man came out, pausing at the top of the steps with a look of utter disdain on his face.

"It's Siegfried," I hissed. "He'll see me. Run."

It was too late. He looked in our direction as he came down the front steps. "Ah, Lady Georgiana. We meet again. What a pleasant surprise." His face didn't indicate that the surprise was in any way pleasant, but he did bow slightly.

I grabbed at my coat and held it tightly around me so that my maid's uniform didn't show. I was horribly conscious of the scratch on my cheek and my hair in disarray. I must have looked a fright. Not that I wanted Siegfried to find me attractive, but I do have my pride.

"Your Highness." I nodded regally. "May I present my friend Belinda Warburton-Stoke?"

"I believe we have had the pleasure before," he said, although the words didn't convey the same undertones as with most young men who had met Belinda. "In Switzerland, I believe."

"Of course," Belinda said. "How do you do, Your Highness. Are you visiting London for long?"

"My aunt has just arrived from the Continent, so of course I had to pay the required visit, although the house she has rented—what a disaster. Not fit for a dog."

"How terrible for you," I said.

"I shall endure it somehow," he said, his expression suggesting that he was about to spend the night in the dungeons of the Tower of London. "And where are you ladies off to?"

"We're going to lunch, at the Savoy," Belinda said.

"The Savoy. The food is not bad there. Maybe I shall join you."

"That would be lovely," Belinda said sweetly.

I dug my fingers into her forearm. I knew this was her idea of having fun. It certainly wasn't mine. I decided to play a trump card.

"How kind of you, Your Highness. We have so much to talk about. Have you been out riding recently—since your unfortunate accident, I mean?" I asked sweetly.

I saw a spasm of annoyance cross his face. "Ah," he said, "I have just remembered that I promised to meet a fellow at his club. So sorry. Another time maybe?" He clicked his heels together in that strangely European gesture, and jerked his head in a bow. "I bid you adieu. Lady Georgiana. Miss Warburton-Stoke." And he marched down Park Lane as quickly as his booted feet would carry him.

Chapter 3

Belinda looked at me and started to laugh. "What was that about?"

"He fell off his horse last time we were together, at that house party," I said, "after he had boasted how well he could ride. I had to say something to stop him from coming to lunch with us. What on earth were you thinking?"

Belinda's eyes were twinkling. "I know, it was rather naughty of me but I couldn't resist. You in your maid's uniform and Prince Siegfried at the Savoy—how utterly scrumptious."

"I thought you were supposed to be my friend," I said.

"I am, darling. I am. But you have to admit that it would have been a riot."

"It would have been my worst nightmare."

"Why should you care what the odious man thinks? I thought the whole idea was to make sure that he would rather fall on his sword than marry you."

"Because he is liable to report back to the palace, especially if he noticed I was dressed as a maid, and even more especially if he put two and two together and realized he'd just spotted me cleaning his house. And if the palace found out, I'd be shipped off to the country to be lady-in-waiting to Queen Victoria's one surviving daughter and spend the rest of my days surrounded by Pekinese and knitting wool."

"Oh, I suppose you do have a valid point there." Belinda tried not to smile. "Yes, that was rather insensitive of me. Come along, you'll feel better after a jolly good lunch at the Savoy." She started to drag me down Park Lane. "We'll take a cab."

"Belinda, I can't go to the Savoy dressed like this."

"No problem, darling." Belinda yanked me sideways into Curzon Street. "My salon is only just around the corner. We'll just pop in there and I'll lend you something to wear."

"I couldn't possibly wear one of your dresses. What if I damaged it in some way? You know what I'm like. I'd be liable to spill something on it."

"Don't be silly. You'll be doing me a favor actually. You can be a walking advertisement for my designs when you mingle with your royal relatives. That would be a coup, wouldn't it? Couturiere by appointment to the royal family?"

"Not the culottes," I said hastily, my one modeling disaster dancing before my eyes. "Some normal kind of garment that I can wear without tripping over it or looking like an idiot."

Belinda gave her delightful bell-like laugh. "You are so sweet, Georgie."

"Sweet but clumsy," I said gloomily.

"I'm sure you'll grow out of your clumsiness someday."

"I hope so," I said. "It's not that I'm perpetually clumsy. It's just that I'm always clumsy at the wrong place and the wrong time, in front of the wrong people. It must have something to do with nerves, I suppose."

"Now why should you be nervous?" Belinda demanded. "You're just about the most eligible young woman in Britain, and you're quite attractive and you have that delightfully fresh and virginal quality to you—speaking of which, anything to report on that front?"

"My virginity, you mean?"

Two nannies, pushing prams, turned back to glare at us with looks of utter horror.

Belinda and I exchanged a grin. "This conversation should probably wait for somewhere a little less public," I said and bundled her into the doorway of the building that housed her salon. Once upstairs in her little room she had me try on several outfits before settling on a light brown georgette dress with a filmy gold short cape over it.

"Capes are so in fashion at the moment and it goes so well with your hair," she said, and it did. I felt like a different person as

I stared at myself in her full-length mirror. No longer gawky but tall and elegant—until I came to my feet, that is. I was wearing sensible black lace-up maid's shoes.

"The shoes will have to go," she said. "We can pop into Russell and Bromley on the way."

"Belinda—I have no money. Don't you understand that?"

"The shoes have to complement the outfit," she said airily. "Besides, you can pay me back when you're queen of somewhere. You never know, you might end up with a maharaja who will weigh you in diamonds."

"And then lock me away in a harem. No, thank you. I think I'll settle for a less wealthy Englishman."

"So boring, darling. And so completely sexless." Belinda stepped out onto the street and hailed a taxicab, which screeched to a halt beside her. "Russell and Bromley first," she said, as if this were normal behavior. For her it was. For me it still made me feel like Cinderella.

It took Belinda half an hour to select a pair of gold pumps for me, then it was off to the Savoy. Belinda chattered merrily and I found my spirits lifting. The cab swung under the wonderfully modern streamlined portico of the Savoy and a doorman leaped forward to open the door for us. I swept inside, feeling sophisticated and glamorous, a woman of the world at last. At least until my cape, flowing out behind me as I entered, got caught in the revolving door. I was yanked backward, choking, and had to stand there, mortified, while the doormen extricated me and Belinda chuckled.

"Did you know that you design dangerous clothing?" I demanded as we went through to the grill. "That's twice now that one of your garments has tried to kill me."

Belinda was still laughing. "Normal people seem to have no trouble with them. "Maybe they are secretly communist garments, sworn to destroy the house of Windsor."

"Then I definitely won't let you sell one to my cousins." I readjusted the cape so that the clip was no longer digging into my neck as we reached the entrance of the grill.

"You have a reservation, miss?" the maitre d' asked.

"I'm Belinda Warburton-Stoke and I'm here to lunch with Lady Georgiana Rannoch," Belinda said sweetly as money passed discreetly from her hand to his, "and I'm terribly afraid that we have no reservation . . . but I'm sure you'll be an absolute angel and find us a little corner somewhere. . . ."

"Welcome, my lady. This is indeed an honor." He bowed to me and escorted us to a delightful table for two. "I will send the chef out to give you his recommendations."

"I must say it is useful to have a name," I said as we were seated.

"You should make use of it more often. You could probably get credit anywhere you wanted, for example."

"Oh no, I'm not going into debt. You know our family motto—Death Before Dishonor."

"There's nothing dishonorable about debt," Belinda said. "Think of the death duties your brother was saddled with when your father shot himself."

"Ah, but he sold off half the estate, the family silver and our property in Sutherland to pay them off."

"How boringly noble of him. I'm glad I'm

just landed gentry and not aristocracy. It comes with less weight of ancestors' expectations. My great-great-grandfather was in trade, of course. Your crowd would have nothing to do with him, even though he could buy the lot of 'em. Anyway, I quite enjoy the vices of the lower classes—and speaking of vices, you never did tell me . . ."

"About what?"

"Your virginity, darling. I do hope you have finally done something to rid yourself of it. Such a burden."

Unfortunately blushes really show on my fair skin.

"You have finally done it, haven't you?" she went on in her loud bell-like tones, eliciting fascinated stares from all the surrounding tables. "Don't tell me you haven't! Georgie, what's the matter with you? Especially when you have someone who is ready, willing and oh so very able."

The poor young man who was busy pouring water into our glasses almost dropped the jug.

"Belinda," I hissed.

"I take it that the rakish Darcy O'Mara is still in the picture?"

"He's not, actually."

"Oh no. What happened? You two seemed so awfully chummy last time I saw you."

"We didn't have a row or anything. It's just that he's disappeared. Not long after the infamous house party. He just didn't call anymore and I've no idea where he's gone."

"Didn't you go and look him up?"

"I couldn't do that. If he doesn't want me, then I'm not about to throw myself at him."

"I would. He's definitely one of the most interesting men in London. Let's face it, there are precious few of them, aren't there? I am positively dying of sexual frustration at the moment."

The chef, now standing at our table, pretended to be busy straightening the cutlery. Belinda ordered all sorts of yummy things—an endive salad with smoked salmon and grilled lamb chops accompanied by a wondrously smooth claret, followed by a bread and butter pudding to die for. We had just finished our pudding, and coffee had been brought to the table, when a braying laugh could be heard across the grill, a sort of "haw haw haw." A young man got up from the table in question, still shaking with merriment. "What a riot," he said and started to walk in our direction.

"Now you see what I mean about there being no interesting men in London," Belinda muttered. "This is the current flower of British manhood. Father owns a publishing house but he's utterly useless between the covers."

"I don't think I know him."

"Gussie Gormsley, darling," she said.

"Gussie Gormsley?"

"Augustus. Father is Lord Gormsley. I'm surprised he's not on your list of eligibles. Must be the publishing connection. No trade in the family and all that." She waved at him. "Gussie. Over here."

Gussie was a large, fair young man who would have made an ideal rugby forward. His face lit up with pleasure when he saw Belinda.

"What-ho, Belinda old bean," he said. "Long time no see."

"Just back from the Med, darling. Have you met my good friend Georgiana Rannoch?"

"Not Binky's sister? Good God."

"Why do you say good God?" I asked.

"I always thought—well, he'd always given us to think that you were a shy, retiring little thing, and here you are absolutely dripping with glam."

"Georgie is probably the most eligible woman in Britain," Belinda said, before I could stammer anything. "Men are positively fighting over her. Foreign princes, American millionaires."

"No wonder Binky kept you a secret," Gussie said. "I must introduce you to old Lunghi." He turned and waved back toward his table in the corner.

"Lunghi who?" Belinda asked.

"Lunghi Fotheringay, old bean." Of course he pronounced the second name "Fungy." One does.

"Lunghi Fungy? What a scream," Belinda said. "Why is he called Lunghi?"

"Just back from India, you know. Showed us a snapshot of himself with a bit of cloth wrapped around his loins and someone said, what do you call that, and he said a lunghi, and then we realized how funny it was. So Lunghi Fungy he became." He gestured again. "Over here, old man. Couple of delectable young fillies I want you to meet."

I felt myself blushing with all eyes in the Savoy on me, but Belinda turned on her brilliant smile as Mr. Fotheringay approached. He was slim, dark and serious looking. Not bad, in fact.

Introductions were made and then Gussie said, "Look here, there's going to be a bit of a shindig at our place next week. You two wouldn't like to come, would you?"

"Love to, if we're free," Belinda said. "Anyone interesting going to be there?"

"Apart from us, you mean?" the dark and brooding Lunghi asked, gazing at her seriously. It was quite clear in which of us his interest lay. "I can assure you we are the most fascinating men in London at the moment."

"Unfortunately that seems to be so," Belinda agreed. "London is singularly devoid of fascination at present. We'll take them up on it, then, shall we, Georgie?"

"Why not?" I replied, trying to indicate that such invitations were commonplace.

"See you there then. I'll pop invitations into the post so that it's official and all that. It's Arlington Street—that big modern white block of flats beside Green Park. St. James's Mansions. You'll know it by the sound of jazz emanating from it and by the disgruntled looks on the faces of the neighbors."

Belinda and I rose to leave. "There you are. Good things happen when you're with me," she said as she paid the bill without a second glance. "And he was certainly impressed with you, wasn't he?"

"With your outfit, more likely," I said. "But it could be fun."

"One of them might do, you know."

"For what?"

"Your virginity, darling. Really you are so dense sometimes."

"You said that Gussie was useless between the covers," I pointed out.

"For me. He might be all right for you. You won't expect too much."

"Thanks all the same," I said, "but I've decided to wait for love. I don't want to end up a bolter like my mother."

"Speak of the devil," Belinda said.

I looked up to see my mother entering the room.

She stood in the doorway of the Savoy

Grill, pretending to be taking in the scene, but really waiting until everyone in the place had noticed her. I had to admit that she did look an absolute vision in flowing white silk with just enough touches of red to be startling. The cloche hat that framed her delicate face was white straw with red swirls woven into it. The maitre d' leaped forward. "Your Grace, how delightful," he muttered.

My mother hasn't been Her Grace since many husbands ago, but she smiled prettily and didn't correct him. "Hello, François. How lovely to see you again," she said in that melodious voice that had charmed audiences in theaters around the world before my father snapped her up. She started across the room and then she saw me. Those huge blue eyes flew open in surprise.

"Good heavens, Georgie. It is you! I hardly recognized you, darling. You look positively civilized for once. You must have found a rich lover."

"Hello, Mummy." We kissed, about an inch from each other's cheeks. "I didn't know you were in town. I thought you'd be in the Black Forest at this time of year."

"I came over to meet—a friend." There was something coy in her voice.

"So are you still with what's-his-name?"

"Max? Well, yes and no. He thinks so. But one does tire of not being able to chat occasionally. I mean the sex is still heavenly, but one does enjoy a good conversation and for some reason I simply can't learn German. And all Max likes to talk about is shooting things. So I have taken a quick flit over to London. Ah, there he is now." I saw a hand waving from a far corner of the restaurant. "Must fly, darling. Are you still at dreary old Rannoch House? We'll have tea or something. Ciao!"

And she was gone, leaving me with the usual disappointment and frustration and so many things left unsaid. You've probably guessed by now that as a mother she hasn't been too satisfactory. Belinda took my arm. "I don't know why you are adamant about not ending up like your mother. She does have a wardrobe to die for."

"But at what cost?" I said. "My grandfather thinks that she's sold her soul."

A taxicab was hailed for us. We climbed in. I stared out of the window and found that I was shivering. It wasn't just the meeting with my mother that had unnerved me. As we were getting into the taxi, I think I spotted Darcy O'Mara walking into the Savoy, with a tall, dark-haired girl on his arm.

Chapter 4

"You're very quiet," Belinda commented during the taxi ride home. "Did the food not agree with you?"

"No, the food was divine," I said. I took a deep breath. "You didn't happen to notice Darcy coming into the Savoy as we left, did you?"

"Darcy? No, I can't say I did."

"Then I may be imagining things," I said. "But I could swear it was he, and he had a young woman on his arm. A very attractive young woman."

"Ah well," Belinda said with a sigh. "Men

like Darcy are not known for their spaniel-like devotion, and I'm sure he has healthy appetites."

"I suppose you're right," I said and sat for the rest of the cab ride in deepest gloom. It seemed that my stupid reticence had robbed me of my chance with Darcy. Did I really want him? I asked myself. He was Irish, Catholic, penniless, unreliable and in every way unsuitable, except that he was the son of a peer. But the image of him with another girl brought almost a physical pain to my heart.

What's more, those fleeting meetings with my mother always left me frustrated and depressed. So much I wanted to say to her and never a moment to say it. And now it seemed she might be moving on to yet another new man. It was the vision of ending up like her that had made me cautious about surrendering to someone like Darcy in the first place. I wasn't sure that I had inherited her flighty nature, but I was sure I had definitely inherited those stalwart Rannoch traits. And Death Before Dishonor was our family name!

I let myself into Rannoch House, still

wearing Belinda's stylish outfit, my maid's uniform and the clompy shoes now in a Harrods carrier bag. I had tried to make her take back the clothes she had lent me, but she had insisted that it was going to be good advertising and all I had to do was to hand her card to anyone who complimented me. I suppose she was right in a way, although she obviously thought I saw my royal relatives more frequently than I really did. As far as I knew, the next time I would set eyes on the king and queen would be at Balmoral, whither I was summoned each summer, Castle Rannoch being but a stone's throw away. And at Balmoral it was strictly Highland dress.

I stepped into the gloom of the front hall and noticed a letter lying on the mat. I picked it up expectantly. Post was a rarity as hardly anybody knew I was in London. Then I saw what it was and almost dropped it. From the palace. Hand delivered.

I went cold all over. From Her Majesty's private secretary. *Her Majesty hopes that you will be able to take tea with her tomorrow, June 7th. She apologizes for the short notice but a matter of some urgency has arisen.*

My first thought, of course, was that Siegfried had recognized the maid's uniform and had promptly visited the palace to tell them the awful truth. I'd be sent to the country and—"Wait a minute," I said out loud. She might be Queen of England and Empress of India and all that, but she can't force me to do anything I don't want to. This isn't the Middle Ages. She can't have my head cut off or throw me into the Tower. I'm doing nothing wrong. I know that cleaning houses is a little beneath my station, but I'm earning an honest living. I'm not asking anybody to support me. I'm trying to make my way in the world at a difficult time. She should be proud of my enterprise.

Right. That's that, then. That's exactly what I'll tell her.

I felt much better after that. I marched upstairs and took off Belinda's creation. Then I sat at my desk and wrote out a bill, for half the agreed amount, to the Dowager Countess Sophia, with an explanation about the maid's sudden aversion to London dust.

**Rannoch House
Tuesday, June 7, 1932**

>**Diary,
>Lovely bright morning. Buck House today. Tea with queen. Not expecting much to eat. Really, royal protocol is too silly. May have to distract HM and gobble down a quick cake this time. I wonder what she wants. Nothing good, I fear. . . .**

When I was dressing to go to tea at the palace, I wasn't feeling quite as brave anymore. Her Majesty is a formidable woman. She is small and may not appear too fierce at first glance, but remember my great-grandmother, Queen Victoria. She was small and yet a whole empire trembled when she raised an eyebrow. Queen Mary doesn't have quite that power, but one look at that ramrod straight back and those cold blue eyes with their frank, appraising stare, can turn the strongest person to a jelly. And she doesn't like to be crossed. I stared at the clothes in my wardrobe, trying to decide what would make the best impression. Not too worldly, so definitely not Belinda's creation. I have some fairly smart formal dresses, but my summer day clothes are sadly lacking. The dress I liked best was made of cotton. It needed a proper ironing and I had not yet mastered the use of the iron. I ended up with more creases than I started with, not to mention a scorch or two. And now was not a good time to practice. In the end I opted for simplicity and went with a navy suit and white blouse. Rather like a school uniform but at least I looked neat, clean and proper. I topped it off with my white straw hat (nothing like my mother's stylish little number) and white gloves, then off I went.

It was a warm day and I was rather red in the face by the time I reached the top of Constitution Hill. I dabbed at my face with my eau de cologne-soaked hanky before I walked past those guardsmen. The visitors' entrance is on the far side of the palace. At least a visitor like myself, arriving without benefit of state coach or Rolls, can enter through a side gate. I crossed the forecourt, feeling, as I always did, that eyes were watching me and that I'd probably trip over a cobble.

I was received with great civility and ushered upstairs, the royal apartments being one floor up. Luckily I didn't have to face the grand staircase with its red carpet and statues, but was taken up a simple back stair to an office that looked as if it could have been any London solicitor's. Here Her Majesty's secretary was waiting for me. "Ah, Lady Georgiana. Please come with me. Her Majesty is awaiting you in her private sitting room." He seemed quite cheerful, jolly even. I was tempted to ask him if Her Majesty had inquired about the train service to deepest Gloucestershire. But then maybe she hadn't disclosed to him why she had summoned me. He may have known nothing about aunts with Pekinese dogs.

Thank heavens we're not Catholic, I thought. At least they can't lock me away in a convent until a suitable groom is found. That made me freeze halfway down the hall. What if I was ushered into the sitting room only to find Prince Siegfried and a priest awaiting me?

"In here, my lady," the secretary said. "Lady Georgiana, ma'am."

I took a deep breath and stepped inside. The queen was seated in a Chippendale armchair in front of a low table. Although she was no longer young, her complexion was flawless and smooth, with no sign of wrinkles. What's more, I suspected she didn't need the help of the various expensive preparations my mother used to hang on to her youthful looks.

Tea was already laid, including a delicious array of cakes on a two-tiered silver and glass cake stand. Her Majesty held out a hand to me. "Ah, Georgiana, my dear. How good of you to come."

As if one refused a queen.

"It was very kind of you to invite me, ma'am." I attempted the usual mixture of curtsy and kiss on the cheek and managed it this time without bumping my nose.

"Do sit down. Tea is all ready. China or Indian?"

"China, thank you."

The queen poured the tea herself. "And do help yourself to something to eat."

"After you, ma'am," I said dutifully, knowing full well that protocol demands that the guest only eats what the queen eats. Last time she had chosen one slice of brown bread.

"I really don't think I'm hungry today," she said, making my spirits fall even further. Did she realize what torture it was to sit and stare at strawberry tarts and éclairs and not be able to eat one?

I was about to say that I wasn't hungry either, when she leaned forward. "On second thought, those éclairs do look delicious, don't they? We'll forget about our figures for once, shall we?"

She was in a good mood. Why, I wondered. Was this a good-bye tea before she announced some awful fate for me?

"How have you been faring since I saw you last, Georgiana?" she asked, fixing me with that powerful stare.

I had been trying hard to take a bite of éclair without getting any cream on my upper lip. "Well, thank you, ma'am."

"So you stayed in London. You didn't go to the country after all, or home to Scotland."

"No, ma'am. I had been planning to keep Sir Hubert company when he returned home from the Swiss hospital, but he has decided to complete his recovery at a Swiss sanitarium and there was little point in going home to Scotland." (Sir Hubert was my favorite former stepfather and had been seriously injured during a mountaineering expedition in the Alps.)

"And are you fully occupied in London?"

"I keep myself busy. I have friends. I lunched at the Savoy yesterday."

"It's always good to be busy," she said. "However, I do hope that there is more to your life than luncheons at the Savoy."

Where was this leading? I wondered.

"At this time of crisis there is so much that needs to be done," she went on. "A young woman like yourself, as yet unencumbered with husband and children, could do so much good and set such a fine example. Helping out in soup kitchens, giving advice on sanitary conditions to mothers and babies in the East End, or even joining the health and beauty movement. All worthy causes, Georgiana. All worth devoting time and energy."

This wasn't going to be too bad then, I thought. She clearly expected me to stay in London if she was suggesting I help mothers and babies in the East End.

"Excellent suggestions, ma'am," I said.

"I am patron of several worthy charities. I will find out where your services would be most appreciated."

"Thank you." I really meant it. I would actually quite enjoy helping a charity to do good. And it would give me something else to do between house cleanings.

"We'll put that suggestion to one side for now," Her Majesty said, taking a sip of China tea, "because I am hoping to enlist you as a coconspirator in a little plan I am devising."

She gave me her frank stare, her clear, blue eyes holding mine for a long moment.

"I am desperately worried about my son, Georgiana."

"The Prince of Wales?" I asked.

"Naturally. My other sons are all proving satisfactory in their own ways. At least they all seem to have a sense of royal duty in which David is hopelessly lacking. This American woman. From what I hear, his fascination for her shows no sign of abating. She has her claws into him and she is not going to let go. Of course at the moment the question of marriage cannot arise, because she is married to someone else, poor fool. But should she divorce him—well, you see what a predicament that would be."

"His Highness would never be allowed to marry a divorced woman, would he?"

"You say never allowed, but should he be king, who could stop him? He is then the titular head of the church. Henry the Eighth rewrote the rules to suit himself, didn't he?"

"I'm sure you're worrying needlessly, ma'am. The Prince of Wales might enjoy the playboy life at this moment but when he becomes king, he'll remember his duty to his country. It is inbred into all members of the family."

She reached across and patted my hand. "I do hope you are right, Georgiana. But I can't sit idly by and do nothing to save my son from ruin and our family from disgrace. It is time he married properly, and to a young woman who can give him children of the proper pedigree. A forty-year-old American simply won't do. To this end, I've come up with a little scheme."

She gave me that conspiratorial look again.

"Do you know the Bavarian royal family at all?"

"I have not met them, ma'am."

"Not related to us, of course, and unfortunately Roman Catholic. They are no longer officially the ruling family, but they do still enjoy considerable status and respect in that part of Germany. In fact there is a strong movement to restore the monarchy in Bavaria, thus making them strong allies against that ridiculous little upstart Herr Hitler."

"You are planning a match with a member of the Bavarian royal family, ma'am?"

She leaned closer to me, although we were the only two people in the room. "They have a daughter, Hannelore. A beauty by all reports. She is eighteen years old and has just left the convent where she has been educated for the past ten years. Should she have a chance to meet my son, what man could fail to be attracted to an eighteen-year-old virginal beauty? Surely she would make him forget about the Simpson woman and return to the path of duty."

I nodded. "But where do I come into this, ma'am?"

"Let me explain my little scheme, Georgiana. If David felt that he was being forced to meet Princess Hannelore, he would dig in his heels. He has always been stubborn, ever since he was a little boy, you know. But should he glimpse her, across the room, should it be hinted that she is promised to someone else—a lesser princeling—well, you know how much men enjoy the chase. So I've written to her parents and invited her to come to England—to bring her out into society and improve her English. And I have decided that she shouldn't stay with us at the palace." She looked up at me with that piercing stare. "I've decided she should stay with you."

"Me?" It was lucky I hadn't been sipping tea at the time. I should have spluttered all over the Chippendale. As it was, it came out as a squeak and I forgot to add the word "ma'am."

"What could be more pleasant for a young girl than to stay with someone her own age and of suitable rank? As you say, you mingle with friends. You dine at the Savoy. She will have a lovely time doing what young people do. Then, at the right intervals, we'll make sure that she attends the same functions as my son."

She went on talking easily. The blood was pounding through my head as I tried to come up with the words to say that there was no way I could entertain a young lady of royal blood in a house with no servants and in which I was living on baked beans.

"I may count on you, mayn't I, Georgiana?" she asked. "For the good of England?"

I opened my mouth. "Of course, ma'am," I said.

Chapter 5

I staggered out of Buck House as if in a dream. Well, nightmare, actually. In a few days from now a German princess was coming to stay at my house, when I had no servants and certainly no money to feed her. Queens never thought about little things like money. It probably never crossed her mind to inquire whether I had the funds to entertain a royal guest or whether I might like some help in that department. And even if she had promised me an allowance to help with the entertaining, that still neglected the fact that I had no maids, no butler, and worse still, no cook. Germans, I knew, liked their food. Baked beans and boiled eggs, which were the sum of my repertoire to date, simply would not do.

Why had I not spoken up and told the queen the truth? After the fact, it seemed quite silly that I had agreed to something so preposterous. But with those steely eyes on me, I simply didn't have the nerve to refuse her. In fact I had followed in the footsteps of countless antiques dealers who had never intended to let the queen walk off with one of their prized pieces and yet had found themselves graciously handing it over to her.

And now I had no idea what I was going to do next. I needed to talk to somebody, somebody wise who would see a way out of my predicament. Belinda would be no good. She'd think it was all a huge joke and be eagerly waiting to see how I handled it. But then she really couldn't imagine how penniless I was. She had come into a small private income on her twenty-first, which enabled her to buy a mews cottage and keep a maid. She also made money from her dress designs, to say nothing of her gambling winnings. To her, "broke" meant going without champagne for a few days.

Oh, God, I thought. What if this princess expects fine wines and caviar? What if she expects something other than baked beans and tea?

Then suddenly I had a brain wave. I knew the one person in the world to whom I could turn for help—my grandfather. Not the Scottish duke whose ghost now haunts the ramparts of Castle Rannoch (playing the bagpipes, if one is to believe the servants, although this does take a stretch of the imagination, as he couldn't play them in life). I'm talking of my nonroyal grandfather, the former policeman. I hurried to the nearest tube station and soon I was heading through the East End of London out to the eastern suburbs of Essex and a neat little semidetached house with gnomes in the front garden.

I went up his front path past a pocket handkerchief–sized lawn and two meticulously kept rose beds under the watchful eye of the gnomes and knocked on Granddad's front door. Nobody answered. This was an unexpected setback. It was six o'clock and I had felt sure that he couldn't afford to dine out. Fighting back my disappointment, I was about to go home. Then I remembered his mentioning the old lady who lived next door. "Old bat" was his actual term of description for her, but in a fond way. Maybe she might know where he had gone. A shiver of worry went through me. He hadn't been very well last winter and I hoped that he wasn't in hospital.

I knocked on the second front door and waited. Again no response. "Damn," I muttered, then glanced up to notice a net curtain twitching. So someone was there and watching me. As I turned to go, the front door opened. A large, round woman wearing a flowery pinny stood staring at me.

"Wot do you want?" she demanded.

"I came to visit my grandfather," I began. "I'm Georgiana Rannoch and I wondered if—"

She gave a great whoop of delight. "I know who you are. Blimey, what a turnup for the books. I never thought I'd have royalty on the doorstep. Am I supposed to curtsy or something?"

"Of course not," I said. "I just wondered

if you knew where my grandfather might be. I came all the way to see him and—"

"Come on in, ducks," she said, almost hauling me inside. "I'll tell you where your granddad is. In my living room, having his tea, that's where he is. And you're more than welcome to join us. Plenty for all."

"That's very kind of you," I said.

"Don't mention it, love. Don't you mention it," she said expansively.

"I'm sorry, I don't know your name."

"It's 'uggins, love. Mrs. 'ettie 'uggins."

I thought that this was a rather unfortunate choice of name for someone who dropped aitches, but I smiled and held out my hand. "How do you do, Mrs. Huggins."

"Pleased to meet you, I'm sure, your 'ighness."

"I'm not a highness, just a lady, but Georgiana will do splendidly."

"You're a proper toff, miss, that's what you are," she said. She was halfway down the hall when my grandfather appeared.

"What's going on, Hettie?" he asked. Then he saw me and his face lit up. "Cor, strike me down. Ain't you a sight for sore eyes," he said. "Come and give your old grandfather a kiss."

I did so, enjoying the carbolic soap smell of his skin and the roughness of his cheek.

"I almost went home," I said, "but then I remembered your speaking of your next-door neighbor so I thought I'd just try, on the off chance. Then when Mrs. Huggins didn't answer her door to start with—"

"She's a bit jumpy right now," my grand-father said. "On account of the bailiffs."

"The bay leaves?" Images of Mediter-ranean casseroles swam into my head.

"That's right. She don't want nothing to do with them and they keep coming round."

I was rather confused by this state-ment. Why this irrational fear of bay leaves? Where did they keep coming around? In stews? In which case why couldn't she remove them?

"Bay leaves?" I asked. "What is so terri-ble about bay leaves?"

"They're trying to throw me out, that's what," Mrs. Huggins said. "Just because I fell a bit behind with the rent when I was poorly and had to pay the doctor."

Light finally dawned and I blushed at my stupidity. "Oh, bailiffs. Oh, I see."

"She don't own her house like I do," my grandfather said. "She weren't lucky enough to have a daughter who did right by her, were you, Hettie love?"

"I got four daughters and they all married rotters," she said. "It's me who's had to help them out, not the other way around."

"Any sons, Mrs. Huggins?" I asked before this conversation turned completely maudlin.

Her face went blank. "Three boys," she said. "All killed in the war. All three within a few days of each other."

"I'm so sorry."

"Yeah, well, there's not much we can do about it now, is there. Wishing won't bring them back. So I tries to muddle through as best I can. And enough of gloomy talk. Come on in and take a load off your feet, love."

She propelled me through into a tiny dining room. Not only did it have a table and four chairs in it, but armchairs on either side of a fireplace, and a sideboard with a radio on it.

"I hope you don't mind being in 'ere," she said. "We don't use the front parlor, except on special occasions. Sit down, ducks. Go on."

She motioned to a chair. I sat experiencing the feeling of unreality that always came over me in normal houses. I had grown up in a castle. I was used to rooms bigger than this whole house, corridors long enough to practice roller skating and great whistling drafts of cold air coming from chimneys large enough to roast an ox. A room like this reminded me of the play cottage that my cousins Elizabeth and Margaret had in their garden.

"I've just come from tea at the palace," I said as my thoughts returned to the royal family.

"The palace, well, I never." Mrs. Higgins looked at my grandfather with awe on her face. "I'm afraid you won't get nothing posh here, just good plain food."

I looked at the tea table. I had expected something similar—thin sliced bread, little cakes—but this was not tea as I knew it. Slices of ham and cold pork, half a pork pie, a wedge of cheese, a big crusty loaf, pickled onions and a dish of tomatoes graced the table, as well as a moist brown fruitcake and some little rock buns.

"This is some tea," I said.

"It's what we usually have, ain't it, Albert?"

My grandfather nodded. "We don't have no dinner at night, like the posh folks do. We have our dinner in the middle of the day and then this is what we have in the evening."

"It looks awfully good to me," I said and happily accepted the slices of ham he was putting onto my plate.

"So what brings you down Essex way?" my grandfather asked as we ate. "And don't tell me you was just passing."

"I came because I need your advice, Granddad," I said. "I'm in a bit of a pickle."

"Is there a young man involved?" he asked with a worried glance at Mrs. Huggins.

"No, nothing like that. It's just . . ." I looked up at Mrs. Huggins, sitting there all ears. I could hardly tell her why I had come but I couldn't drag him away without seeming rude. The matter was solved when he said, "You can say what you want in front of Hettie. She and I don't have no secrets, at least only the ones concerning my lady friends."

"Get away with you." Hettie chuckled and I realized that their relationship had progressed since I had last visited.

"It's like this, Granddad," I said, and related the whole conversation with the queen. "So I've no idea what to do next," I said. "I can't entertain a princess, but I dare not face the queen and tell her the truth either. She'd be so horrified that I'm slumming without servants that I know she'd send me off to the country to be some royal aunt's lady-in-waiting." My voice rose into a wail.

"All right, love. Don't get yourself into a two-and-eight about it."

"A what?"

"Two-and-eight. Cockney rhyming slang for a state. Haven't you never heard that before?"

"I can't say that I have."

"Well, she wouldn't, would she?" Mrs. Huggins demanded. "They don't use no rhyming slang at the palace."

Granddad smiled. "This wants a bit of thinking about," he said, scratching his chin. "How long is this foreign princess coming for?"

"I've no idea. The queen did mention

that she'd want us to come to Sandringham and there are house parties that we should attend."

"So it might only be for a week or so?"

"Possibly."

"Because I was thinking," he said. "I know where I might be able to supply you with a cook and a butler."

"You do? Where?"

"Us," Granddad said, and burst out laughing. "Me and Mrs. Huggins. She's a fair enough cook and I could pass as a butler when needed."

"Granddad, I couldn't expect you to be my servant. It wouldn't seem right."

"Ah, but you'd be doing us a bit of a favor yourself, love," he said, with another glance at Mrs. Huggins. "You see it might be useful to be away from home if that bailiff is going to show up again with an eviction notice. He has to deliver it in person, don't he?"

"But I couldn't afford to pay you."

"Don't you worry about the money right now, my love," Granddad said. "We don't need paying, but you will need enough money to feed this young woman."

"She's probably going to expect the

best," Mrs. Huggins agreed. "I'd say it was wrong of the queen to expect you to pay for this out of your own pocket."

"She just doesn't think of such things," I said. "The royal family never has to consider money. They don't even carry money with them."

"Nice for some," Mrs. Huggins said with a knowing nod to my grandfather.

Granddad scratched his chin. "I was thinking that you should write to your brother and ask him for some help. He owes you a big favor, after all."

"You're right, he does, but he's awfully hard up too."

"Then tell him you're bringing the princess home to Scotland. From what I know of your snooty sister-in-law, she'd do anything rather than have to entertain visiting royalty at her house."

"Granddad, that's a brilliant idea," I said, laughing. "Absolutely brilliant. And I'll remind Binky he promised to send me my maid as well. Oh, Lord, I'm sure the princess will expect someone to dress her."

"I ain't volunteering to dress no princesses," Mrs. Huggins said. "I wouldn't have no clue how them fancy clothes do up and my rough 'ands will probably scratch her delicate skin."

"If Binky sends my maid from Scotland as he promised, then she can wait on the princess," I said. "I've become quite used to doing without a maid myself."

"So when is this likely to start?"

"Within the next few days," I said. "Oh, dear. I'm not looking forward to it at all."

"Don't get yourself in a two-and-eight." Granddad patted my knee. "It will all work out. You'll see."

Chapter 6

Our butler up at Castle Rannoch has become hard of hearing recently. It took a good five minutes before I could make him understand that I did not want to speak to Lady Georgiana, but that I *was* Lady Georgiana. Eventually the telephone was grabbed by none other than my sister-in-law, Fig.

"Georgiana?" She sounded startled. "What's wrong now?"

"Why should something be wrong?"

"I trust you wouldn't be squandering money on a telephone call with the current telephone rates being so astronomically high, unless it were a real emergency," she said. "You are telephoning from Rannoch House, I take it?"

"I am, and it is something rather urgent." I took a deep breath. "I wondered whether you were going to be home for the next few weeks."

"Of course we're going to be home," she snapped. "Summer holidays are simply beyond our means these days. No longer can one think of jaunting off to the Med for the summer. I shall probably take little Podge to stay with his grandparents in Shropshire, but apart from that, it will strictly be a case of attempting to amuse ourselves at Castle Rannoch, however dreary that prospect may sound."

"That's good news, actually," I said, "because I am going to suggest a way to liven things up for you. I'm planning to bring a party of Germans to stay with you."

"Germans? With us? When?"

"The end of this week, I believe."

"You're going to bring a party of Germans to us this week?" Fig's usually impeccable upbringing showed definite cracks. A lady is brought up never to show her emotions. Fig's voice had become high and shrill. "How many Germans?"

"I'm not sure how big a retinue the princess will be bringing with her."

"Princess?" Now she was definitely rattled.

"Yes, it's all very simple really," I said. "I had tea at the palace yesterday and Her Majesty asked me if I'd be good enough to host a visiting Bavarian princess—"

"You? Why you?"

It irked Fig considerably that I was related to the king and she was not, especially since my mother was of humble birth and an actress to boot. The closest Fig ever came to royal chumminess was an evening or two at Balmoral.

"Her Majesty felt that the palace might be rather stuffy for a young girl and that she would have more fun with someone closer to her own age. I would have been happy to comply in normal circumstances and play host at Rannoch House, but as you know, I no longer have an allowance from my brother and thus can afford no staff, so I don't see how I can entertain anyone, especially a princess."

"Then why didn't you tell Her Majesty that?"

"Tell her that I'm living at the family home with no staff because my brother refuses to pay for them? How would that look, Fig? Think of the family name. The disgrace of it." Before she could answer this I went on brightly, "So that was when I came up with the brain wave. I'll just bring them all up to you in Scotland. They'll have a rattling good time. We can organize some house parties for them, and excursions to the sea, and then make up a shooting party when the season starts in August. You know how much Germans love shooting things."

"August?" Fig's voice had now risen at least an octave. "You are expecting them to stay until August?"

"I have no idea how long they plan to stay. One does not go into trivial details with Her Majesty."

"I am expected to feed a party of Germans until August? Georgiana, do you have any idea how much Germans eat?"

"I don't see any other alternative," I said, thoroughly enjoying this conversation so far.

"Tell the queen that you can't do it. Simple as that."

"One does not say no to the queen, Fig. And if I told her I couldn't do it, I'd have to explain why and there would be a horrible fuss. As I said, this could all be solved quite simply. I'd be quite happy to entertain the princess at Rannoch House, were I given the means to do so. Her Majesty did mention inviting us to Sandringham for part of the time, and of course there would be plenty of house parties to keep Her Highness entertained, so the expense shouldn't be too terrible. All Binky would have to do is to reinstate my allowance for a little while and send me down the maid he promised."

"Georgiana, if didn't know you better, I'd say you were trying to blackmail me," Fig said coldly.

"Blackmail? Oh, good gracious, no. Nothing like that. I just wanted to remind you both that you do owe me a small debt of gratitude for what I did for Binky. Had I not uncovered the truth about who had really killed Gaston de Mauxville, I rather fear that Binky would be languishing in a jail cell. He could even have been hanged by now, leaving you to bring up little Podge and run the estate single handedly. The use of one maid seems like a trifle in return."

There was a pause. I could hear Fig breathing. "We did ask your maid, Maggie," she said at last, "but as you know, she was reluctant to leave her mother, given her mother's current state of health. And there really isn't anybody else suitable. Mrs. Hanna, the laundress, has a daughter, but she is proving most unreliable. She slopped soup down Lady Branston's front the other day."

I almost commented that it would be hard to miss Lady Branston's front.

"If my allowance were reinstated, I could hire a temporary maid locally in London. My friend Belinda has a very suitable girl. I could use the same agency."

"But what about the rest of the staff?" Fig sounded desperate now. "You can't entertain a German princess with only one maid. Who will cook for you? Who will serve?"

"Ah, well, I do happen to know where I can borrow a temporary cook and butler— from friends who are going abroad, you know. So it's really only a maid, and the question of food. One does need to feed guests."

There was a long pause. "I must speak to Binky about this," Fig said. "Times are hard, Georgiana. I don't need to tell you that. I'm sure you pass bread lines in the city every day."

"I do, but I don't think you're exactly down to the level of queuing up for bread, are you, Fig?"

"No, but we jolly well have to live off the estate these days," she said hotly. "No more sending down to Fortnum's for the little treats that make life worth living. Binky has even given up his Gentlemen's Relish and you know how he adores it. No, it's simple, humble country food for us now."

"Too bad it's not hunting season," I said. "If it were, you could shoot enough deer to keep the Germans fed. I understand that they love venison."

"I'll talk to Binky," she said hastily. "I do understand that we shouldn't let down the family name to Her Majesty or to foreigners."

I replaced the mouthpiece with great satisfaction.

The next morning two letters arrived in the early post. One was from Binky, instructing me that he was having a modest amount transferred to my bank account, which was all he could spare at such short notice and such a difficult time, but which he hoped would prove enough to cover my temporary financial needs. Underneath Fig had added, *Make sure you double-check references for any staff you bring into OUR HOME and keep the silver locked up!!* The other letter was from the palace. Her Royal Highness Princess Hannelore would be arriving on Saturday's boat train. That gave me two days to turn my house into the sort of home fit for a princess, install my grandfather and Mrs. Huggins as butler and cook, and hire a maid for myself.

I sent for my grandfather and Mrs. Huggins then got to work immediately opening up the rest of the house. Since I moved in, I had been using my bedroom, the kitchen and the small morning room. The rest of the house remained shrouded in dust sheets. Now I went to work furiously dusting, sweeping floors and making beds. I got through with only minor mishaps. I did manage to knock the leg off a prancing horse statue, but I don't think it was Ming or anything and I found the glue to stick it back on again. Oh, and I dropped a sheet I was shaking out of the window onto a passing colonel. He wasn't too happy about it and threatened to report me to my mistress.

By the time Granddad arrived, I was exhausted. He and Mrs. Huggins toured the house without comment and I realized that they probably had no idea how much I had accomplished and thought that the house looked like this all the time. But then my grandfather stopped, his head on one side like a bird. "Don't tell me you made this bed up by yourself?"

"Of course I did. And cleaned the whole rest of the house too."

"Well, I never," Mrs. Huggins said. "And you a lady and all."

She looked rather dismayed when she saw the size of our kitchen, and even more dismayed when she saw the empty larder. I told her to make a list and stock up with food.

"I've no idea what a German princess would eat, ducks," she said. "And I can't make no foreign muck. No frog's legs and garlic and things."

"That's French," Granddad said. "Germans like their dumplings."

"You just cook what you are used to, Mrs. Huggins," I said. "I'm sure it will be perfect."

Secretly I was beginning to have serious doubts that it would be perfect. Granddad and Mrs. Huggins were lovely people, but what could they possibly know of the formality of court life? Then I reminded myself that the princess was straight from a convent. She probably had little idea of court life herself. Having settled in my butler and cook, I went to look for a maid. This was not going to be as easy as I had hoped. It seemed that all of the very best servants had fled to the country with their respective masters and mistresses. The agency promised to have some girls ready for me to interview by Monday or Tuesday—by which time they could have checked their references. When I asked if they might have someone who could fill in for the weekend, the refined lady behind the desk looked as if she were about to have a heart attack.

"Fill in?" she demanded. "For the weekend?" She winced as if each of these words were causing her pain. "I am afraid we do not handle that sort of thing." By that she implied that I had requested a stripper straight from the Casbah.

So that left me in a bit of a pickle. A princess, arriving from the Continent, would not expect to have to run her own bath, or hang up her own clothes. She probably wouldn't even know how to do either of those things. She wouldn't expect the cook to pop up from the kitchen and do it either. I needed a maid, and I needed one rapidly. I did the only thing I could think of and went posthaste to Belinda's little mews cottage in Knightsbridge.

"I need a big favor," I gasped as her maid showed me into the ultramodern sitting room with its low Scandinavian furniture and art deco mirrors. "I wondered if I could possibly borrow your maid for the weekend." (Binky would have been horrified to hear me using such awful Americanisms as the word "weekend," but for once I had no choice.)

"Borrow my maid?" She looked stunned.

"But darling, how could I possibly survive without my maid? I have to go to a party on Saturday night. Who would lay out my things? And she has Sundays off. No, I'm afraid that wouldn't work at all."

"Oh, dear," I said. "Then I'm doomed. I have a German princess arriving and only the most basic of staff."

"Last time I was at Rannoch House you had no staff at all, so things must be looking up," she said.

"I really have no staff this time—I've dragged my grandfather and his next-door neighbor up from Essex."

"Essex?" Her eyes opened wider. "You are expecting them to know how to wait on a princess?"

"It's better than nothing. The queen foisted this on me and I'm trying to do my best. Besides, the princess has just been let out of a convent. It can't be worse than that, can it?"

Belinda's face lit up. "How screamingly funny, darling."

"It's not funny at all, Belinda. It will probably be a disaster and I'll be banished to the country."

"But why is HM foisting a princess on you? Are they redecorating Buck House or something?"

"She, er, thinks the princess would have a better time with someone her own age," I said, not revealing the true reason, which was to hitch her up with the Prince of Wales. Belinda was part of the smart set and might well bump into the prince. And I didn't think she could be trusted not to spill the beans.

"I hope she's not expecting a good time with the bright young things," Belinda said, "because you don't exactly move in those circles, do you, darling?"

"If her family has taken the trouble to keep her shut away in a convent for most of her education, I rather suspect they'd like her to avoid the smart set," I said.

"Very wise. You have no idea what kind of thing is going on nowadays," Belinda said, crossing her long legs to reveal delicious white silk stockings. "The prince was at a party with another boy last night."

"The Prince of Wales?" I asked, horrified.

"No, no. He likes old hags, we know that. Prince George, I mean. The youngest son. They were passing around a snapshot of him wearing his Guardsman's helmet and nothing else."

She broke into giggles. I wondered if his mother knew anything of this, or whether he was one of the sons who was doing well in her eyes.

"I'd better go," I said. Somehow I couldn't bring myself to laugh. It was all becoming somewhat overwhelming.

"Don't forget Gussie and Lunghi's party next week, will you?" Belinda said as she escorted me to the door. "It should be tremendous fun. Gussie's father's got pots of money so I gather there will be a band and heaven knows what else."

"I don't know if I'll be able to go if I'm stuck with a princess," I said.

"Bring her along, darling. Open her eyes to what fun people we British are."

I didn't think Her Majesty would approve of the sort of parties Belinda thought were fun, and I walked home feeling as if I were about to sit for an exam for which I hadn't studied. I wondered if it would be too awful to come down with a sudden case of mumps, and thus foist the princess on to the palace instead.

Then, of course, that good old Rannoch blood won out. A Rannoch never retreats. I'd heard that often enough during my upbringing at Castle Rannoch. Who could forget Robert Bruce Rannoch, who, after his arm had been hacked off, picked up his sword with his other hand and went on fighting? I shouldn't retreat from a little thing like a visiting princess. With my head held high I marched to my destiny.

Chapter 7

Rannoch House
Saturday, June 11, 1932

> **Diary,**
> **German princess due to arrive today.**
> **Sense impending doom.**

On the way to Victoria Station to meet the boat train, I nearly lost my nerve and had to give myself a severe talking to. She is a young girl, fresh from school, I told myself firmly. She will be enchanted with the big city, and with everything about London. She will be thrilled to be alone with such a young chaperone. All will be well. She'll only stay a few days and the queen will be pleased.

Thus encouraged by this little talk, I made my way across the station, past the hissing steam engines, the shouts and toots of whistles, to the platform on the far right where the boat trains come in. As that great fire-breathing monster pulled into the station, puffing heavily, something occurred to me. I had no idea what she looked like. I was told she was a pretty little thing, but that was about it. Would she look German? How exactly did Germans look? I had met plenty when I was at school in Switzerland but people of fashion usually dressed from Paris and were indistinguishable by race.

I stationed myself at a point where all those disembarking would have to pass me and waited. I approached several young women only to be met with suspicious glances when I asked if she was a princess. The platform cleared. She hadn't come. She's changed her mind and stayed home, I thought, and a great wave of relief swept through me. Then through the clearing smoke I saw a party of three women, standing together and waving arms as they negotiated with a porter. There was a stout elderly woman, a young girl and a third woman, plainly dressed, dark, sallow and severe-looking. The young girl was enchantingly pretty— very blond with long hair twisted into a braid around her head, and wearing a navy linen sailor suit. The elderly woman was wearing an unmistakably German cape—gray and edged with green braid, plus one of those little Tyrolean hats with a feather in the side.

I hurried up to them.

"Are you, by any chance, Princess Hannelore?" I asked, addressing the young one.

"*Ja.* This is Her Highness," the old woman said, bowing to the pretty girl in the sailor suit. "You are servant of Lady Georgiana of Rannoch?" She spat out the words with a strong German accent while giving me a critical stare. "We wait for you." (Of course, she said "Vee vait.") "You are late."

"I am Lady Georgiana. I have come personally to meet Her Highness."

The older lady recoiled and gave a bobbing curtsy. "*Ach, Verzeihung.* Forgive me. Most honored that you come to meet us in person. I am Baroness Rottenmeister, companion to Her Highness."

Oh, Lord. It had never occurred to me that there would be a companion! Of course there would. How dense of me. What king would send his daughter, newly released from the convent, across from the Continent without a chaperone?

"Baroness." I bowed in return. "How kind of you to bring the princess to visit us. Will you be staying long?"

"I stay wiz princess. She stay. I stay. She go. I go," she said.

Oh, golly. And I hadn't made up a second good bedroom. How and when was I going to do that without being noticed?

"May I present Her Royal Highness, Princess Maria Theresa Hannelore Wilhelmina Mathilda?" Baroness Rottenmeister gestured with a black-gloved hand. "Highness. I present Lady Georgiana of Glen Garry and Rannoch."

The pretty young girl held out her hand. "Hiya, doll," she said in a sweet, soft voice.

I was confused. Wasn't Huyerdahl a Norwegian name? What had it to do with German?

"Huyerdahl?" I repeated.

A big smile crossed her face. "Howya doin', doll?"

"Doll?"

The smile faded. "Is that not right? I speak real good modern English. I'm the bee's knees, no?"

"Highness, where did you learn this English?" I asked, still perplexed. "They taught it in the convent?"

She giggled wickedly. "The convent? No. In our village" (she said "willage") "is good cinema and they show many American films. We climb out of convent window at night and go see movies. I see all gangster films. George Raft, Paul Muni—you seen *Scarface*?"

"No, I'm afraid I haven't seen *Scarface*."

"Real good movie—lots of shooting. Bang bang, you're dead. I love gangsters. Is there much shooting in London?"

"I'm glad to say there is very little shooting in London," I said, trying not to smile because she looked so earnest.

"Gee. That's too bad," she said. "Only shooting in Chicago then?"

"I fear so. London is quite safe."

She sighed in disappointment.

"So where do you want me to shift this lot then?" the porter asked impatiently.

"Your chauffeur waits for us outside?" Baroness Rottenmeister asked.

"I have no chauffeur in London," I said. "We'll take a taxicab."

"A taxicab? *Gott im Himmel.*"

"Taxicab. I like this." Hannelore looked excited. "My jewelcase, Irmgardt."

"I have not been presented to your friend," I said, nodding to the third woman of the party.

"Not friend. Zis is Her Highness's personal maid," Baroness Rottenmeister said coldly.

I beamed at her. She'd brought her own maid. Of course she'd brought her own maid. What normal person wouldn't? I was saved.

"Come. Vee go find taxicab," the baroness said imperiously and swept ahead of us.

Princess Hannelore sidled up to me. "Vee gonna ditch de old broad. Vee gonna have great time, you and me, babe, yeah?"

"Oh yes. Definitely." I smiled back.

When the taxi pulled up outside Rannoch House even Baroness Rottenmeister looked impressed. *"Ja,"* she said, nodding her thick neck. "Fine house. Is *gut.*"

Hannelore looked around excitedly. "Look," she whispered. A man was crossing Belgrave Square carrying a violin case. "He's a gangster."

"No, he's a violin player. He stands on the corner and earns pennies by playing the violin. I told you, there are no gangsters in London."

Hannelore took in the leafy square, a crisply starched nanny pushing a pram while a small girl beside her pushed an identical doll's pram. "I like London," she said, "even if no gangsters."

"Even if there were gangsters, I don't think you'd find them in Belgrave Square," I pointed out. "This is one of the most respectable addresses in London. Only a stone's throw from Buckingham Palace."

"Vee go meet king and queen soon?" Hannelore asked. "I'm real tickled to meet those old guys."

I could see some rapid English lessons would be needed before we met those "old guys."

I rang the doorbell, to alert my extensive staff that we had arrived. It was opened by my grandfather, wearing tails. I nearly fell over backward.

"Good afternoon, your ladyship." He bowed earnestly.

"Good afternoon, Spinks," I replied, trying not to grin. "This is Princess Hannelore with her companion, Baroness Rottenmeister, who will be staying here with us too, and her maid."

"Yer Highness. Baroness." Granddad bowed to them.

"Our trusty butler, Spinks," I said and as we entered I beheld a rotund figure in a smart blue uniform with starched white apron.

"And our housekeeper, Mrs. Huggins, my lady," Granddad said.

Mrs. Huggins dropped a curtsy. "Pleased to meet yer, I'm sure," she said.

"There are bags to be brought in from the taxi," I said, almost squirming with embarrassment. "Would you please take them straight up to the princess's bedroom. Oh, and we'll have to make up a bedroom for the baroness."

"Bob's yer uncle, me lady," Granddad said.

"Irmgardt, Mrs. Huggins will help make up a bedroom for you after you have helped with the bags," I said.

The maid stared at me blankly.

"She speaks no English," the baroness said. "She is a particularly stupid girl."

"Then please explain to her in German."

German instructions were rattled off. Irmgardt nodded dourly and went to retrieve the bags from the taxi.

"I go and see which bedroom I like," the baroness said. "I have many requirements. Must be quiet. Must not be too cold or too hot. Must be near bathroom." And before I could stop her, she stalked up the stairs.

Princess Hannelore looked at me. "She's a pain in the ass, right?"

Then she must have noticed that I looked shocked. "Highness, that's probably not an expression you should use," I said gently.

"Is bad word?" she asked innocently. "What is wrong about calling her a donkey?"

"It's not that sort of ass," I explained.

"Okey dokey," she said. "And we must be good pals. I am not Your Highness. My friends call me Hanni."

"Honey?" I asked because this was how she pronounced it.

"That's right."

"And I'm Georgie," I said. "Welcome to London."

"I know I'm gonna have a swell time," she said.

At that moment Baroness Rottenmeister came sweeping down the stairs again. "I choose room I vant," she said. "Quiet. Away from street. Your maid will make my bed for me."

"My maid?" I glanced out into the street where Mrs. Huggins and Granddad were wrestling with a mountain of cases. "I'm afraid she is not . . ."

"But she has already said she will do this for me right away. A sweet girl."

I looked up the stairs and almost fell over backward. Belinda was standing there, in a jaunty maid's uniform that looked as if it came straight out of a French farce. "All taken care of, your ladyship," she said in her best Cockney voice.

Chapter 8

By dinnertime my guests were installed in their rooms. They had taken hot baths (my grandfather having stoked the boiler up to full strength). The table was laid in the dining room with white linens and polished silver. Belinda had slipped away to go to her party, promising she'd try to come back the next day, if her hangover wasn't too terrible. Good smells were coming from the kitchen. It seemed as if this might work out after all.

"I hope your cook understands that I have a delicate stomach," Baroness Rottenmeister said as she came down to dinner. "I eat like a sparrow for the sake of my health."

Since she was of impressive girth, I privately questioned this remark. Hanni looked delightful in a pink evening gown trimmed with roses. I even began to feel hopeful that she would indeed catch the Prince of Wales's eye and all would be well with the future of the British monarchy. Maybe I'd be given a new title as a thank-you gift. Marchioness of Belgravia? And maybe it would come with property— my own estate, Lady of the Isle of somewhere or other. I'm sure there are still islands around Scotland waiting to be given away to the right person. With these happy thoughts I led my guests through to dinner.

"It's very cold in here," the baroness said. "Why is there no fire?"

"It's summertime. We never light fires after the first of May," I replied.

"I shall catch a chill," the baroness said. "I have a most delicate chest."

Her chest could in no way be described as delicate and she was wearing a fur wrap over her black evening gown. She also didn't appear to be concerned that her charge, Princess Hanni, was décolleté and wearing the lightest silk, from which she appeared to be suffering no ill effects.

Food arrived via the dumbwaiter. My grandfather served the plates.

"What is this?" The baroness poked experimentally with her fork.

"Steak and kidney pud," said Granddad. "Good old solid British grub."

"Steakandkidkneepood? Grub?" the baroness demanded. "Grub is word for insect, *ja*?"

"Cockney word for food, Yer Highness," my grandfather said.

"I do not think I shall like this," the baroness said, but she tried a small taste. "Not bad," she said, and promptly wolfed down everything on her plate.

When the pudding course arrived she looked puzzled. "There is no soup? No fish? No fowl? No salad? How am I supposed to keep my strength with so little to eat?"

"I live alone and have become used to eating simply," I said. "When we are invited to the palace to dine with the king and queen, I'm sure they will serve all of those courses."

"But until then I must suffer, I suppose," she said with dramatic resignation.

"I thought it tasted real swell," Hanni said. "Better than food at the convent. Nuns always make penance."

The dessert was placed in front of us. "And what is this now?" the baroness asked.

"Spotted dick and custard," Granddad said. "One of Mrs. Huggins's specialties."

"Spotted dick?" The baroness prodded it suspiciously. "You mean duck?"

"No, dick." Granddad caught my eye and winked.

"Duck I know. Dick I do not know," the baroness said.

I had to stare down at my plate for fear of laughing. "It's just a name," I said. "An old traditional name for a suet pudding."

"Suet? So bad for my digestion." But she ate it, clearing her plate before any-one else and not refusing seconds. "I sup-pose I have to eat something," she said with resignation. "Do all English noble families eat so simply?"

"There is a depression," I said. "We try to live simply when the ordinary people are having such a hard time."

"I see no point in being of noble birth if one can't eat well," she said. "We have so few privileges left."

"I like spotted dick," Hanni exclaimed. "And tomorrow you show me London and we go to parties and dance and have good time."

I thought that any good time might be severely restricted by Baroness Rotten-meister but wisely kept silent. Then, when the baroness excused herself for a few moments, Hanni hissed at me, "We have to get rid of pain in ass. She will not let me have good time. We should take her out."

"Take her out where?"

Hanni grinned. "You know. Take her out. Waste her. Bang bang. Curtains."

"Hanni, I don't think we're going to be able to waste the baroness, but I agree she's not going to make things pleasant for us."

"Then we must plan way to make her go home."

"How?"

"Make it not nice for her here. She likes to eat. Serve her very little food. And she likes to be warm. Open all windows. Make it cold. And she likes hot baths. Turn off hot water."

I looked at her in amazement. "For someone straight from the convent, you are quite devious," I said.

"What means devious?"

"Sneaky."

"Oh, like pulling a fast one," she said, beaming. "Yeah. Sure thing, baby."

"*Ach, dass ist gut.* You young ladies make friends. I like this," said the baroness as she reentered the room.

After coffee I escorted my guests up to bed. The baroness needed more blankets and complained that her room was damp and she was sure she saw a spider in the corner.

"I'm sorry. This house is very damp, even in summer," I said. "And I'm afraid there are often spiders. Although not many poisonous ones."

"Poisonous spiders? In London?"

"Only sometimes," I said.

And where was my maid to help her? she demanded. I explained that the maid had the night off.

"Night off? You allow servants out on Saturday night? Unheard of. In Germany

A Royal Pain   103

our servants are there when we need them."

I finally got her settled in and popped in to see how Hanni was faring. She was sitting at her dressing table while her maid, Irmgardt, brushed out her long golden hair. Truly she looked like a princess from a fairy tale.

"Hanni, I'm going to have to watch you carefully," I said. "You may break a lot of hearts in London."

"What am I to break?" she asked with that lovely innocent smile.

"Hearts. Lots of Englishmen will fall in love with you."

"I hope so," she said. "I'm gonna be hot sexy dame. You can give me tips."

"I don't know about that." I laughed nervously. "I'm supposed to be keeping my eye on you. And I certainly don't know much about being hot and sexy."

"But you are not still wirgin?" she asked.

"Werging?"

"You are voman of vorld. Not wirgin."

"Oh," I said. "I see. Well, yes, I am still a virgin, I'm afraid."

"This is not good," she said, wagging a finger at me. "Young girl like me. Eighteen years old. Men like that I am virgin. But old like you, is not good. Men think there is something wrong with you."

"I'm not that old," I said. "I won't be twenty-two until August."

But she didn't look convinced. "We must do something for you. Pretty damned quick."

"You sound like my friend Belinda."

"Belinda? I like this Belinda. I will meet her soon?"

I couldn't say "You already have, hanging up the baroness's clothes." "I'm sure you will," I said instead. "She and I are great friends. But she really is a woman of the world. If you want to know anything, ask her."

"Maybe she will find me hot sexy guy?"

"Your Highness, I rather think that you'll be expected to save yourself for marriage," I said. "You'll be expected to make a good match with a prince."

"But princes are so dull, don't you think?" she asked.

This was not a good sign. She was supposed to fall hopelessly in love with the Prince of Wales.

"We have some awfully entertaining

princes in England," I said. "You'll meet them soon."

In the middle of the night I woke up and lay there, wondering what had awoken me. Then I heard it again, the creak of a floorboard. One of my guests using the bathroom, I surmised, but I got up in case they couldn't find the light switch. I had just opened my door a few inches when I gasped: a dark figure was coming up the stairs from the ground floor. Before my heart started beating again, I recognized it was Irmgardt, Hanni's maid. She didn't notice me, but tiptoed right past and kept on going, up the next flight of stairs to the servants' quarters.

What had she been doing downstairs? I wondered. Obviously not fetching something for her mistress, or she would have brought it to her bedroom. I didn't notice anything in her hands but Fig's words about locking up the family silver did spring to mind. Surely a royal maid would have been well vetted before she was allowed to accompany a princess. Maybe she had just been looking for something as simple as a glass of water. I closed my door and went back to sleep.

Next morning I passed along Hanni's instructions to my grandfather and Mrs. Huggins. Cut back on the food and turn down the hot water. They were reluctant to do this. "What, and have them think I don't know how to cook proper?" Mrs. Huggins demanded. "I'm proud of my cooking, I am."

"And I don't want that old dragon coming after me because there's no hot water," Granddad said. "She's already waved her stick at me a couple of times."

"Tell her it's an old and eccentric boiler system in the house and it's unpredictable whether we have hot water or not. Tell her in England we are used to cold baths. My brother, the duke, takes them all the time."

"I hope you know what you're doing, ducks." Granddad shook his head. "You wouldn't want her complaining to the queen that you're not treating them proper."

"Oh, I don't think she'd do that," I said, but I wasn't sure. I rather had a feeling that this was a lost cause. Baroness Rottenmeister struck me as one of those noble creatures who will not flinch from her duty, however horrible it is. Rather like my ancestors, of course. Oh, God. I hope she doesn't have Rannoch blood!

Sunday, June 12

Diary,
Pouring with rain today. Have no idea how to entertain visiting princess plus escort. Hanni seems nice enough and should be easy. Baroness will be another matter.

On Sunday morning the baroness, Irmgardt and Hanni had to go to mass. I sent them off in a taxicab. The baroness was horrified that I wouldn't be joining them. "In England we're all C of E," I said. "Church of England," I added when she clearly didn't understand. "The head of the church is the king, my cousin. We don't have to go every Sunday if we don't want to."

"You are relation of head of church? A nation of heathens," she said and crossed herself.

When they returned, Mrs. Huggins was about to cook bacon, eggs and kidneys for breakfast but I insisted on porridge.

"This is breakfast?" the baroness asked.

"Scottish breakfast. It's what we eat at home at Castle Rannoch."

She prodded it with her spoon. "And what goes with it?"

"Nothing. Just porridge. In Scotland we eat it with a little salt."

She sighed and pulled her shawl more closely around her. Luckily the weather was cooperating for once. The brief summery spell had been replaced by usual English summer weather. It was raining cats and dogs and was distinctly chilly. Even I looked longingly at the fireplace and almost relented about lighting fires. But I knew what was at stake and bravely sought out a woolly cardigan. There was no sign of Belinda all morning. I suspected that the party had not ended until the wee hours and rising early for her meant around eleven.

Mrs. Huggins absolutely insisted on cooking a roast for Sunday lunch. "I don't want them foreigners to think we don't do things proper in England," she said. "We always have a joint on a Sunday." But I did persuade her not to do too many roast potatoes to go with it, but a lot of greens.

And for pudding something light. She suggested junket. Perfect.

The baroness ate her meat rapidly. "Good *Fleisch*," she said. "*Fleisch* is healthy." But I noticed she didn't attack the great mound of greens with the same enthusiasm, nor did she like the junket.

"Yoonkit?" she asked. "What means yoonkit?"

It had never been a favorite of mine. I always associated it with invalid food but I managed to give an impression of someone eating with gusto. After lunch it was too wet for a walk, so we sat in the cavernous drawing room while the wind whistled down the chimney. The baroness napped in an armchair. Hanni and I played rummy.

"Does nobody come to call? No visitors?" the baroness demanded, as she stirred during her nap. "Life in England is very dull."

"I think the rain is stopping." Hanni looked out of the window. "We go for walk. You show me London."

We left the baroness snoozing in her armchair.

"Let us walk through the beautiful park,"

Hanni suggested. "Very romantic place, no?"

So we walked through Hyde Park, where drops dripped on us from the horse chestnut trees and Rotten Row was sodden underfoot. The park was almost deserted until we came to Speakers' Corner. There a small crowd was gathered around a man standing on a packing case.

"The workers will rise up and take what is rightfully theirs," he was shouting, while around him other earnest young men were carrying signs saying, *Join the Communists. Make the world a better place. Down with monarchy. Equality for all. Up the workers.*

Hanni looked at them with interest. "They can say this and not be arrested?" she asked.

"This is called Speakers' Corner. You can say what you like here, however silly it is."

"You think communists are silly?" she asked.

"Don't you?"

"I think it would be nice if all people had money and houses and enough food."

"And you think the communists could deliver that? Look at the mess in Russia."

"I don't know," she said, then gave a little squeak as her glove dropped onto the wet ground. Instantly one of the young men lowered his sign and leaped for her glove.

"There you are, miss," he said, handing it back to her with a charming bow.

"Thank you very much." Hanni blushed prettily. "Your friend speaks very well," she told him.

He beamed at her. "Are you interested in coming to one of our meetings? We hold them at St. Mary's Hall in the East End. You'd be most welcome."

"You see. Communists are nice people, no?" Hanni whispered as he retrieved his sign. "He was handsome guy."

I had to agree he was handsome, even though he was wearing a threadbare tweed jacket and hand-knitted pullover. The interesting thing was that he spoke like a gentleman.

At that moment there was the tramp of boots and a group of young men wearing black shirts, adorned with an emblem of a lightning bolt, marched up to the communists.

"Go back to Russia where you belong," one of them shouted. "England for the English."

"We're as bloody English as you are, mate, and we've a right to speak here," the man shouted from his platform.

"You're a bunch of intellectual pansy boys. You're no bleedin' use to anybody," one of the blackshirts jeered and leaped up to push him from the platform. Suddenly a scuffle broke out around us. Hanni screamed. The young man she had spoken to tried to fight his way through the melee toward her, but he was punched by a large thuggish blackshirt. Suddenly a strong arm grabbed me around the waist and I found myself being propelled out of the skirmish. I looked up to protest and found myself staring at Darcy O'Mara.

"Over here, before things get ugly," he muttered and steered Hanni and me away into the park, just as the sound of police whistles could be heard.

"Those hooligans can't stop free speech in Britain. We'll show them the right way," someone was shouting as the police waded in to break up the fight.

I looked up at Darcy. "Thank you. You arrived at the right moment."

"Ah well, didn't you know I'm your guardian angel?" he asked with that wicked grin. "What on earth were you doing at a communist rally? Are you about to trade Castle Rannoch for a peasant's hovel?"

"We were only there by accident," I said. "We went for a Sunday afternoon stroll and Hanni wanted to know who was shouting."

Darcy's gaze turned to Hanni. "A friend of yours?" he asked. "I don't believe we've met."

"Highness, may I present the Honorable Darcy O'Mara, son and heir of Lord Kilhenny of Ireland. Darcy, this is Her Highess Princess Hannelore of Bavaria," I said. "She's staying with me at Rannoch House."

"Is she, by George." I saw his eyes light up. "Delighted to make your acquaintance, Your Highness." He gave a very proper bow, then lifted her outstretched hand to his lips. "I'd volunteer to escort you ladies back to Belgrave Square but unfortunately I'm already late for an appointment. I look forward to seeing you again soon, now that I'm back in London. Your Highness. My lady." Then he melted into the by-then considerable crowd.

"Wow, holy cow, hubba hubba, gee whiz. That was some guy," Hanni said. "Don't tell me he's your main squeeze!"

"My what?"

"Your honey. Your sugar. Isn't that right word?"

"In England we're a little less colorful with our language," I said.

"So you say it?"

"Boyfriend? Escort?"

"And is he?"

"Obviously not anymore," I said with a sigh.

Chapter 9

Rannoch House
Monday, June 13, 1932

Monday morning—cold and blustery again. More porridge for breakfast. Mrs. Huggins wasn't particularly good at porridge and it was like gooey wallpaper paste. I ate mine with expressions of delight. I thought the baroness might be beginning to crack.

"When will king and queen invite us to palace?" she asked hopefully.

"I couldn't say," I said. "It depends how busy they are."

"Is most irregular that princess not received at palace by king," she said; then she added, "The food at palace is good?"

"They are also trying to eat simply," I replied, knowing that they were.

"And where is your maid?"

"I'm afraid she hasn't returned from visiting her mother."

"Servants in England have no idea of duty. You must dismiss her instantly and find a good reliable German girl," the baroness said, waving her stick at me.

At that moment the post arrived, bringing two letters. One was indeed from the palace, inviting us to dinner on Tuesday evening. The other had been forwarded from my post office box and was from a Mrs. Bantry-Bynge, one of my regular customers in the house-cleaning business. Every now and then Mrs. Bantry-Bynge abandoned Colonel Bantry-Bynge and popped up to town, apparently to see her dressmaker but really for a tryst with a frightful slimy man called Boy. I had been called upon to make up the bedroom for her on several occasions now. It was easy work and she paid generously. Buying my silence, Belinda called it.

But Mrs. Bantry-Bynge needed my services this Wednesday. She would be spending Wednesday night in town, dining with friends. Oh, bugger, I muttered. It is not a word that a lady ever says out loud, but one has been known to mutter it out of earshot in times of severe crisis. How on earth was I going to find an excuse to leave Hanni and the baroness for several hours? Maybe somebody at the palace dinner party might be persuaded to invite Hanni out for a spin in a Rolls, or maybe I could prevail on Belinda, wherever she was.

I was just showing my guests the dinner invitation to the palace when there was a knock on the front door and in swept Belinda herself, looking startling in a silver mack.

"My dears, it's raining cats and dogs out there," she said as my grandfather-turned-butler helped her off with the coat. "Positively miserable, so I thought I'd better come straight to you and cheer you up with good news."

"How kind of you," I said, "but you haven't met my guests."

I led her into the morning room and presented her.

"Miss Belinda Warburton-Stoke," I said. "A great pal of mine from school."

"How do you do." Belinda executed a graceful curtsy.

"How strange." The baroness stared at Belinda. "You bear a strong resemblance to somebody."

"I have relatives all over the place," Belinda said breezily. "How are you enjoying London so far?"

"So far it has been raining and we have sat alone in this house," the baroness said.

"Oh, dear. You'll be taking them out today, won't you, Georgie?"

"Yes, I thought maybe the National Gallery, since it's raining, or the peeresses' gallery at the House of Lords."

"Georgie, how positively gloomy for them. Take them shopping. Take them to Harrods or down Bond Street."

"Oh, *ja*. Let us go shopping." Hanni's face lit up. "This I like."

"All right," I said slowly, wondering if royal protocol would force me to buy things for the princess. "We'll go shopping."

Belinda opened her handbag. "Georgie, I came to see you because the invitation arrived this morning."

"Invitation?"

"To Gussie's party, darling. Here." She handed it to me. It was impressively large.

Augustus Gormsley and Edward Fotheringay invite you to an evening of merriment, mayhem and possible debauchery at St. James's Mansions, Wed., June 15th, 8.30 p.m.

This was most tiresome. I really wanted to go, but I shouldn't take a visiting princess to an evening of possible debauchery, and I could hardly go off and leave her.

"I don't think I can go," I said. "I mean, I couldn't leave Her Highness."

"Bring her along," Belinda said cheerily. "Give her a taste of the London smart set. I understand that a prince or two might be in attendance."

"I really don't think—," I began, but Hanni peered over my shoulder and gave a squeak of delight.

"Young men and dancing," she exclaimed. "Yes, this I should like."

"Good, then it's all settled then. Wednesday at eight," Belinda said. "I'll call for you. Must fly, darling. I'm working on a new design."

I escorted her out into the hall.

"You were running an awful risk," I

hissed at her. "The old dragon almost recognized you."

"Nonsense, darling. One never recognizes servants. They are invisible."

"You were a scream, pretending to be my maid."

"I did a jolly good job too, I can tell you. And sorry about yesterday. I fully intended to come, but the truth was that I didn't get back to my own bed until five (he was divine, darling), and then I simply slept until five in the afternoon, when it was time to wake up for another party. So being a maid simply fell by the wayside."

"That's all right. The princess has a maid with her who has been press-ganged into looking after both of them. And Binky has sent me a little money to engage a new maid for myself and the agency is supposed to be rounding up suitable girls."

"Choose one who isn't talkative," Belinda said. "Nothing is worse than waking up in the morning to chatter, chatter when they bring in the tea. And then you never know to whom she will spill the beans about certain people who stayed the night. One does have a reputation of sorts, you know."

"That wouldn't apply to me," I replied. "My maid might die of boredom."

"Things will change, you'll see. You've only been here a couple of months. Once you're in with our set it will be party after party. And this little do of Gussie Gormsley's is just the thing. Everyone will be there, I can assure you."

"Are you sure I should bring the princess to a wild party?"

"Oh yes." Belinda grinned. "What better way to introduce her to life outside the convent? So until then"—she kissed my cheek—"toodlepip."

And she was gone, running down the front steps and out into the rain.

Baroness Rottenmeister insisted on coming with us to Harrods. I was rather reluctant to go there, as Harrods had been the site of one of the humiliations of my life. I had served behind the cosmetics counter for all of three hours before being sacked. But today I would be going as myself, accompanied by a princess and a baroness. I didn't anticipate any problems.

Hanni was like a small child in a toy shop the moment she entered the store. She danced from counter to counter uttering little squeaks of joy. "Oh, look. Rings. Necklaces. And lovely handbags. Oh, look, lipsticks." I had to admit that her vocabulary was quite impressive in this area and I wondered how she would have encountered English words like "cosmetics" at the convent. Maybe there were interludes between gang fights in those American movies. Maybe the gangsters' molls talked about their cosmetic preparations. We passed from accessories to the dress department.

"Oh, zat is a beautiful dress. I must try it on." Hanni was almost embracing it and a shop assistant was bearing down with a gleaming look in her eyes. "I have no sexy dress to wear to party. Just boring German dresses." She glanced at the tag. "It is only twenty-five pounds."

"That is the belt, madam," the assistant said, appearing miraculously behind her. "The dress is three hundred guineas."

"Three hundred. Is that much?" Hanni asked me innocently.

"Much," I said.

"I try anyway." She beamed at the assistant, while I tried to think of a way to tell her I had no money without general embarrassment. Perhaps the baroness had her checkbook with her.

"Is the young lady visiting from abroad?" the assistant asked me.

"She is Princess Hannelore of Bavaria," I said and noticed the woman's demeanor change instantly.

"Your Highness. What an honor. Let me bring you some other dresses to try on."

We spent a happy half hour, with Hanni looking more delightful in each successive dress and me feeling more ill at ease about who was expected to pay for them.

"I believe you've seen all our evening gowns now, Your Highness," the assistant said.

Hanni waved her arms expansively. "I will take them all," she said.

"No, you can't." The tension burst forth from me, louder than I had intended.

"Of course not," the assistant said, beaming at Hanni. "One would never expect you to have the inconvenience of carrying the dresses with you. We will have them delivered in the van this afternoon."

"Does the baroness have money from your father to pay for these dresses?" I asked.

"I do not." The baroness almost spat the words.

"Then I'm afraid you can't have them," I said.

"We will telephone my father." Hanni was pouting. "He will want me to have fashionable dress for meeting king and queen, not boring German dress."

"German dress is not boring," the baroness said, her face now beetroot red. "You should be proud to wear German dress. Come, Hannelore. We go now."

I gave the shop assistant a remorseful smile as Hanni was ushered out. We had almost reached the front entrance of the store when I felt a tap on my arm. It was a man in a frock coat and he was frowning. "Excuse me, madam, but were you intending to pay us now for the princess's purchase or should we send a bill?"

"Her purchase?" The dresses were surely still hanging in the fitting room.

"The handbag, madam." He indicated Hanni's arm, which was now tucked through the strap of a delightful white kid purse. "Fifty guineas."

"Your Highness?" I grabbed Hanni before she stepped out into the street. "I think you forgot to put back the handbag you were examining."

Hanni stared down at her arm in surprise. "Oh yes. So I did." And she handed it back to the floorwalker with a sweet smile. I sat in the taxi home watching Hanni as she pouted. Had she really forgotten the handbag or was she intending to sneak it out of the store?

"I must marry a rich man very soon," Hanni declared. "And so must you, Georgie. Will there be rich men at the party we go to?"

"Yes, I think there will."

"Good. Then we will each choose one." She paused, thoughtfully. "Will the beautiful man who saved us yesterday be there, do you think?"

"I don't think so," I said, hoping that he wouldn't. I had seen Darcy's eyes light up when he saw Hanni. "And men are not described as beautiful. They are handsome."

"He was beautiful," Hanni said wistfully.

I had to agree that he was. Probably the most beautiful man I was ever going to meet.

Chapter 10

That night Mrs. Huggins served toad in the hole and rice pudding. It was nursery food at its plainest and the baroness stared in horror when it was put before her.

"Toad in 'ole?" she asked, imitating Granddad's Cockney. "Toad? This is like frog, no? You bake frog in this pooding?"

"It's just a name," I said, although I was so tempted to let her think she was eating a baked toad. "We have a lot of quaint names for our food in English."

"I like toad in 'ole," Hanni said. "It tastes good."

And so it did. Like a lot of plain food, toad in the hole is delicious if well cooked, and I've always had a weakness for sausages.

"If is not frog, then what is it?" the baroness demanded of my grandfather.

"It's bangers, ducks," my grandfather said, smiling at Hanni. Those two had set up an immediate bond.

"You mean ducks that have been shot?" the baroness asked. "It does not taste like duck."

"Not ducks. Bangers," Grandfather said patiently.

"He means sausages. English sausages."

"But this is food for peasants," the baroness said.

"I like," Hanni muttered again.

The baroness went to bed early in a huff, muttering "no bathwater, no heat and toads to eat," all the way up the stairs.

I was still pondering how I was going to slip out to carry out my assignment with Mrs. Bantry-Bynge on Wednesday morning. Then, overnight, a brilliant idea struck me. I hadn't heard from the agency about my new maid. I could claim I was going to interview candidates for the post. This brilliant scheme was frustrated by a telephone call while we were eating breakfast on Tuesday morning. It was the domestic agency; they had found a highly suitable person for the position if I might have the time to interview her.

"I'm afraid I must leave you to your own devices this morning," I said as I came back into the breakfast room. (It was kippers this time. The baroness complained about the bones.) "But I have to go and interview a new maid."

"What happened to your other maid?" the baroness asked. "Where has she gone? I thought she was good."

"Good, but unreliable," I said. "She went out on Saturday night and didn't turn up again. So I took your advice and decided I had to let her go."

She nodded. "*Gut.* One must be firm at all times with servants."

"So if you will excuse me, I need to interview her replacement. Maybe you would like to take a tour of the National Gallery. There are fine paintings there, I believe."

"It is raining too much," the baroness

said. "And the princess needs to rest before our dinner at the palace. She must look her best."

"But I feel fine," Hanni complained. "I want to go see London. Meet people. Have a good time."

"The princess will rest," said the baroness. "She will write letters home."

"Okay." Hanni sighed.

I set off for the domestic agency feeling as if I were about to sit for a stiff examination. Hiring servants wasn't something I did every day—in fact I'd never done it before.

"I believe we have finally found a suitable maid for you, my lady." The woman at the desk was quite intimidating in her immaculate gray suit and white jabot. A cross between a hospital matron and school headmistress and with an air of more refinement than I could ever hope to achieve. She looked distinctly pleased with herself. "This is Mildred Poliver."

A woman in her forties rose to her feet and dropped a curtsy. "I am delighted to make your acquaintance, your ladyship. It would be an honor to serve you."

"I'm sure you'd like to ask Miss Poliver

some questions," the headmistress lady said.

"Oh yes. Of course." I tried to sound efficient and breezy, as if I interviewed servants on a regular basis. "Um—what experience do you have, Miss Poliver?"

"I have been a leedy's maid for twenty-naine yahrs," she said in the sort of refined accent that those born to the lower classes seem to think sounds upper-class. "My last position was with Brigadier Sir Humphry Alderton. Do you know the Humphry Aldertons by any chance?"

"Not personally."

"A faine family. Very refained."

"So why did you leave?"

"They were returning to India and I had no wish to go to that country. I can't abide the heat, you see."

"I see."

"Mrs. Humphry Alderton gave me a glowing reference. It is here, should you wish to see it."

I glanced over it. *Mildred is a gem. Don't know what I'll do without her . . .*

"This looks quite satisfactory," I said.

"Miss Poliver would naturally expect a

wage commensurate with her experience," the dragon said.

"How much did you receive at your last
position?"

"Seventy-five pounds a year, all found. I
require Thursday afternoons and Sunday
evenings free."

"That sounds satisfactory," I said. I was
sure the maids at home got nothing like
seventy-five pounds a year. More like
twenty. I was also calculating that Binky
had given me one hundred pounds to
cover the maid and the expenses of feed-
ing our German visitors, and the baroness
would soon prove expensive to feed. But
then I didn't have to keep Mildred Poliver
after my guests had gone. I could find
some excuse to get rid of her. My honest
nature won out of course.

"I should point out that the position may
only be temporary."

"Temporary?"

"I am not sure how long I am remaining
in London and I do have a personal maid
at Castle Rannoch."

"As it happens, a temporary assignment would suit me to a tee," Mildred said.

"I did so enjoy living in the country and I am not sure how I will like the hustle and bustle of London."

We shook hands and Mildred offered to start that very afternoon.

"That would suit me very well," I said. "We are expected for dinner at the palace tonight."

"The palace? Fancy." The two women exchanged impressed nods.

"Well, of course, your ladyship is related to the royal family, it stands to reason," Mildred said. I could see the wheels of her mind already working. She was going to enjoy boasting about the royal connection. She was probably even hoping that a royal relative might pop in for tea from time to time. I had actually taken an instant dislike to her but could find no way of rejecting her. It's only temporary, I told myself. A Rannoch can handle adversity.

Mildred set off to collect her things and I went home. With Mrs. Huggins's help I prepared a room for her, next to Irmgardt's, up under the eaves. It felt bitterly cold and damp up there and I understood for the first time why Irmgardt always looked so disgruntled. Could I possibly expect Mildred to be satisfied with such surroundings? Maybe she was used to adversity. But then maybe she would only stick it out for a few days, which would suit me well. She arrived not long after, bearing a pitifully small suitcase, and gushed over the impressive nature of Rannoch House's hallway. She was rather more quiet when I took her up three flights to her room.

"It's rather spartan," was all she managed.

"Of course we can make it more comfortable," I said rapidly. I couldn't understand why I was trying to please her. She was rather intimidating.

"And I should point out that my name is Mildred," she said. "I am never called Millie. Never."

"Of course not." I was apologizing again as if I had intended to be on chummy Millie–Georgie terms with her any moment.

I took her on a tour of the house. She approved of my bedroom, but not of the clothes draped over the backs of chairs. "I can tell your ladyship has been without a competent maid for a while," she said. "And the state of your clothes, my lady.

Did your last maid not know how to use an iron?"

"Not very well," I said hastily. "Now, this room next to mine is currently occupied by my guest, Princess Hannelore of Bavaria."

"A princess here. Fancy." I rose in her estimation again.

"She has her own maid, called Irmgardt. We'll see if she's in here and I can introduce you, although she doesn't appear to speak anything but German."

I pushed open Hanni's bedroom door. There was no sign of Irmgardt. Hanni had obviously been writing letters. A piece of writing paper lay on her bedside table, on which someone had written in big letters *C.P.???* The envelope lay beside it. It bore a W.1. postmark. So Hanni did know someone else in London after all.

Chapter 11

Buckingham Palace
Tuesday, June 14, 1932

Diary,
Buck House this evening. Oh, Lord, I hope Hanni doesn't do her gangster impression! I hope everything goes smoothly. Maybe the queen will be so enchanted with Hanni that she'll invite her to stay at the palace instantly. . . .

It felt strange to have a maid dress me for the dinner at the palace. I had become so used to fending for myself that I was embarrassed to stand there like a dressmaker's dummy while Mildred fussed around me, powdering my shoulders, hooking my dress, slipping my feet into my evening shoes and then doing my hair. She despaired about the latter.

"May I suggest a good cut and a permanent wave, my lady? Waves are fashionable these days."

"I'll consider it," I said lamely.

"And what jewelry has your ladyship selected for tonight?"

I hadn't even thought about jewelry. "I don't know. I have some nice pearls."

"Pearls?" She sounded as if I had said a rude word. "Pearls are not worn in the evening, unless, of course, they are exceptional pearls of great size and history. Is your necklace of great size and history? Does it include other precious stones?"

I had to admit that it didn't.

"May I suggest rubies, given the color of the dress," she said.

"I don't own rubies. I do have garnets."

"Garnets?" She actually looked pained.

In the end I handed her my jewel case and let her select. "The good stuff is at home in the vault," I said, trying to redeem myself. "My family worried about burglaries in London."

As I went downstairs to meet my guests I hated myself for letting her upset me. She was, after all, the servant and I the mistress. Why should I care if she thought my jewelry pathetic or my dresses crumpled?

Hanni looked stunning in an evening version of a German dirndl, the baroness fearsome in black with several strings of jet around her neck and a fierce black feathered concoction sticking out of her bun at the back of her head. As we rode to the palace in the taxicab, I gave Hanni a few last-minute warnings. "Please do not talk about gangsters or call Her Majesty a doll, babe or broad," I said.

"Okeydokey," she said happily. "I'll talk like London person now. Your butler, he help me."

This did not sound encouraging, but before I could do any more warning, we were turning in through the palace gate and pulled up in the courtyard. Liveried lackeys leaped forward to open the taxicab door and we climbed out. We were ushered into a brightly lit foyer. "Their Majesties are awaiting you upstairs," we were told.

"Bob's your uncle. We go up the apples and pears here," Hanni said loudly and brightly and started to ascend the broad marble stair decorated with gilt and statues.

"Maybe you shouldn't try to talk like a London person," I whispered.

"Apples and pears is not right?"

"Not for the palace. At least not for this palace. At the Hammersmith Palace it would be fine."

"Which palace?" she asked.

"Never mind. Just listen to what I say and try to use the same words."

At the entrance to the gallery we were announced and stepped into a room already full of people, most of whom I didn't know. The king and queen were standing at the far end, looking remarkably regal even though this was classed as an informal evening with no tiaras or sashes. The queen held out a white-gloved hand and greeted us warmly.

"Hannelore, my dear, we've so been wanting to meet you. How are you enjoying London so far?"

I held my breath, waiting for Hanni to answer in gangster or Cockney terms.

Instead even she seemed a little awestruck. "I like very much," she said. "And I too am wanting to meet the lovely English queen and see the lovely palace."

"We must show you around on another occasion," the queen said.

"This I would like." Hanni beamed at them. So far so good.

"I do hope our sons are going to join us for dinner," the queen said. "I would so like you to meet them."

As if on cue the Prince of Wales sauntered up and gave his mother a peck on the cheek. He looked terribly dashing in his dinner jacket and black tie. (White tie and tails were reserved for formal occasions.)

"I'm glad you could come after all, David," the queen said.

"Just popped in but I can't stay long," he said. "I'm dining with friends."

"David, how tiresome. I particularly asked you to come and meet our guest from Germany. Princess Hannelore."

The prince nodded and spoke a few words in German to Hanni, who responded with a charming blush.

"I had hoped that my second son, the

Duke of York, and his wife would be able to join us," the queen said, "but apparently one of their daughters is not well and they thought it wiser to stay home."

"He stays home because his daughter has the sniffles," David said with a derisive snort. "He positively wallows in domesticity these days. Hardly ever goes out. The devoted papa, you know."

"At least he has given me grandchildren," the queen said sotto voce as the prince turned away. "May I remind you that we don't have an heir yet."

"Don't start that again, for God's sake," the prince muttered back to her, then raised his voice. "In fact I think that's my cue to exit. Princess, Georgie, I bid you adieu for now." He nodded briefly to Hanni and me and disappeared into the crowd as the queen gave me a despairing look.

Hanni was taken around to be introduced to the guests by an elderly general who seemed rather smitten with her while I stood beside the queen.

"How are we ever to bring them together?" she asked me. "You must take her to the smart parties that David attends."

"I don't get invited to smart parties, ma'am," I said. I wasn't sure that the mayhem and debauchery of the following night should be mentioned. "And besides, if the Prince of Wales goes to a party, he is likely to be accompanied by the American lady."

"Woman," the queen corrected. "Certainly no lady. But I suppose you're right. She has him in her clutches and she's not going to let go. We'll have to think of something, Georgiana. You have a good brain. You come up with a plan."

"The Bavarian lassie is definitely charming," the king muttered to his wife as he drew close to her. "Did the boy seem interested?"

"Can't say that he did," she replied curtly.

"That boy will be the death of me," the king said as he moved off again.

As the royal couple greeted more guests, the baroness reappeared, beaming, with Hanni in tow. "I have found good friend here," she said. "Come. You must meet."

We were taken through the crowd.

"My good friend Dowager Countess

Sophia," Baroness Rottenmeister said proudly, "and her nephew, Prince Siegfried."

I mumbled something and prayed for the dinner gong, or at least a large earthquake, while I waited for doom to fall. Any minute now she'd shriek, "But she came to clean my house!"

Apparently Belinda had been right and servants really are invisible, because she greeted me quite pleasantly. Siegfried chatted away in German to Hannelore, who insisted on answering him in her broken English. Hope rose in my heart. Maybe those two might make a match and I'd be off the hook. Knowing his predilection for boys, I didn't think it would be a very satisfying marriage for Hanni, but she didn't seem to possess many scruples. She probably wouldn't mind taking a lover or two.

Then the gong sounded and we were led in to dinner. I was seated next to Siegfried and had to listen to his account of how he had shot the world's largest wild boar in Bohemia. "As big as a bus with tusks as long as this," he exclaimed, almost knocking over a glass. As I nodded and muttered occasionally, Hanni's high, clear voice floated down the table to me. "*Ja,* I am liking the English food. The spotted dick and the bangers and the toad in the 'ole. They're the bee's knees."

She wasn't close enough to kick.

"How fascinating," said an elderly viscountess as she peered at Hanni through her lorgnette.

"Maybe in wintertime you come visit Romania and we go shoot wild boar," Siegfried was saying to me.

"Princess Hannelore likes shooting things," I said, bringing her into this conversation. "Don't you, Hanni?"

"Yeah, bang bang. Shooting is fun."

And they were off, discussing guns. Siegfried looked rather puzzled when Hanni mentioned machine guns and violin cases, and I had to explain that she was talking of a shoot-out in a gangster film. They seemed to be getting along splendidly. Unfortunately the queen wasn't equally delighted. As we ladies withdrew while the men passed the port and lit up cigars, she drew me to one side.

"Siegfried seemed to be paying her too much attention," she said. "We can't let that happen. You must show more enthusiasm for him, Georgiana. Men like to be flattered. And as for Hannelore, I'm counting on you to find a way to bring her and my son together."

She had just moved away to talk with another guest when the baroness came barreling down on me, still beaming. "Vonderful news," she said. "My kind friend the Dowager Countess Sophia has invited me to stay at her house. She has a good German chef and central heating and plenty of hot water. I shall take Hannelore and stay there."

Oh, dear. I didn't think the queen would approve of Hanni being under the same roof as Siegfried. My life seemed to be one continual stepping out of the frying pan and into the fire.

Chapter 12

Fortunately Hanni flatly refused to move to the dowager countess's house.

"But I like it with Georgie," she said. "The queen wishes I stay with Georgie."

"But Your Highness needs a chaperone," the baroness said. "What would your father say?"

"Georgie will be my chaperone. And Irmgardt will stay to look after me."

The baroness went to say something, looked hard at me, then closed her mouth again. I could tell she was torn between her duty to the princess and the good food and warmth that awaited at the

dowager countess's house. Finally she
nodded. "Very well. But you must not
leave London without me and I insist that
I accompany you to all official functions.
Your father would expect it."

And so it was settled. Baroness Rottenmeister would move out the very next
morning. I went to bed feeling optimistic
for the first time in weeks. I awoke to a
bump, a yelp and someone creeping
around my room. I sat up, terrified. "Who's
there?" I asked.

"Sorry, m'lady," said a voice from over
near the window, and a curtain was drawn
back, revealing Mildred. "I was bringing up
your morning tea, but I'm not yet familiar
with the layout of your furniture and I
bumped into your dressing table. It won't
happen again, I promise."

She came across to the bed and
placed a tray on my bedside table. The
tray contained a cup of tea with a biscuit
beside it. "When should I run your ladyship's bath?" she asked.

I was beginning to see that this maid
business might have some advantages.
At home at Castle Rannoch we had never

indulged in luxuries like tea in bed. I was
contemplating lying there, reading the
Times and sipping tea, when I remembered that I had a busy morning ahead of
me: I had to see the baroness suitably
transported to Park Lane and clean Mrs.
Bantry-Bynge's house. How on earth was
I going to manage that?

"And what are your ladyship's social
engagements for today?" Mildred asked.
"What outfit may I lay out for you?"

I could hardly say that I was going to
sweep floors and wear a maid's uniform.
"Oh, nothing special. A skirt and jersey. I
can select them myself when I've had my
bath."

"Certainly not, my lady. I am here to
give service and service I shall give."

I sighed as she brought out a linen
skirt and a silk blouse. Both had already
been miraculously cleaned and pressed.
Somehow, somewhere I was going to
have to change from the clothes Mildred
wanted me to wear into my uniform.

"You may run my bath now, Mildred," I
said. "I have a morning visit I must pay"—
then I remembered the happier news of

the day—"and the baroness will be leaving us, so maybe you could assist Irmgardt with her packing."

I bathed, dressed and put my maid's uniform into a carrier bag, then I went downstairs to find my guests already at breakfast. In honor of the baroness's departure Mrs. Huggins had made bacon and kidneys and the baroness was devouring them as if she had been starving for months. "At last. Good *Fleisch*," she said, smacking her lips.

I hoped the *Fleisch* wasn't so good that she had changed her mind about moving in with the dowager countess.

"I'm afraid I have to go out for a while this morning," I said. "I expect Hannelore would like to accompany you to Park Lane to make sure you are comfortably settled."

"Where do you go?" Hanni asked.

"Oh, just to visit a friend."

"I come with you," Hanni said firmly. "Is boring with old broads."

Oh, dear. "I'm afraid the friend I'm going to visit is very elderly herself," I said. "Bedridden, in fact, and not very well. I visit out of duty, once a month."

"I can come and make her happy,"

Hanni said. "Old women in bed like to see young smiling faces."

"Not this one. She only likes to see people she knows. Otherwise she becomes confused. And of course she has a rash, but I don't think it's catching." I heard a gasp from the baroness.

"Princess Hannelore will come with me," she said.

"Good idea." I heaved a sigh of relief. "I will call to escort you home in time for a rest before the party."

"I am thinking it is my duty to come to this party with Her Highness," the baroness said.

This day was turning into one complication after another.

"I'm afraid you would have a most disagreeable time," I said. "It will be young people and jazz music."

"Highly unsuitable," the baroness muttered. "I don't think her father would approve."

"My father wants me to meet young people," Hanni said.

"Young people of good family," I added. "And I promise to watch over the princess at all times."

The baroness snorted but I think was relieved to get out of an evening of jazz, not to mention debauchery. I offered my maid's services to help her pack, my butler to summon a cab and transport her luggage, and then I slipped down to the servants' quarters to change into my maid's uniform and slip out through the servants' entrance without being seen.

"So your little plan worked, did it?" my grandfather asked. "The old Kraut is off?"

"Yes, thank goodness. I told her you'd summon a cab and take down her luggage for her."

"Is she taking that maid, that Fireguard person, with her?" Mrs. Huggins poked her head around the kitchen door.

"No, Irmgardt is the princess's maid. She'll obviously be staying here," I said.

Mrs. Huggins sighed. "Gives me the willies, that one does. Drifting in and out like a black shadow, staring at you with a face that could curdle milk."

"She can't help her face, Mrs. Huggins, and she doesn't speak English, which must make it hard for her."

"I've tried teaching her English words but she don't seem too eager to learn.

Thick as a plank, if you ask me. And downright unfriendly."

"I don't suppose the Germans think more kindly of us than we do of them," Granddad said. "But she won't even take her meals down here with us. Puts her food on a tray and then takes it up to her room. What with her and your Miss Lah-dee-dah . . ."

"Mildred, you mean?"

"Frightfully posh, she is. If she sticks her nose in the air any higher, she'll fall over backwards," Mrs. Huggins said.

I had to laugh. "Yes, she is rather annoying, isn't she? But it won't be for long, I promise. It's no easier for me, I can assure you. At least we're getting rid of the baroness. And I have to go out, I'm afraid."

I slipped into the downstairs cloakroom, changed into my maid's uniform and crept out of the tradesmen's entrance when no one was looking. I had to get through my assignment at Mrs. Bantry-Bynge's as early as possible. Mrs. B-B was not due until the afternoon, but I had once encountered her gentleman friend. He had been rather too friendly and I had no wish to fight him off again. I assumed that men such as he were not early risers so I hoped to complete my work unmolested. I took the bus to Regent's Park and had the whole thing done before noon, without any embarrassing encounters with men in blazers, then I went home to change out of my maid's uniform before I went to Park Lane to collect Hanni.

When I arrived home I was greeted by my grandfather.

"The princess isn't back yet, is she?" I asked.

He had a strange look on his face. "No," he said. "But there was a telephone call for her while you were out. It seems the piece of jewelry she saw this morning at Garrard's is ready to be delivered. They pointed out that they require C.O.D. for an item of that price. Apparently it's emeralds." He watched me wince. "That young lady needs watching," he said.

"You can say that again." I sighed. "Yesterday she tried to sneak a handbag out of Harrods. Now I suppose I'll have to explain to Garrard's that there has been a mistake. I just hope she didn't have it engraved."

"That's what happens if you keep girls locked away in a convent," Granddad said. "They go off the rails when they get out. If I were you, I'd let the queen know what you're going through, and ship Her Highness back to Germany. Nothing good ever did come out of that country!"

"Beethoven. Mendelssohn. Handel," I pointed out, "and Moselle wine. And I thought you'd taken a fancy to the princess."

"She seemed a nice enough little thing," he agreed. "But she still wants watching. She don't think like you and me."

I suffered an embarrassing interview at Garrard's, during which I had to hint that madness ran in the princess's family, then I went to Park Lane to bring Hanni home.

"But Siegfried escorted her back to your house immediately after luncheon," the baroness exclaimed. "I don't understand."

"She probably just went for a walk," I said. "It is a lovely day."

"That girl needs a good spanking," the baroness said. "I should not have let her out of my sight. Perhaps I should come back to your house after all. I am neglecting my duty."

"I'll go and find her right away and keep a closer watch on her," I said. "I'm sure there is nothing to worry about."

Of course I wasn't at all sure. I didn't mention the Garrard's episode. My grandfather was right. The sooner she was shipped back to Germany, the better.

I had no idea where to look for her and had visions of her rifling Harrods or buying up Bond Street at this very moment. I walked around aimlessly for a while then came home to find that Hanni had returned and was resting. She had fallen asleep and looked positively angelic. My opinion of her softened. She was, after all, a very young girl in the big city for the first time. She just didn't know the rules yet.

Chapter 13

Belinda called for us at eight. She was wearing the outfit she had made me model for Mrs. Simpson—black silk trousers with a white backless top. Stunning on her, of course—an utter disaster on me. I felt positively dowdy in my flowing taffeta panels made by our gamekeeper's wife. Hanni wore the same pale pink affair she had worn to dinner the first night. She looked the way a princess should look in fairy stories. I half expected to see her followed by dwarves.

We could hear the party in full swing as we pulled up in the taxicab outside St.

James's Mansions. The deep thump thump of a jazz beat and the wail of saxophones floated down into the refined air of Arlington Street, making a pair of old gentlemen, on their way to their club, wave their canes and mutter about the youth of today and what they needed was a stint in the colonies or a good war in Africa. The flat was in one of the big modern blocks that overlook Green Park. We rode in the lift to the sixth floor and as the doors opened, we were hit by the full force of the sound. This was no gramophone recording. They had a full jazz band in there!

The front door was unlatched and Belinda didn't wait to be invited in. She went straight in and motioned for us to follow her. We stood in the square marble entrance hall, overwhelmed with the level of music. An archway led to the main living room. The lights were low and a smoky haze hung in the air, but I got an impression of white walls, low chrome furniture and highly modern paintings. At least I think they were paintings. To me they looked as if someone had hurled paint at a canvas and then jumped around on it. The carpet had been rolled back and the parquet floor was packed with gyrating couples. A colored jazz band took up most of the dining alcove. There was a bar in the hallway, with a steady procession of young people in the most fashionable evening clothes passing to and fro with cocktail glasses.

The only parties I had been to in my short and dull life had been the coming-out balls during my season, all taking place in well-lit and well-chaperoned ballrooms—at which the strongest concoctions had been punch with a hint of champagne. Apart from those there were the Christmas parties at Castle Rannoch with Scottish reels and bagpipes, plus the odd summons to Balmoral for the royal equivalent. But nothing like this. This was the sort of sinful, smart party I had dreamed of. And now I was here, I was overcome with awkwardness.

Belinda plunged right in, sailing up to the bar. "What are we making tonight, darlings?" she asked. "Can we manage a sidecar? Oh, and make it a double while you're about it, there's an angel."

She looked back at Hanni and me, still standing just inside the front door.

"Come on. What are you drinking?"

"I try some moonshine," Hanni said. "That is what Edward G. Robinson drinks."

"Hanni, this is England. Drinking is legal here. We don't need moonshine," I said.

At that moment the dance number ended and Gussie Gormsley came out of the drawing room, dabbing at his face with a red silk handkerchief. "My God, it's like a Turkish bath in there," he said. "A drink, my good man, and rapidly." Then he saw us and looked genuinely pleased. "Hello, Georgie, hello, Belinda. You came. Splendid. Hoping you would." Then his eyes moved to Hanni. "And who is this delightful creature?"

"This is Princess Hannelore of Bavaria," I said. "She's staying with me. I hope you don't mind that we brought her along."

"Not at all. Delighted. Most welcome, Princess."

"Call me Hanni," she said, graciously extending a hand to him.

"Hanni, this is one of our hosts, Augustus Gormsley," I said.

"Call me Gussie, everyone else does. And we're having a positively royal evening. Half the crowned heads of Europe will be here before the night is over. But where are my manners? You ladies need a drink before I introduce you."

He went up to the bar and handed us something pink with a cherry in it. "That will put hair on your chest," he said.

"But I do not wish hair on my chest," Hanni said, causing a general laugh.

"I'm sure your chest is absolutely beautiful the way it is," Gussie replied, studying it earnestly. "Come on in and meet people."

"It's awfully loud," Belinda said. "I'm surprised the police haven't shown up yet."

"Already been and gone, old thing," Gussie replied with a grin. "And we have the helmet to prove it. We did send the poor chap off with ten quid to keep him happy, however."

He took Hanni and me by the arm and steered us into the drawing room. "Look what I just found out in the hall," he called to Lunghi Fotheringay.

Introductions were made. Lunghi made a beeline for Hanni and steered her out to the balcony to see the view.

"He doesn't waste any time, does he?" Gussie said, looking a little disappointed. "Now, let's see. Who do you know?"

"I'm sure nobody," I said. "I don't exactly mix with the smart set."

"Nonsense," Gussie said. "I'm sure you know old Tubby, don't you? Tubby Tewkesbury? Everyone knows old Tubby."

A large, red-faced fellow turned at the sound of his name. That face lit up when he saw me. "What-ho, Georgie. Didn't expect to see you at a bash like this. In fact, I haven't seen you since you came out. Down in London for a while, are you?"

"I'm living here now. Attempting to make my own way in the world."

"Splendid. That is good news. Although you don't want to get mixed up with this lot. They'll lead you down the road to perdition, you know."

"Ah, but think of the fun she'll have along the way," Gussie said. "Come on, drink up."

The band struck up again and Tubby dragged me onto the dance floor. His gyrations were even more dangerous than those around us and I was lucky to come out of the dance with no black eyes or broken toes. "Another drink, I think," he said, as the sweat ran down his face. "Same for you, old thing?" and he took my glass for a refill before I could answer.

I stood alone, looking around the room, trying to recognize faces in the dark, and found myself looking directly at a face I knew only too well.

"Mother!" I exclaimed. "What are you doing here?"

"Having fun, darling, the same as you," she said. She was reclining in one of the low leather armchairs, a cigarette holder held nonchalantly in one hand, a cocktail glass in the other. "Dear Noel insisted on bringing me."

"Noel?"

"Noel Coward, darling. You must have heard of Noel. Everybody knows Noel. He writes the most divine plays and acts in them too. So talented. And he positively adores me."

"Mummy, so he was the man who was making you think of ditching Max?"

She laughed. "Oh no, no, no. He doesn't adore me in that way, I assure you, darling. But he's trying to persuade me to return to the stage. He wants to write a play especially for little *moi.* Isn't that touching?"

"Don't tell me you're actually thinking of returning to the stage?"

She looked coy. "Noel has been absolutely begging me. And I have to admit, it might be fun."

"You should take him up on his offer," I said. "You can't go on relying on men to support you for the rest of your life, you know."

She laughed, that wonderfully melodious peal that made heads turn throughout a room. "You are so sweet. If I were desperate I believe I'm still officially married to a deadly dull Texan millionaire and I could go and live on a ranch for the rest of my days. If not he, then several others are lining up for the position, you know. But as it happens, I'm not desperate. I do have a teeny bit tucked away for a rainy day, and that sweet little villa outside Cannes that Marc-Antoine gave me."

"Marc-Antoine?"

"The French racing driver who was so tragically killed at Monte Carlo. I truly believe I could have been happy with him for the rest of my life." An expression of grand tragedy covered her face, then the smile broke through again. "Well, maybe not. All those exhaust fumes. So bad for the complexion."

"So you're seriously considering going back on the stage?"

"I'm sorely tempted," she said. "But I can already hear the whispers: 'She started off as a duchess and it's been all downhill from there on.'"

"As if you worry what people say," I said. "There must have been a good deal of talk during your life."

She laughed again. "You're right. To hell with what people say. And speaking of what people say, you missed the grand entrance of the evening."

"Grand entrance and it wasn't yours?"

"The Prince of Wales, darling, with the dreadful American woman clinging to his arm."

"He brought her here with Mr. Simpson in tow?"

"He did indeed."

"The queen will be furious," I said. "Where are they now?"

My mother was positively gloating. "The spider-woman took one look at me and announced that the party wasn't her thing. 'You didn't tell me that the riffraff would be here, David,' she said and stalked out."

"Damned cheek."

"That's what I thought, considering I have legitimately been a duchess and she hasn't risen above the rank of American housewife. But they left and I stayed, which I consider a victory, darling." She sat up, suddenly alert. "Ah, there Noel is now, darling. Noel, have you brought me another drink, my sweet?"

The suave and elegant figure whom I recognized from the pages of countless magazines glided toward us with a glass in each hand and an ebony cigarette holder balanced between his fingers. "Your wish is my command, as you well know," he said. "Here's to us, darling, the two most beautiful and talented people in the room."

"And may I introduce my daughter, Georgiana?" My mother gestured to me.

"Don't be ridiculous, you are not old enough to have a daughter out of nappies."

"You are such a flatterer," she said. "You know I positively adore you."

"Not as much as I adore you."

I looked around to escape from this orgy of adoration and beat a tactful retreat toward the hallway. Hanni was standing surrounded by a group of young men.

"I like English parties," she said to me as I joined them.

Noel Coward reappeared, having apparently torn himself away from my mother. He eyed us both appraisingly. "What lusciously virginal apparitions," he said. "So ripe and absolutely begging to be deflowered instantly. I almost feel I should take up the challenge myself, if it wouldn't make a certain person insanely jealous."

I thought for a moment that he was referring to my mother, but I saw him glance across the hallway to where a man was leaning against the wall, watching him with a frown on his face. I reacted with surprise as I recognized the person. It was the king's youngest son, Prince George, currently an officer in the Guards. He noticed me at the same moment and came over to me.

"Georgiana. What a pleasant surprise." His hand firmly gripped my elbow and he steered me away. "For God's sake don't mention to my parents that you saw me here, will you? There would be a frightful row. You know what father is like."

"My lips are sealed, sir," I said.

"Splendid," he said. "Let me get you a drink."

I accompanied him to the bar. Noel Coward had now taken over at the piano. He was singing, in that peculiar clipped, bored voice of his, "It's a silly little ditty, and it really isn't pretty, but one really can't be witty all the time. . . ."

"I get another drink too." Hanni had appeared beside us at the bar. "I like cocktails." She pronounced it in the American manner—"cacktails."

"They are rather delicious, aren't they?" I agreed. They did seem to be slipping down remarkably easily.

"And so many sexy guys," she said. "The dark one. He said his name was Edward, but everyone is calling him Lunghi."

"It's a nickname, because he's just come back from India."

"India?"

"Yes, a lunghi is apparently what they wear there."

"Ah. He is sexy guy, don't you think?"

"Yes, I suppose he is." I looked around for him and then froze. Lunghi was now perched on the arm of my mother's chair and she was gazing up at him. As I watched, he took the cherry from his glass and placed it in my mother's mouth. I was wondering how to distract Hanni from this embarrassing scene but she had already given an excited little squeak. "And there is the man from the park."

Chapter 14

My heart leaped. I was sure she meant
Darcy, but instead, standing in the doorway was the young man from the communist rally. He was not wearing threadbare
clothes tonight, however, but a dinner
jacket like everyone else. He looked positively civilized. Hanni rushed straight up to
him. "Hiya, baby. What a kick to see you."

"Roberts just walked in," I heard Gussie
say to Lunghi. "Did you invite him?"

"Had to, old chap. He's harmless
enough, isn't he? Pretty much house-
trained. Won't pee on the carpet."

"Yes, but, I mean to say . . . Roberts

and the prince at the same party. Shows how broadminded we are, what?"

"Who exactly is this Roberts?" I asked Gussie. "Hanni and I saw him at a communist rally in Hyde Park."

"Doesn't surprise me at all. Terribly earnest is our Sidney. Good causes and rights for the masses and all that. Of course he came from the masses, so one can understand, I suppose."

"He's a GSB," Lunghi added, coming to stand beside us. "But a good enough chap, in his way."

"GSB?" I asked.

"Grammar School Boy," Gussie said, grinning. "He was at Cambridge with us, on a scholarship. Terribly bright. He got me through Greek."

"Hanni seems to like him," I commented as I saw them dancing together.

"I don't think the King of Bavaria would approve if his daughter went to live in a semidetached in Slough," Gussie muttered to me.

I laughed. "You're an awful snob."

Noel Coward's song finished to a burst of laughter and applause. Gussie took a long draw on his cigarette. "Born to it, my dear. Snobbery is in the blood, like hunting, as you very well know."

The band struck up another dance number and the floor filled with couples again. Tubby Tewkesbury stumbled past us clutching an empty glass. "Dying of thirst. Need refill," he muttered.

"Now, he'd make a good match for some poor girl," Gussie said. "Rolling in money, the Tewkesbury family. And of course he'll inherit Farringdons. You should snap him up."

I looked at the sweating back of Tubby's neck. "I don't think I could marry anybody just to inherit something."

"Plenty of girls do," he said. "Plenty of boys do it too. Money is a useful commodity, isn't it, Tubby, old bean?"

"What?" Tubby turned blurry eyes onto us and tried to focus.

"I said money comes in useful at times."

"Oh, rather." Tubby beamed. "If I were penniless, I'd never be invited to parties like this. No girl would dance with me. As it is I have a hard enough time . . . want to hop around again, Georgie? This one's a foxtrot, I think. I can manage that."

"All right."

He gave me a pathetically grateful smile. He was a nice enough boy. A lot of them were. So why couldn't I be practical and settle down as the Marchioness of Tewkesbury in that lovely old house?

In the middle of the dance I was aware of someone standing in the doorway, watching me. I looked around and Darcy was leaning nonchalantly against the doorpost, smoking a black cigarette while he studied me with amusement. I went on dancing, horribly conscious of Tubby's big, sweaty hand on my back, undoubtedly leaving a mark on the taffeta, and of his scary wiggles that passed for moving to the music. I forced myself to carry on chatting merrily and thanked him kindly when the dance was over.

"Now that's what I call charity," Darcy murmured, coming up behind me.

"He's a nice enough chap," I said. "And rich, and has a lovely family home. The ideal match for someone like me."

Darcy still looked amused. "You can't tell me you're seriously considering it?"

"I don't know. I could do worse. He has some redeeming qualities."

"Apart from the money and the house?"

"He's loyal, like a British bulldog. You can rely on someone like Tubby. He's not here today and gone tomorrow like some people." I gave him a meaningful stare.

"Ah, well, I'm sorry about that, but something came up unexpectedly and I've been out of town for a while." Darcy looked uncomfortable.

"Something with long dark hair and good legs. I saw her at the Savoy with you."

"Well, actually," he began but got no further as Hanni burst in, almost flinging herself upon Darcy.

"It is the kind man who saved my life in the park," she said. "I kept telling Georgie that I wanted to meet you again. Now my wish has been granted. I am so happy!"

She was gazing up at him with such open admiration that I thought that no man could resist. Darcy certainly couldn't. "I came to the party hoping to run into you again, Your Highness," he said. "What are you drinking?"

"Cocktails. I just love cocktails," she said. "The ones with cherries in them. You can get me another one. My glass is empty."

And off they went together. Lunghi Fotheringay had now taken over at the cocktail shaker. Interested though I was in observing how Hanni would handle flirting with the two young men she seemed to fancy at the same time, I was not going to stand in the hallway like a wallflower. I made my way back toward the dancing. There was no sign of Belinda anywhere, nor of my mother, Noel Coward or Prince George. The band was playing a lively syncopated number and couples were dancing wildly. I picked out Tubby leaping around shaking like a large jelly, then I noticed Hanni and Darcy come into the room and start dancing together. After a few moments the beat changed to a slower tempo and Hanni draped herself all over him. He didn't seem to be objecting.

Suddenly I felt horribly alone and out of place. What was I doing here? I didn't belong with the smart set and I certainly didn't want to stay and watch Hanni seducing Darcy, or vice versa. The effect of at least four cocktails was beginning to make itself felt. As I started to move toward the door, the whole room swung around alarmingly. This is terrible, I thought.

I can't be drunk. I tried to walk in a controlled manner as I fought my way through
the crowd and out to the balcony. There I
leaned on the rail, taking great gulps of
fresh air. Far below me Green Park
stretched out in darkness, and the noise
of the traffic along Piccadilly seemed
muted and far away. It took me a while to
realize I wasn't alone out there. Sidney
Roberts, the earnest communist, was
standing at the rail beside me, staring out
into the night.

"Terribly stuffy in there, isn't it?" he said.
"And loud too. Not really my thing at all but
old Lunghi insisted that I come and he
was dashed good to me at Cambridge, so
I thought why not?" I could see that he
had also been drinking quite a bit and had
reached the maudlin phase. "Being a
communist is a worthy cause, you know,"
he went on, more to himself than to me. "I
mean, it's not right that people like Gussie
and Lunghi can fritter a few thousand
pounds on a party while the masses are
out of work and starving, and one should
do something to make the world a fair
place. But the communists are so deadly
dull. No parties. No laughter. Hardly any

booze. And just occasionally one longs for fine wines and beautiful women."

"You're really one of us at heart," I said, laughing. "A true communist would be happy with a pint of bitter on Saturday nights."

"Oh, dear, do you think so?" He looked worried. "I'm not so sure. Even in Russia there are those who eat caviar. We just need a form of government that doesn't come from the ruling classes. Representation by the people and for the people."

"Isn't that what they have in America? I can't say it's working well there."

He looked worried again.

"Besides, the British would never accept anything too extreme," I said. "And most people like things the way they are. The crofters on our estate love being part of the Rannoch family. They enjoy serving us."

"Has anyone actually asked them?" he demanded, then drained the rest of his glass.

"They could leave any time they wanted," I said hotly. "They could work in a factory in Glasgow."

"If there was any work for them."

"What's going on out here?" Gussie

appeared with a drink in either hand. "Not interrupting a tryst, am I?"

"No, an argument about communism," I said.

"Too serious. No earnest talk allowed tonight. Strictly reserved for merriment and mayhem. What you need is another drink, old chap."

"Oh, no, thanks. I'm not much of a drinker," Sidney Roberts said. "I've already had enough."

"Nonsense. There is no such word as enough," Gussie said. "Go on. Take it. Down the hatch."

"I really shouldn't, but thanks all the same," Sidney said as Gussie tried to force it on him.

"If he doesn't want it, then I'll do him a favor and drink it for him." Tubby had come out onto the balcony. His face was now beetroot red and he was sweating pro-fusely. Not a pretty sight, in fact. He grabbed the nearest glass from Gussie and drained it in one swig. "Ah, that's what I needed," he said. "Hair of the dog."

"I think you've had enough, old man," Gussie said. "You are seriously blotto."

"Not me. Cast-iron stomach. Never met

a drink I didn't like," Tubby said with a distinctly slurred chuckle. Then he swayed, lost his balance and staggered backward.

"Look out!" Sidney shouted as there was a splintering sound and part of the railing collapsed.

As if in slow motion Tubby fell backward off the balcony—arms and legs spread like a starfish, his mouth and eyes opened wide with surprise—and disappeared into the night.

Chapter 15

For a second the three of us stood there, frozen with the horror of what had just happened.

"We must call an ambulance," I said, trying to make my legs obey me and walk back into the room.

"No bloody use calling an ambulance," Sidney said. "We're six floors up. The poor chap's a goner."

Gussie looked as if he might vomit any second. "How could that have happened?" he said. "How could it have happened?"

"He did weigh an awful lot," I said, "and

he fell against the railing with all his weight."

"Oh, my God," Gussie said. "Poor old Tubby. Don't let them know in there what happened."

"They'll have to know. You'll have to call the police," I said.

"You saw it. It was an accident," Gussie said. "A horrible accident."

"Of course it was. You're not to blame."

"It's my party," Gussie said bleakly. "I shouldn't have let people out on the balcony drunk."

I took his arm and led him back inside.

"What's up?" Darcy grabbed my arm as I stumbled past. "Are you all right? Have you been drinking too much?"

"That chap I was dancing with," I whispered. "He just fell off the balcony. Gussie's gone to phone the police."

"Holy Mother. Then we'd better get Her Highness and yourself out of here while there is still time," Darcy said.

"But I should stay to answer questions," I said. "I saw him fall."

"You were out there alone with him?"

"No, Gussie was out there, and a chap called Sidney Roberts. It was horrible. He'd had far too much to drink. He staggered backward against the railing and it collapsed and he just went over."

"You're as white as a sheet." Darcy took my arm. "You need a good stiff brandy."

"Oh, no more alcohol, thank you. I've already drunk too much."

"All the more reason for spiriting you out of here. You don't want that to get back to the palace, do you?"

"No, but wouldn't it look odd if we fled?"

"Certainly not. You didn't push him, did you?"

"Of course not, but I know my duty . . ."

"Then you stay if you feel you must but someone should get the princess out of here. I'll take her home if you like."

"Oh no," I said. "I'm supposed to be chaperoning her. I wouldn't trust you to behave yourself. I've seen you looking at her."

"Just being friendly to foreigners." Darcy managed a grin. "Come on, let's go and find her before the police arrive."

We split up and looked around the flat. She wasn't in the main drawing room. I pushed open the door to the kitchen. It was as modern as the rest of the flat, with white painted cabinets and a large, impressive refrigerator. Several people were seated at the kitchen table and they looked up as I came in. Hanni was one of them. I went over and took her arm. "Hanni, we have to go home now. Come along quickly."

"I don't want to leave. I like it here. These nice guys are going to let me try what they are doing," Hanni said.

I stared at the table. It looked as if someone had spilled a line of flour across it.

"Get her out of here," Darcy hissed, taking Hanni by the arm.

"But I want to stay. I'm having fun," she complained loudly. It was clear that the drink was affecting her too.

"You wouldn't be having fun in prison, I assure you," Darcy said as he dragged her out of the door.

"What do you mean?" I whispered. "Why should Hanni go to prison?"

"My dear, you are a complete innocent, aren't you?" Darcy said. "They were sniffing cocaine in there. Hardly the sort of party the queen had in mind for her. And you can't afford to have your names plastered all over the front page of tomorrow's newspapers."

"Why would they put our names in the newspapers?" Hanni demanded.

I went to say something but saw Darcy's warning look.

"If the police raid the party," he said quickly. He steered a swaying Hanni toward the lift.

She was crying now. "I don't want to go home. I want to stay and drink cocktails," she was whimpering.

"What about Belinda?" I hadn't actually seen her since I arrived.

"Belinda can take care of herself, I guarantee," Darcy said. He bundled us into the lift, then quickly found us a cab.

"Are you not coming with us?" Hanni asked with obvious disappointment as Darcy gave the driver our address.

"No, I think I'd better go my own way," Darcy said. "I've a couple of things I should be doing. But I'm sure we'll meet again soon, Princess." He took her hand and kissed it, but his eyes met mine as his lips remained on her hand.

"I'll be seeing you soon," he said. "Take care of yourself, won't you?"

"That was fun," Hanni said as we drove off. "Why did we have to leave? I would have liked a police raid. Like Al Capone. Will the police have machine guns?"

"No," I said. "In England the police don't carry guns at all."

"How silly," she said. "How do they catch the crooks?"

"They blow a whistle and the crooks give themselves up," I replied, thinking that this did sound rather silly.

"But Mr. O'Mara says he will see us again soon. That is good news, no?"

"Yes, I suppose it is," I replied mechanically. I stared out of the window, watching the lights of Piccadilly flash past us. The shock of Tubby's death, mixed feelings about Darcy, combined with the effect of those cocktails, was just beginning to hit me. I felt that I might cry at any moment. I fled to my room as soon as we got home.

"Was it a good party, my lady?" Mildred rose from the shadows.

I leaped a mile. "Mildred, I didn't expect you to stay up so late. You didn't have to wait up for me."

"I always wait up to help my ladies undress," she said primly. I stood there and let her undress me like a little girl. She was just brushing out my hair when we heard raised voices from the next room. Mildred raised an eyebrow but said nothing.

"Will that be all, my lady?" she asked, putting the hairbrush back on my dressing table.

"Thank you, Mildred. It was good of you to stay up so late," I said.

As she opened my door to leave, Irmgardt came out of the princess's room next door and stomped past with a face like thunder. I suspected that the princess had revealed a little too much of what went on at the party. Suddenly I was overcome with tiredness. I got into bed, curled into a tight ball in my bed and tried to sleep.

∞≈∞

The next morning's *Times* had a small paragraph reporting the tragic death of Lord Tewkesbury's son, who plunged from a balcony after too much to drink at a Mayfair party. Fortunately the report didn't mention whose party, nor who had been on the guest list. I was still reading the *Times* in bed when my grandfather appeared at my door.

"There's a geezer downstairs what wants to see you," he said.

"What sort of geezer?"

"Says he's a policeman."

"Oh, Lord." I leaped out of bed and tried to put on my dressing gown. My head felt as if it were being hit with a large hammer. Oh, Lord, so this was a real hangover.

"Have you been doing something you shouldn't?" Granddad asked.

"No. I expect it's about the party last night. Some poor chap fell off the balcony. I saw it happen."

"That can't have been very nice for you. Drunk, was he?"

"Completely. Tell the policeman I'll be down immediately."

On my way out of my door I bumped into Mildred. "My lady, I should have been instructed to fetch you. It is quite unseemly for your butler to go into your room. Let me help you dress before you receive company."

"It's not company, Mildred. It's a policeman. And I'm respectably covered up, you know."

"A policeman?" She looked as if she might swoon.

"Nothing I've done." I dodged past her and went downstairs.

My grandfather had put the policeman

in the morning room and given him a cup of tea. He rose as I entered and I was dismayed to see it was none other than Inspector Harry Sugg. I had encountered him once before and the memory was not a pleasant one.

"Ah, Lady Georgiana. We meet again," he said. "And again under tragic circumstances."

"Good morning, Inspector." I offered my hand and received a limp handshake, before sitting opposite him on an upright gilt chair. "Please forgive the attire. I wasn't expecting visitors this early."

"It is after nine o'clock." He repositioned himself on the sofa and crossed his legs. "The rest of the world has been out and working for hours."

The thought crossed my mind that he'd have got on like a house on fire with Sidney Roberts. They could have shared their communist sympathies.

"But then the rest of the world doesn't stay up at parties until all hours," he added.

Ah. So he did know I had attended the party last night. No point in denying it then.

"I imagine you're here to take my statement about the horrible accident."

"That's exactly why I'm here. It seems you made a quick getaway before the police arrived last night. Why exactly was that, miss?"

He still hadn't learned that one addressed the daughter of a duke as "my lady" and not "miss," but I had come to think it was deliberate in his case. I chose to ignore it.

"I should have thought it was perfectly obvious. I was extremely distressed by what I had seen. Kind friends put me in a taxi."

"And what had you seen?"

"Mr. Tewkesbury" (I couldn't remember his first name. I'd only ever known him as Tubby. And in my early morning fogged state I couldn't remember whether he was the Honorable Mr. or Viscount something) "fell from the balcony. I was out there. I saw the whole thing."

"Can you describe it for me?"

I went through the whole scene, relating word for word what had happened. When I had finished he nodded. "Well, that corresponds exactly with what Mr. Roberts told us. The other chap, Gormsley, must have been blotto by that time. He couldn't even remember who had been out on the balcony."

Dear Gussie, I thought warmly. Trying to protect me from involvement.

"There had been a lot of drinking going on," I agreed. "Poor Tubby was completely squiffy. That's why he fell over in the first place."

"And the balcony railings actually collapsed?"

"Yes. I heard them splintering. He was a big chap, you know."

"All the same, I presume they build railings to withstand big chaps leaning on them, and it is a new block."

I looked up. "What are you hinting?"

"Nothing at this stage. From what you and Mr. Roberts tell me, we can call it a horrible accident and close the books then?"

"Definitely," I said. "A horrible accident, that's exactly what it was."

"And you can swear that nobody gave him a shove?"

"A shove? Of course not. Why would anyone give him a shove?"

"Extremely rich young fellow, so I understand. People have been known to do a lot of things for money."

"The only person near him was Gussie Gormsley and he's also an extremely rich young fellow."

"There's also jealousy, over a woman?"

"Nobody would be jealous of Tubby," I said. "And besides, I saw the whole thing. Nobody touched him. He took a drink, lost his balance and fell."

The inspector rose to his feet again. "Well, that seems to be that then. Thank you for your time, your ladyship. There will obviously be an inquest in the case of unnatural death. You may be called upon to make a statement. We'll let you know when that will be."

"Certainly, Inspector," I said. "Glad to help."

I remembered to ring the bell to summon my grandfather.

"The inspector is leaving now," I said.

At the doorway Harry Sugg paused and looked back at me. "Strange, isn't it, that you've been involved in two deaths so close together."

"Not involved in either, Inspector," I

said. "A witness, that's all. An innocent bystander, in the wrong place at the wrong time."

"If you say so, miss." He took the hat that Granddad had given him, tipped it to me then put it on his head. "Thank you for your time."

And he was gone. I got the impression that Inspector Sugg would dearly have loved it had I really been involved.

"Miserable-looking bloke he was," Grandfather said. "Did he want a statement from you about the party?"

"Yes. He wanted to make sure that Tubby wasn't pushed."

"You saw the whole thing, did you?"

"I did. It was just a horrible accident. Tubby was very drunk and very large."

I felt tears welling up again. I hardly knew Tubby, but he was a harmless fellow and he didn't deserve such a horrible fate.

"So silly, these young people, aren't they? Drink too much, drive too fast. Think they'll live forever. You'll be wanting your breakfast now, I expect."

"Oh, goodness. I don't feel like food at all," I said. "Some black coffee, please, and maybe some dry toast."

"Mrs. Huggins will be disappointed. She was looking forward to cooking real food now that the baroness has gone. What about the little lady? Is she up yet?"

"I haven't seen her yet. We got home very late. I expect she'll want to sleep in."

Granddad looked up the stairs then moved closer to me. "You want to watch that one," he said. "She may prove to be more trouble than she's worth."

"What do you mean by that?"

"Oh, don't get me wrong. She's a nice enough little thing. You can't help liking her, but there's something not quite right with her."

"What are you saying?"

"It's just a feeling I have. I've observed a lot of people in my time as a copper on the beat. Made plenty of arrests, and I think she's a wrong-un. Trying to pinch a handbag from 'arrods. Ordering herself jewels from Garrard's. Ordinary folk don't do things like that."

"Well, she is a princess, Granddad. And she is just out of the convent. She probably hasn't a clue about money and thinks that things she wants miraculously appear in front of her."

Granddad frowned. "I don't care who she is, princess or fishmonger's daughter, she should know right from wrong. And I tell you something else. I think I caught her using the telephone yesterday. I picked up the downstairs extension and I'm sure I heard a click, as if the upstairs receiver had been put down."

"Maybe she was just calling the baroness."

"If she was, why not ask your permission first? And why hang up when she thought someone was listening? She knows we don't speak Kraut."

"I don't mind if she uses the telephone."

"Your brother will mind if she's calling home to Germany," Granddad pointed out.

"Oh, golly, yes. Fig would be livid."

He leaned closer to me. "If I was you, I'd tell the queen you've bitten off more than you can chew with her and send her packing. They can decide at the palace what to do with her. If you don't, I get the feeling she'll lead you up the garden path."

At that moment the front doorbell rang again.

"Blimey, we are popular this morning, aren't we?" Granddad adjusted his tails and started toward the front door. "And you'd better get yourself out of sight. Standing in the hallway in your dressing gown—what will people think?"

I darted for the nearest doorway, then stopped when I recognized the voice.

"I know it's dashed early, but I had to talk to her ladyship before the police show up on her doorstep. Would you tell her it's Gussie? Gussie Gormsley."

I reappeared. "Hello, Gussie. I'm afraid you're too late. The police beat you to it."

"Well, that's a bally nuisance," he said. "I didn't like to wake you and I'd no idea they'd show up at the crack of dawn. No sense of propriety, those fellows. They were dashed rude last night too. Hinted to me that someone might have given poor Tubby a shove, or had been fiddling with the railings. 'Look here,' I told them, 'Tubby hadn't an enemy in the entire world. Everyone liked old Tubby.' I tried to keep you out of it, you know."

"I gathered that. Thank you for trying."

"Would have worked too, but that blasted idiot Roberts, with his lower-class morality, had to go and blurt out that you were on the balcony with us. Then, of course, they wanted to know why you'd done a bunk."

"Actually I wanted to stay, but Darcy thought I should get the princess away so that there was no making of an international incident."

"Oh, right. Good thinking. Darcy O'Mara, you mean?"

"Yes."

"Was he at the party last night?"

"Yes, he was."

"Didn't notice him. Don't think I invited him."

"He probably gate-crashed. He often does," I said.

"Friend of yours?"

"In a way."

He frowned. "Rum fellow. Irish, isn't he? Went to a Catholic school and Oxford, but we won't hold those against him. He plays a decent game of rugby. Father's an Irish peer, isn't he?"

"That's right."

"Don't think I'd quite trust the Irish," Gussie said. "I'd better be off, then."

"Thank you for coming," I said. "And for trying to protect me. It was very sweet of you."

"Not at all. Dashed awful thing to have happened, wasn't it? I can tell you I felt quite green myself. Poor old Tubby. I still can't quite believe it." He started to walk toward the front door, then turned back. "Look here, I gather that some fellows at my party were doing a little more than drinking, if you get my meaning. You saw them in the kitchen, didn't you? If the police question you again, I'd rather you conveniently forgot that. I'd hate to get the family name in the papers in any way mixed up with drugs."

"I understand," I said. "And frankly I had no idea what was going on. I thought they'd spilled flour on the table."

Gussie laughed. "That's a good one. I like you, Georgie. You're a great girl. I hope we can meet again soon. In happier circumstances, I mean."

"I hope so too."

"Is the princess staying with you long?" he asked wistfully.

So that was it. It wasn't me he wanted to meet again soon. It was Hanni.

Chapter 16

No sooner had Gussie departed than Hanni came down the stairs, looking fresh and bright and lovely. No sign of a hangover, and yet she had definitely consumed as many cocktails as I.

"Hello, Georgie. I'm not too late for breakfast, am I? I'm starving. Can we have proper English breakfast now that pain in ass is no longer here?"

"Hanni, that expression really isn't suitable. If you must say something you can say 'pain in the neck.'"

"Neck is better than ass?"

"Definitely. I'll tell Mrs. Huggins you want breakfast."

We went through into the breakfast room and I nibbled at a piece of buttered toast while Hanni attacked a huge plate of bacon, eggs, sausages, kidneys, the works.

"When can we go to another party?" Hanni asked between mouthfuls. "It was such fun. I like the music and the dancing and the cocktails were the bee's knees." She sighed happily. "And the sexy guys too. When can we go see Darcy again? I think he has the hot pants for me. He stayed beside me a long time last night. He wanted to know all about me—my home and the convent and my dreams for the future. He was really interested."

"I don't think you should take Darcy too seriously," I said.

"But he would make good match for me. He is Catholic. Good Irish family. My father would be happy."

"No, your father wouldn't be happy," I said, trying to keep my face calm. "His family is penniless, for one thing, and Darcy is not the type who settles down with one woman. He'll be tired of you by this time next week."

But as I said it, I couldn't help wondering. Did Darcy see the princess as a good bet for his future? Did he fancy himself as Prince of Bavaria with a handsome income for life? He was clearly opportunistic and he might not want to let such a catch as Hanni get away. The queen would be furious, I thought, and then a small voice in my head whispered that I wouldn't be too happy about it either.

"So where do we go today?" Hanni asked. "More shopping? I like London shops. Or lunch at the Savoy? Your friend Belinda said you met Gussie and Lunghi at lunch at the Savoy. I would like a place where I get good food and meet guys."

I began to think that Granddad was right. The princess was rapidly turning into more than I could handle. The small stipend from Binky certainly wouldn't cover outings like lunch at the Savoy and I couldn't risk letting Hanni loose in any more shops.

"You agreed to have lunch with Baroness Rottenmeister at the Park Lane house," I reminded her. "And this morning

I think we should take in some British culture," I said. "I am supposed to be educating you. I'm taking you to the British Museum."

"Museum? But museums are full of old stuff. We have crummy old stuff in Germany. I like modern things."

"You may be a future queen," I said. "You need to know your history. British Museum and no arguing."

"Okay," Hanni said with a sigh.

I went upstairs to have my bath and get dressed. Mildred insisted on my wearing decent clothes, and a strand of pearls.

"I'm only going to a museum, Mildred," I said.

"It doesn't matter, my lady. You are a representative of your family and your class every time you set foot outside your front door. My previous ladies never went out unless they looked like aristocrats. The ordinary public expects it."

I sighed and let her attempt to brush my hair into fashionable waves. "And I'm sure you haven't forgotten, my lady, but I did request Thursday afternoons off."

"Oh, absolutely," I said with relief. "Go and enjoy yourself."

"I will indeed, my lady. I often take in a matinee of a show."

Feeling like a dowdy forty-year-old in my suit and pearls, I came out of my room and tapped on Hanni's door. "Ready to go?" I asked, pushing the door open.

Irmgardt looked up at me with her usual sullen blank expression. She was in the process of hanging up the princess's ball gown.

"Is the princess ready to go out?" I asked. "Princess? Downstairs?" I gestured.

She nodded. *"Ja."*

Poor Hanni, I thought. I bet she didn't choose such a maid. Irmgardt was obviously an old family retainer who had been sent to keep an eye on Hanni by the palace. And she had given her little charge a good talking to the night before. I wondered if it would have any effect.

As I turned to leave, I glanced at the bedside table. There were some letters on it, including the strange sheet of paper with *C. P.* printed on it. And now somebody had slashed an angry red cross through the initials.

I stood staring at it. The angry red slash was quite out of character for Hanni. And I knew nobody called C.P. And anyway, her private mail was none of my business. I closed the door behind me and went downstairs.

◦✂◦

Hanni enjoyed riding on the top of a bus down Oxford Street. It was a lovely summery day, with a warm breeze in our faces, and the crowds below us looked happy and festive.

"Selfridges," Hanni exclaimed. "What is this?"

"Another department store, like Harrods."

"When can we go there?"

"One day, maybe," I said, and decided that I should write to the queen to find out how long I was to be saddled with the princess. It was about time someone else took over the responsibility.

I was glad when we reached the more sedate area of Bloomsbury and I led Hanni up the steps of the British Museum. She clearly wasn't interested in the Egyptian mummies or the Roman statues and wandered around mechanically with a bored expression on her face. I was tempted to give in and take her somewhere more fun like the zoo or a boat on the Serpentine.

We reached the Roman jewelry. "Look, Hanni," I said. "This should be more in your line. These fabulous emeralds."

I looked up from the glass case and she had gone.

The little minx, I thought. She's given me the slip. I had to catch her before it was too late. I hurried through one gallery after another, but the museum was a huge, rambling place. There were groups of schoolchildren to negotiate on the stairs, so many places she could hide, and I realized that my chances of finding her were slim.

"So she's run off," I told myself. She's eighteen years old and it's broad daylight. Why should I be so worried? The worst she'll do is to go shopping on Oxford Street. Yes, and try to shoplift again, and get arrested, I thought. And then what would the queen say?

Drat Hanni, I muttered, and was stomping down the main staircase when I saw her coming up toward me.

"I've been looking for you," she said. "I thought you went without me."

"No, we just mislaid each other," I replied, feeling guilty about my uncharitable thoughts. "But all is well. We've found each other."

"You're right. All is well," she said. "All is very well." She was glowing with excitement. "Something really good just happened. I met the guy from the party last night. Isn't that great?"

"Which guy?" I asked.

"You know, the serious one we met in the park. Sidney. He was here looking for an old book. He told me he works in a bookshop, you know. That is interesting, no?"

I should not have thought of Hanni as the bookshop type—nor the Sidney type. My first thought was that anyone working in a bookshop could not afford to feed and entertain Hanni. But I rapidly came to the conclusion that a bookshop was definitely healthier than parties and cocktails, not to mention cocaine. And he wasn't Darcy.

"Yes, that is interesting," I said. "Where is this bookshop?"

"He said it is in the old part of the city. It's an old, old bookshop. Sidney said the famous writer Charles Dickens used to visit it often. He has invited me to visit it too. He said it has much history. We can go, *ja*?"

"I don't see why not. It's definitely educational."

"Good, then we go tomorrow." Hanni nodded firmly. "Today is no use because Sidney will be here, studying boring old books all day."

"And you are expected at lunch with the baroness," I added.

She rolled her eyes. "Pain in neck," she said. Then her expression softened. "Sidney is nice boy, don't you think?"

"A little too serious for you, I'm afraid," I admitted.

"He is a communist," she said. "I never met a communist before. I thought they were all wild and fierce like in Russia, but he seems gentle."

"I'm sure he's a good person, and he is definitely idealistic. He likes the ideal of a communist society, but it would never work in reality."

"Why not?" She turned those innocent blue eyes on me.

"Because people are people. They are not willing to share equally. They always try to grab what they can. And they need to be led by those born to rule."

"I do not agree with this," she said. "Why should my father be a king, just because he was born to be king?"

"I suppose it does help if one is brought up to rule."

"Sidney is from lower classes, but he would make a good leader," she said.

I thought how easily she was swayed by a pair of earnest gray eyes. If she met a handsome fascist tomorrow, she'd be in favor of whatever it was he believed.

Hanni chatted excitedly all the way back to Park Lane. I found myself half hoping, half dreading that Prince Siegfried would be present at lunch and that Hanni would fall for him. At least he was suitable. Then I rationalized that she was acting like any typical eighteen-year-old straight from a girls' establishment. She wanted affirmation that she was attractive to young men—and at this moment it didn't matter if they were suitable young men or not.

Siegfried was not at lunch. The meal seemed to go on forever, with course after heavy course—the dowager countess's German cook producing dumplings and cream with everything. The baroness smacked her lips and wolfed down everything she was offered. I kept my head down, tried to say as little as possible and prayed with every moment that the dowager countess wouldn't suddenly realize she had seen me sweeping her floors.

I was glad when it was over.

"Now can we visit sexy guys?" Hanni asked. "We go and say hi to Darcy or to Gussie and Lunghi?"

"I hardly think the latter is appropriate," I said without thinking.

"Why?" Hanni turned innocent blue eyes on me.

"Because, er"—I remembered I hadn't told her the truth about what happened the night before—"one of the guests was taken ill and died." I hoped this half truth would suffice. "They are very upset about it," I added. "They won't want to entertain visitors."

"Darcy then? He could take me out to dinner tonight."

I was tempted to tell her the truth about Darcy's financial situation but instead I said, "Hanni, you must learn that a young lady should never be forward. It is not up to you to make the first move. You have to wait for a young man to ask you out."

"Why? This is silly," she said. "If I want to go on date with a young man, why can't I ask him?"

She did have a point. Maybe if I hadn't been so reticent with Darcy he might not have drifted into the arms of whoever the girl with the long dark hair was, and he would not have been flirting with Hanni last night. I remained firm, however, and decided to distract Hanni with a visit to the theater. I picked a light musical comedy by Sigmund Romberg, called *The Student Prince.* This was probably a mistake as it was all about a prince falling in love with a simple girl. In the end he renounces her for his duty. Hanni wept all the way home. "So sad," she kept on murmuring. "I would never give up the man I loved for my duty. Never."

Chapter 17

Rannoch House
Friday, June 17, 1932

Diary,
Blustery day. White clouds, blue sky. It would have been a good day to go riding at home. Instead I have to take Hanni to meet a man at a bookshop. This chaperone business is tiring.

When she came down on Friday morning, I had visions of a repetition of last night's play. Hanni was clearly excited about seeing Sidney again. "I don't care if he is only a commoner," she kept saying. She ate sparingly at breakfast and paced until it was time to leave the house. I was still not too familiar with the geography of London and went downstairs to ask Granddad how I'd get to Wapping.

"Wapping, ducks?" he asked. "Now what would you be doing there?"

"Going to a bookshop."

"A bookshop in Wapping?" he said.

"That's right. It deals in old and rare books. Where is it?"

"Not the best area. Down by the river. Docklands. I wouldn't have thought they went in for much reading there. Where is this place?"

"It's off Wapping High Street, near a pub called the Prospect of Whitby."

Granddad was still frowning. "I seem to remember that them communists hold meetings in a hall around there. You want to be careful, my love. I hope you're not thinking of taking the princess to a place like that."

"She's the one who wants to go. She's met a young man . . . he's a communist and he works in this bookshop."

Granddad made a tut-tutting noise and shook his head. "She wants watching, that one."

"He's perfectly civilized for a communist,

Granddad. He went to Cambridge and he seems terribly nice and earnest. And it is broad daylight."

Granddad sighed. "I suppose it is a weekday. People are working. They're not likely to have one of their punch-ups on a Friday morning. When they have their meetings, there's often a right brawl afterwards. The blackshirts and them go at it."

"I'm sure we'll be quite safe, and knowing Hanni, she'll be bored quite quickly in a bookshop."

"Just make sure you don't dress too posh," my grandfather warned, "and watch out for pickpockets and anyone who makes improper suggestions."

I passed on his advice to Hanni and we left the house in simple cotton skirts and white blouses—two young women on an outing to the city. We rode the tube to Tower Hill Station. I pointed out the Tower of London to Hanni, but she expressed little interest in London history, and dragged me forward like an impatient dog on a leash. It was a long, complicated walk to reach Wapping High Street. Roads twisted, turned and dead-ended between tall brick warehouses and docks. Exotic smells of spices, coffee and tea competed with the less savory odor of drains and the dank smell from the river. Barrows clattered past piled high with goods. Finally we came upon the high street. The bookshop was in a small alleyway off the busy street. It was still paved with cobblestones like a scene from an old painting. To complete the picture a beggar sat on the corner, rattling a couple of pennies in a tin cup in front of him. His sign read, *Lost leg in Great War. Spare a penny.* I felt awful and rummaged in my purse for sixpence, then changed my mind and gave him a shilling.

"God bless you, miss," he said.

There were only three shops in the alley. One was a cobbler (boots, shoes and umbrellas repaired like new!), another, halfway down on the left-hand side, was a Russian tearoom with a couple of sad-looking, down-at-heel men sitting in the window, conversing with dramatic gestures. The bookshop was at the dead end of the alley. Haslett's Bookshop. Established 1855. Specializing in Rare Books and Socialist Literature. An interesting combination since I suspected not too many communist workers collected first editions. Now that we had reached the door, Hanni hung back shyly and let me go inside first.

A doorbell jangled as the door closed behind us. The peculiar musty, dusty, moldy smell of old books permeated the air. Dust motes hung in a single shaft of sunlight. The rear of the shop dissolved into darkness, with mahogany shelves, crammed with books, towering up to a high ceiling. It was like stepping back in time. I almost expected an old Victorian gentleman with muttonchop whiskers and tails to come out to greet us. Instead the shop appeared to be deserted.

"Where can everyone be?" Hanni asked as we stood, taking in the silence. "Sidney said he would be here."

"Maybe he's somewhere in the back helping a customer," I suggested, peering past her into the dark interior.

"Let's go find him."

Hanni went ahead of me. The shop was like a rabbit warren, with passages between shelves twisting and turning. We passed dark little side aisles and negotiated boxes of pamphlets on labor unions and workers' rights. There was a Russian poster on the wall with happy, brave-looking workers building a bright future. Next to it was a shelf of first edition children's books. A delightful mixture. At last we came to a narrow stair twisting up to our right.

"Maybe they are upstairs," Hanni suggested. She started up the dark little stairway. I was about to follow her when I heard the bell jangling on the front door.

"My dear young lady, can I help you?" a voice called. Its owner was not unlike my vision of the Victorian gent—white whiskers, faded blue eyes, paisley waistcoat. Alas no tails, however. "I am so sorry." He continued, shuffling toward me. "I just stepped away for a moment. I had to hand-deliver a book. But my assistant should have been here to take care of you. I am Mr. Solomon, the shopkeeper. Now, how may I assist you?"

Hanni had already disappeared up the stairs. I returned to the old man.

"We were actually looking for your assistant, if you mean Mr. Roberts. He had promised to show us around your shop today."

"Mr. Roberts. A fine young man. A truly noble soul," he said. "Yes, he should be here somewhere. He's probably found a book that interests him and he's sitting somewhere, oblivious to the rest of the world. We'll go and seek him out, shall we?"

"My companion already went upstairs," I said.

"Yes, that's a likely place for him. He's writing a book on the history of the labor movement and we have a Russian section up there he's probably perusing. After you, my dear."

He motioned for me to go up the stairs ahead of him. They were steep and narrow and they turned two corners before we emerged at the upper level. This floor was even darker and mustier, with a lower ceiling and shelves stacked so closely together that one almost had to squeeze between them. Anemic electric lights hung here and there but did little to dispel the gloom.

"Hanni?" I called. "Where are you?"

There was no answer.

"Hanni? Mr. Roberts?"

At last a little voice said, "Over here. I'm over here."

I followed the voice to a side aisle. Hanni didn't look up or turn as we came toward her. Instead she stood like a statue, staring down at her hand with a look of utter surprise on her face. The hand held a long, slim knife, its blade coated in something dark and sticky. My gaze went beyond her to the white object on the floor. Sidney Roberts lay there on his back, his eyes open, his mouth frozen in a silent yell of surprise and pain. A dark stain was slowly spreading across the white front of his shirt.

Chapter 18

"My God, what have you done?" The old gentleman pushed past us to Sidney Roberts's body. "Sidney, my boy."

Hanni looked up at me with frightened eyes. "I found it on the floor," she said, holding out the knife to me. "I came around the corner and my foot kicked something. I bent to pick it up and . . . and I saw what it was. Then I saw Sidney lying there. I didn't do it."

"Of course you didn't," I said.

"Then who did?" Mr. Solomon demanded. He knelt beside Sidney and felt for a pulse.

"Is he . . . dead?" Hanni asked.

Solomon nodded. "I feel no pulse. But he's still warm. And the blood is still spreading. It can only just have happened."

"Then the murderer might still be in the shop." I glanced around uneasily. "Is there another way out?"

"No, there's only the front door."

"Then we should go downstairs immediately and call the police," I said. "He could be hiding anywhere. Come, Hanni."

She was still staring at the knife in her hand. "Here," she said and handed it to me.

"I don't want it!" My voice rose in repulsion as I felt the cold stickiness of the knife touch me. "Put it back on the ground where you found it. The police will want to know."

"I'm not sure where it was." She sounded as if she was about to cry. "It was about here, I think."

I replaced it on the floor and Mr. Solomon ushered us gallantly in front of him down the stairs.

"Alas, I have no telephone," he said. "I keep meaning to have one installed but my customers prefer to write to me."

"So where is the nearest telephone?" I demanded.

"I'm sure they have one at the accountant's opposite the tearoom. I'll go. You two young ladies should probably wait outside."

"But what if the murderer tries to make a break for it?" Hanni asked with a trembling voice. "We can't stop him."

"Of course you can't. Why don't you come with me to the accountant's if you feel safer. Or better still, wait in the tearoom." Mr. Solomon sounded as confused and upset as I felt.

"Yes, that's a good idea," I said. "We'll wait in the tearoom. Hanni looks as if she could do with a cup of tea." I rather felt as if I could do with a cup myself. I couldn't stop shivering.

We let the front door close behind us and followed Mr. Solomon over the cobbles. "Here's sixpence," I said to Hanni. "Get yourself a cup of tea. I'm going to see if I can find a constable before the murderer can escape."

"Don't leave me." Hanni grabbed my arm. "I'm scared. There are spots of blood on my dress, and look at my hands." And she started to cry.

I put my arms cautiously around her because I too had blood on me. "It's all right. I know it is utterly horrible, but don't cry. The police will be here soon and we'll be safe."

"Why would anybody want to kill Sidney?" she asked, brushing away tears. "He was nice, wasn't he?"

"Yes, very nice. You'll feel better after a cup of tea, and you'll be quite safe in the café," I said. "And I won't go far, I promise. See. You can keep an eye on Mr. Solomon from the window."

I watched her safely inside and then I ran back to Wapping High Street. I was just coming around the corner when I bumped into someone.

"Hold on, there, where's the fire?" he said, grabbing me by the shoulders. I went to fight him off until I realized it was Darcy.

"What are you doing here?" I stammered, almost wondering whether I was hallucinating.

"Keeping an eye on you. I called at your house and your butler told me where you had gone. He wasn't too happy about it, so I said I'd go after you to make sure you were all right."

"We're not all right." I heard my voice crack. "We've just found a man murdered. The bookshop owner is calling the police. I have to find a constable."

His hands tightened on my shoulders. "Murdered, you say? Where's the princess? You haven't left her alone, have you?"

"I left her in the tearoom. She was in shock."

"What on earth were you doing in a place like this anyway?"

"Hanni wanted to visit a chap she met at Gussie's party."

"I shouldn't have thought this was a likely location for any of Gussie's friends," Darcy said.

"His name was Sidney Roberts. I don't know if he's exactly a friend of Gussie. They were at Cambridge together. We also met him at the communist rally in the park, when you stepped in to rescue us."

"You say his name *was* . . . ? So that means that he . . ." Darcy looked at me inquiringly.

"Yes. He's the man lying dead upstairs in the bookshop. Somebody stabbed him."

"Holy Mother of God," Darcy muttered

and almost went to cross himself. "And you and the princess found him?"

"Hanni did. She stumbled over the knife lying on the floor."

"You look as if you could do with a cup of tea too," Darcy said. "You're as white as a sheet."

I nooded. "It was awful, Darcy. All that blood and I touched the knife and . . ." I swallowed back a sob.

His arms came around me. "It's all right," he murmured, stroking my hair as if I were a little child. "You're safe now."

I closed my eyes, feeling the warmth and closeness of him, his chin against my hair, the roughness of his jacket on my cheek. I didn't want him to let go of me ever.

"Come on. We'd better get you that tea." He took my arm and led me to the tea-room. Hanni's eyes lit up when she saw him.

"It is Darcy! How did you find us here? You always come at the right moment to rescue us."

"That's me. Darcy O'Mara, guardian angel in disguise."

In the distance came the sound of a

police whistle being blown and a constable came running down the alley. Mr. Solomon appeared from the office across the way, together with several interested clerks. When the constable heard that the murderer might well still be in the bookshop he was not too keen to go inside. He stood at the doorway of the tea shop with Mr. Solomon while Darcy took me to get a cup of tea. We didn't have to wait long. The incessant jangling bell of a police motorcar could be heard, echoing between high buildings. The noise caused several windows to open and brought more people into the alleyway.

The alleyway was just wide enough to accommodate a police motor. It came to a halt. Two plainclothes officers and two uniformed bobbies got out, pushing their way through the growing crowd. I returned to the door of the tea shop.

"Stand back, now. Go back to your business," one of the officers shouted. He saw the bobby standing guard at the doorway. "What have we got here then?"

"They say a man's been murdered and the murderer might still be in the building," the bobby said. "I didn't like to go in alone, sir, so I guarded the doorway to make sure he couldn't get out."

"Quite right," the plainclothes officer said. In spite of the warm day he was wearing the traditional fawn mack and trilby hat, pulled down low on his forehead. His face and mustache were fawn to match the raincoat. He had jowls that gave him a sad bulldog look. Worse still, I now recognized him. None other than Inspector Harry Sugg of Scotland Yard. He spotted me at the same moment and reacted similarly.

"Not you again. Don't tell me you've got something to do with this."

"Princess Hannelore was the one who found the body." I gestured an introduction to the princess inside the tea shop.

"Why on my shift?" he complained. His voice tended to whine at the best of times. "I'm not normally in this part of town. I just happened to be over this way, so they sent me. Are you making a hobby of finding dead bodies?"

"I don't actually enjoy the experience, Inspector," I said. "In fact I feel as if I might be sick at any moment. Someone was getting me a cup of tea."

"All right," Sugg agreed. "Drink your tea, but don't go anywhere. I'll have questions to ask you, and the princess." Hanni looked up at him, wide eyed, from the table at which she was sitting.

"Don't let any of them go anywhere, Collins," Sugg barked. "Stay out here and keep an eye on them. Foreman, James. Come with me."

They pushed past everyone and went into the bookshop. A little later they emerged again. "No sign of anyone in there," Sugg said as he came back into the tearoom. "Which of you is the bookshop owner?"

"I am." Mr. Solomon came forward.

"There didn't seem to be any other exits except for the front door."

"That is correct," Mr. Solomon said.

"You were the one who phoned the police?"

"I was indeed."

"And do you know the identity of the murder victim?"

"Of course I do. He is my assistant. His name is Sidney Roberts. As nice and respectable a young man as you could find. I don't understand how anybody got into my shop to kill him or why they'd do so."

Inspector Sugg turned to look at Hanni and me. "So this young lady found the body? Your full name is . . ."

"This is Her Royal Highness Princess Maria Theresa Hannelore of Bavaria," I said, adopting my most regal tones to make it very clear. "She is a guest of the king and queen. I am chaperoning her around London."

"And what's a visiting princess doing in a place like this, I'd like to know?"

"We met a young man at—the British Museum." I had been about to say "at a party" but I thought it wiser not to remind the police of the occasion of another dead body. "He told the princess about the book-shop where he worked. She accepted his invitation to be shown some rare old books."

Harry Sugg stared hard at me as if try-ing to gauge whether this sounded plausi-ble or not.

"Does Her Highness speak English?" he asked.

"A little," I said before she could answer.

"So tell me, Yer Highness, how you found the body."

Hanni glanced at me for reassurance. "Lady Georgiana and I, we go to visit Sidney." I noticed she had picked up on my words and was speaking as if finding the right words in English was extremely hard for her. "We enter the bookshop. Nobody is there. We look. I find staircase. I go up the stairs in front of Georgie. It is very dark up there. I kick something with my foot. It is long and silver. I pick it up and it is sticky. I see it is horrible knife. And then I see the body lying there." She put her hand to her mouth to stifle a sob.

"And what did you do then?"

"Lady Georgiana and Mr. Solomon come immediately after me. Mr. Solomon sees that Sidney is dead and we go to call the police."

"How long do you think he had been dead, sir?" Inspector Sugg asked Mr. Solomon.

"Not long at all," Mr. Solomon said. "He was still warm. The bloodstain was still spreading. That's why we suspected the murderer might still be on the premises."

"So who else had been in the shop recently?"

"Nobody. Just myself and Mr. Roberts.

A very slow morning. I left Mr. Roberts in charge and I went across the street to hand-deliver a book that had just come in. When I came back, these two young ladies were in the shop."

"Were you gone long?"

"Only a moment."

"And did you pass anybody in the alley-way?"

"The alleyway was deserted."

"Interesting." The inspector turned his attention back to Hanni and me. "Did you ladies pass anybody as you walked down the alleyway?"

"Nobody," I said. "Wait. There was a beggar sitting at the entrance to the alley, and then there were those two men sitting at the window of the tearoom. They haven't moved."

"Beggar, Foreman. Go and check on him and who he's seen," Sugg barked. "And James. Ask those geezers in the tea shop."

The crowd was steadily growing. Darcy handed me a teacup and I drank grate-fully.

"If you don't mind my suggesting, Inspector," Darcy said, "but might it not be wise for me to escort these two young ladies home before the gentlemen of the press get here? This lady is a visiting foreign princess, after all. We don't want to cause an international incident, do we?"

I heard the whisper run through the crowd. Foreign princess. Some of them ran off to fetch their friends. Obviously this was going to be more interesting than the usual back-alley murder.

"And who might you be?" Sugg demanded, apparently not the least concerned about causing an international incident.

"O'Mara is the name," Darcy said with a certain swagger. "I am a friend of the young ladies."

"And I suppose you're also a prince or a duke?"

"Not at all. My father is Lord Kilhenny, Irish peer, if that's what you want to know, but I don't see what that has to do with anything."

"So were you here with the young ladies when they discovered the body?"

"No, I wasn't. I've only just arrived here myself."

"And what made you happen to be in

the same, disreputable part of town? Pure coincidence?"

"Not at all," Darcy said again. "I called on Lady Georgiana and her butler told me where she had gone. He expressed concern, so I did the only decent thing and went to keep an eye on them."

"And exactly why did he express concern?" Sugg was still attacking like a bulldog, shaking and not letting go.

"Isn't that obvious, Inspector? Would you want your innocent daughters wandering through this part of London? These girls have been raised in seclusion. They have little experience of the seedier side of life in the big city."

Sugg stared at him, one eyebrow raised and a half smirk on his lips, then he said, "So you arrived on the scene exactly when?"

"Just before yourself. As I came around the corner into the alley, I met Lady Georgiana, running to find a police constable. She was extremely distressed. I brought her back to have a cup of tea. And now, if it's all right with you, I'd like to take her home. And the princess, naturally."

I was conscious of the growing crowd,

swarming around us, staring with unabashed curiosity. It would only be moments before the first pressmen arrived. "You know where I live, Inspector," I said. "Her Highness is staying with me. If you have more questions for us, we'd be happy to answer them."

Harry Sugg looked from me to Hanni to Darcy and then back again. I think he was trying to decide whether he'd lose face by allowing us to go.

"If these ladies' faces appear on the front page of the newspapers in connection with an East End murder, the king and queen would not be pleased—you can see that, can't you?" Darcy said. "Added to which, they are both clearly suffering from shock."

"I'm not happy about this," Harry Sugg said. "Not at all happy, I can tell you. I know you young things and what you do for thrills. Stealing policemen's helmets, for one thing, and what goes on at your parties. Don't think I don't know about your thrills. Oh, I know right enough." His eyes didn't leave my face as he spoke, then he took a step closer to me so that I was conscious of that fawn mustache dancing up and down in front of my face. "Two bodies in one week. That's a little more than coincidence, wouldn't you say?"

"The other death was a horrible accident," I said. "I was there on the balcony when it happened. Nobody was near him. He fell. An awful accident."

"If you say so, my lady. I just find it strange, that's all. In the police force we are trained not to believe in coincidences. If something looks suspicious, it usually is. And if there's some kind of connection, trust me, I'm going to sniff it out."

"I assure you there is no connection between us and the murdered man, Inspector," I said coldly. "Now if you don't mind, I'd like you to take us home, Darcy, please."

Nobody stopped us as we walked out of the tea shop and forced our way through the crowd to Wapping High Street.

Chapter 19

Nobody spoke much as we sat on the tube back to Hyde Park Corner. I had thought of getting a taxicab, but we couldn't find one in that part of the city and in the end it seemed simpler to take the underground. Even Hanni was unnaturally subdued and didn't attempt to flirt with Darcy once. Darcy escorted us all the way back from the station to Rannoch House.

"You'll be okay now, will you?" he asked.

I nodded. "Thank you for coming to look for us. If you hadn't been there, we'd probably have been off to prison in a Black Maria by now."

"Nonsense. You know how to stick up for yourself pretty well, I'd say."

"I'm very grateful. It is most kind of you to be concerned about us." I held out my hand. I've found that in moments of great duress, I revert to upbringing and become exceedingly proper.

A look of amusement flashed across Darcy's face. "You're dismissing the peasants, are you?"

"I'm sorry, but under the circumstances . . ."

Darcy took my hand and squeezed it. "I understand. Go and have a stiff drink. You'll feel better. You'll feel even better knowing that it's Binky's brandy you're drinking."

At that I managed a smile. As I went to withdraw my hand from his, his fingers closed around mine. "Georgie," he said. He opened his mouth to say more, but Hanni stepped between us. "I also thank you for saving us," she said, and wrapped her arms around his neck, depositing a big kiss on his cheek. I was so shocked I just stood there. Darcy extricated himself, giving me a half-embarrassed smile, and went on his way. I steered Hanni up the front steps.

"What will happen now?" Hanni asked. "I think that man did not believe us that we found poor Sidney dead."

"They certainly can't believe that one of us killed him. What possible motive could we have?" I asked, but even as I said it I saw that there might be motives that the police could unearth. I hadn't forgotten the cocaine at Gussie's party. And I had found Hanni sitting at the table in the kitchen with the cocaine users. What if Sidney were somehow involved with that? If he ran a cocaine ring, or he had not paid his drug debts—I had read that these people were ruthless. Maybe it was not for nothing that he worked in the East End of London, so close to the river. Perhaps the respectable bookshop was merely a front for less respectable activities. Perhaps this inquiry would open a whole can of worms. I felt quite sick as we went into the house.

My grandfather was waiting anxiously for us. I sent Hanni up to her room to lie down before lunch and then I went down to the kitchen, where he was polishing silver, and told him exactly what had happened. He listened with a concerned frown on his face.

"That's nasty, that is. Very nasty. Someone is killed at a party, then a few days later the princess meets someone she had met at that very party again, at the British Museum of all places, and he invites her to a bookstore in a shady part of London and you stumble upon him dead? It all sounds like too much of a coincidence to me."

"That's what the policeman in charge said. But it *was* a coincidence, Granddad. That's the awful thing. I know the first death was an accident. And why on earth would one of us want to kill poor Sidney Roberts? We both spoke with him at the party and he seemed a harmless, earnest kind of chap. Rather sweet, actually. Hanni must certainly have thought so. She seemed rather smitten with him. But we'd only met him on those two occasions. We knew nothing about him, really."

"If I was you, ducks, I'd get on the old blow piece to the palace right away. Let Her Majesty know what has happened and let her decide what to do with the princess." He put down the silver teapot he had been polishing. "I told you that one wanted watching, didn't I? Never did feel quite easy about her."

"Oh, but, Granddad, Hanni had nothing to do with this. She wanted to meet Sidney again because she is a little boy-mad, given her years in the convent. And he was very nice looking. And I think she was intrigued that he was a communist. But that's all."

"I'm not saying she stabbed the poor bloke or nothing. It was just a hunch I had about her. I've seen the type before. Where she goes, trouble follows. You'll be well rid of her, ducks."

"Oh, dear. I have to say that I agree with you. I'll go and telephone the palace right away."

"Have your lunch first." Granddad put an arm around my shoulders. "You look as if you've seen a ghost, you do. Nasty shock, I expect."

"Yes, it was. It was utterly horrible. And then the police and everything . . ." I didn't mean to cry but suddenly I could feel tears trickling down my cheeks.

"There, there. Don't cry, my love," Granddad said, and he enveloped me in a big bear hug. I stood there with my head on his shoulder, feeling the comforting firmness of his arms around me and realizing at the same time how strange this was. I believe it must have been the first time in my life that a relative actually hugged me and comforted me. Oh, to be sure, Nanny had hugged me when I had fallen down as a small child, but my parents had never been there. So this is what it is like for ordinary people, I thought. They care about each other. They comfort each other. I resolved there and then that I would be an ordinary mother to my children and hug them hard and often.

"I'm so glad you are here," I said.

"Me too, my love," he murmured, stroking my hair as if I were a little child. "Me too." Then he released me. "You'd better go and keep an eye on Her Highness before she gets into any more trouble."

"Oh, dear, yes, I suppose I had." I turned back to the stairs.

"Your cook's made one of her famous pork pies," Granddad called after me. "Known for her pork pies, 'ettie is."

I met Hanni coming down the stairs as I emerged through the baize door.

"Is lunch ready? I'm starving," she said, and in truth she looked as if she had just woken from a good night's sleep. She had changed out of the dress with blood on it and looked fresh and innocent. I stood looking at her for a moment, weighing in my mind what my grandfather had said. Was she indeed one of those people who seem to invite trouble, or had the last week been an unlucky one for both of us?

"It's almost ready," I said. "I see you've changed your clothes."

"I fear that dress will have to be thrown away," she said. "Irmgardt is working on it, but I do not think she will be able to remove the blood from the skirt."

"I should go up and wash and change," I said. "I'll be down in a few minutes."

I remembered with relief that Mildred was out for the afternoon. As I started to unbutton my dress I realized that I too still had traces of blood on my hands. I just stood there, looking down at them, fighting back the revulsion. Until recently I had never even seen a dead body. Now in the last few days I had watched two men die. I felt an overwhelming desire to rush to the station and catch the next train to Scotland. Castle Rannoch might be the most boring place on earth, it might contain

Binky and Fig, but it was home. I knew the rules there. I felt secure. But there was the small matter of the princess. Surely the queen wouldn't expect her to go on staying with me after this.

I scrubbed my nails furiously and washed my hands in a way that would have been admired by my fellow Scot Lady Macbeth. Then I changed and went down to lunch. True to Granddad's predictions, Mrs. Huggins had made a delicious pork pie. Hanni tucked into it with gusto. "English food I like," she said.

I had to admit it looked wonderful, served cold with pickled beetroots, lettuce and pickled onions. But somehow I couldn't chew or swallow. I toyed with it, pushed it around on my plate, and only managed a couple of mouthfuls. When it was followed by jam roly-poly with custard, Hanni uttered squeaks of delight and fell upon it. It was a pudding of which I am particularly fond, but again after one or two spoonfuls I couldn't eat any more. I kept seeing the body lying on the floor with the blood soaking through his shirt, and I felt the cold stickiness of that bloody knife in my hands.

"You haven't eaten much," Granddad complained as he came to clear away. "That won't do."

"I'm sorry. I still feel a bit shaky," I said.

"Let me bring you a brandy," he said kindly.

I nodded. "Yes, that might be a good idea."

"I too like brandy," Hanni said brightly. "I too have the shock."

I didn't think she was showing it. She seemed to have bounced back with remarkable resilience, especially considering that this was a chap she was keen on. I thought for a second what I would feel like if it had been Darcy lying there. It was too painful even to contemplate.

Granddad returned with the brandies and coffee. Hanni and I sat chatting about anything but the morning's events, when Granddad appeared in the doorway.

"You have a visitor, my lady."

I rather feared it was a policeman. I stood up. "I'll come to the drawing room."

"No need to get up, darlings, it's only me," Belinda said, bursting in with her usual radiance and wafting hints of Chanel as she approached. "I simply had to come and apologize. My conscience was positively nagging at me."

"Apologize for what?" I asked.

"Why, for leaving you in the lurch at that boring party," she said. "The truth was that I was only there because I had my eye on some chap, so when I saw he had his eye on someone else—well, I decided to cut my losses and head for Crockford's and some productive gambling. Lucky I did, too, because not only did I win a couple of hundred pounds but I met the most divine Frenchman and one thing led to another and to put it bluntly, I've just surfaced from his hotel room. I do hope you managed to find your own way home with no problems."

I almost laughed at the irony of this statement. "Belinda, how do you do it?"

"Keep meeting men, you mean? Sex appeal, I suppose. Raw sex appeal."

"No, I don't mean that. I mean, how do you manage to skate over the surface of life, avoiding all the pitfalls?"

"What are you talking about?" She took off her dinky little straw hat and gloves and perched on a chair beside us.

"May I bring you some coffee, miss?" Granddad asked in his best formal manner.

"How kind." They exchanged a grin.

"You left the party before the poor man was killed?" Hanni asked.

She had obviously put two and two together from our conversations, proving that there wasn't much wrong with her English. "I wanted to find you but Darcy took us away," I said.

"Killed? What man was killed?" Belinda demanded sharply.

"Tubby Tewkesbury. He fell off the balcony."

"How utterly dreadful. Poor old Tubby. What an extraordinary thing to happen. I say, is that why a young man with a camera is standing in the square opposite Rannoch House?"

"Oh, gosh," I exclaimed. "Don't tell me the press is here already."

"Already? It doesn't usually take them days to sniff out a story, you know."

"She means the other man who was killed. Today. Not two hours ago," Hanni chimed in.

Belinda looked at me incredulously. "Another man? Where? When?"

"We went to visit a chap we met at the

party and . . ." I told her the whole story. "It was all rather horrible, actually," I said. "I couldn't eat a bite of lunch."

"Of course you couldn't, darling," she said. "How utterly beastly for you. I must say, you do seem to be a bit of a body magnet this spring, don't you?"

"Don't joke about it, Belinda, please. The first one I didn't mind because he was such a horrible man, but these were two nice, decent boys and they didn't deserve this fate."

Belinda nodded. "I was going to invite you both to a show tonight, but given the circumstances . . ."

"I would like to see a show," Hanni said brightly. "I like London shows. I like the singing and the legs kicking up."

"Use your head, Hanni," I snapped. "If there is already one newspaper reporter standing outside the house, that means they know about this morning. Just think how bad it would look to picture you enjoying yourself at the theater."

Hanni pouted but didn't say anything.

"I'm off to the country tomorrow," Belinda said, "or I'd come and keep you company and fend off the press. I rather fear you're in for another bombardment like last time. Not very jolly for you, I'm afraid."

"Not at all jolly," I said. "The country sounds like a good idea. Maybe I'll suggest it to Her Majesty when I telephone her this afternoon."

"Between you and me, I rather wish I hadn't accepted the invitation now that I've met Louis, but one can't go back on one's word, can one?"

"No, one can't." I looked at her fondly, realizing how nice and solidly British she was in spite of her fast and loose lifestyle.

"So I should be going." She got up. "Ciao, darlings. Cheer up. At least it was someone you hardly knew."

"Don't forget your titfer," Hanni called after her.

Belinda looked back in utter surprise. "My what?"

"Your titfer. Tit for tat. That's how Londoners say hat, isn't it?"

Belinda picked up her hat from the seat. "You should definitely take her to the country before her vocabulary is irretrievably ruined," she said as she went out.

Chapter 20

After Belinda had gone, I suggested that Hanni pay a visit to the baroness, explain to her what had just happened, and ask her advice on how to proceed and what to tell her father. Hanni made a face. "She will be angry that I went to bad part of city. She will be angry that I went to meet boy."

"I can't help it. It must be done. You are a princess, Hanni. You've been away from royal life in a convent, but you have to realize that things have to be done in the correct manner. There is protocol to follow. Your father may wish you to return home immediately."

"Then I will say nothing to baroness. I do not wish to return home."

"Don't be silly," I snapped. "You don't want her to read it for herself in the newspapers, do you? There will be an awful fuss and you'll be in serious trouble."

"All right," she agreed with a dramatic sigh. "I go see old pain in neck."

As soon as she had gone, I put through a telephone call to the palace. I explained the events briefly to Her Majesty's private secretary. He informed me that Her Majesty was not at home, but he would inform her as soon as she returned.

I tried to rest but found it impossible. When I stood behind the net curtains in the drawing room I could see several men loitering across the street, leaning on the railings of the gardens, talking and smoking. One held a camera with a large flash attachment. Oh dear. I needed to take action immediately. I found the telephone number for the baroness, asked to speak to the princess and then instructed Hanni to be sure to take a taxi home. I would make sure one of us was on the lookout for her and she should run straight into the house without talking to anybody.

"The man try to talk to me when I go out," she said. "I tell him I am only the maid."

For all her naïveté and youth, Hanni was sharp when she needed to be. I wondered if I had misjudged her need to be protected in the big city. Then I remembered the incidents at Harrods and Garrard's. And my grandfather's comments. He was a wise old bird and had the experience of years on a city beat.

Hanni arrived home soon afterward and did exactly as I said, running up the steps from the taxi and in through the front door without pausing. "Do you have money for taxi man?" she asked me.

"I'll do it." My grandfather found some money and went out to pay the cabbie.

"So what did Baroness Rottenmeister say?" I asked.

"She was not there. She had gone out."

"So why didn't you stay until she returned?"

Hanni made a face. "I did not wish to see her."

"Did you at least leave her a note?"

Hanni stared at me defiantly. "She will be mad at us. She will want to take me home."

A huge feeling of relief swept over me. At least one good thing would have come from this horrid event. Hanni would go home. I'd be free of her. I could go back to my own, somewhat boring, life.

"I do not wish to go," she said firmly. "I like it here with you, Georgie. I like your butler and Mrs. 'uggins. I like that it is not formal and old-fashioned and full of rules. All my life has been rules, rules, rules."

I did see her point. I felt rather the same way about my upbringing. "I don't know what we're going to do, Hanni," I said. "It seems that the press has found out about us and they will hound us until they get a story. Trust me, I know. I have been through this before. I had to move in with Belinda last time."

"Last time?"

"A man was drowned in our bathtub," I said.

"So you know about dead bodies," she said happily.

"More than I care to."

"Then why don't we move in with Belinda," Hanni said. "I like Belinda. She's hot sexy dame. She can teach me what to do with boys. The nuns taught us nothing.

They said all things with men are sin. Even to think about them is sin."

"From what I've observed you have quite a good idea what to do with boys already," I said, remembering how she draped herself all over Darcy during a slow dance. "And remember you are a princess. It is rather expected that you will stay a virgin until you marry."

"Baloney," she said. An interesting expression that I hadn't heard before. I wasn't even sure whether it was a swear word or not.

"Anyway we are not going to stay with Belinda. She only has one bedroom. I had to sleep on the sofa, which was jolly uncomfortable."

"I'm hungry," Hanni complained. "Let's have tea. I like tea. It is a good meal. When I go home I shall make people have tea in Germany."

"I didn't think that royals had any power to make people do things any longer in Germany," I said, amused by the way she stuck out her little chin.

"This is true, but Herr Hitler, he will soon be our new leader and he likes me. He says I look like good healthy Aryan girl."

She did.

She smiled coyly. "So if I ask him please make everybody in Germany have teatime, he will say, *Jawohl, mein Schatz.*"

I laughed. "All right. Ring for the servants and ask if we can have tea a little early today," I said. "Tell Spinks we'll take it in the morning room. It's more pleasant in there."

We had just sat down to tea and I was in the process of being mother and pouring when Granddad appeared again.

"Sorry to trouble you, my lady," he said in a most formal tone, "but a man from Scotland Yard is here. He would like to speak with you and with Her Highness. I've shown him into the drawing room."

"Thank you, Spinks," I replied, in case the man from Scotland Yard could hear. "Is it Inspector Sugg again?"

"No, my lady. It's his superior this time. Here is his card." He came over and presented it to me.

"Chief Inspector Burnall," I said out loud, then lowered my voice. "He was the one who tried to send Binky to the gallows. And I haven't yet decided whether he is a gentleman or not. I don't recognize the school tie."

"I wouldn't hold that against him. The important question is whether he's a good copper or not."

"He wasn't very bright on the last occasion," I said, "but anything is preferable to the awful Sugg. There's nothing he'd like more than to have me convicted of something. I rather suspect he's a communist."

I got to my feet. "Sorry about this, Hanni, but we have to abandon our tea for now. I'm sure this is just a formality. Nothing to worry about."

With that I put on a bright face and walked into the drawing room with a confident stride. Chief Inspector Burnall was standing by the mantelpiece, examining the Spode figures. He turned as we came in, looking exactly as I had remembered him. He was a tall, erect figure of a man in a well-cut navy suit, unidentifiable school tie (or was it a regimental tie?), with dark hair graying at the temples, and a distinguished-looking face with a neat line of mustache, in the style of Clark Gable. He could equally have passed for an ex–Guards officer, a member of parliament, or a salesman at a gentlemen's clothing store.

"Lady Georgiana." He gave a small, correct bow. "I am sorry to trouble you again today."

"That's perfectly all right, Chief Inspector. This is Her Highness, the Princess of Bavaria. Highness, may I present Chief Inspector Burnall of Scotland Yard."

I just prayed she wouldn't say, "Hiya baby," or worse still, "Wotcha?"

She said nothing, but returned his bow with a gracious nod.

"Please be seated." I indicated the sofa and armchairs.

"I'm sure you realize, Lady Georgiana, that this was a very unfortunate incident that took place at the bookshop this morning."

"It is always tragic when someone dies," I said. "Especially someone so young and with such a promising future before him."

"Uh—quite." He paused, as if not quite sure how to proceed.

"I have been briefed on this matter by Inspector Sugg and I understand that you, Princess, discovered the body."

"I did," she said. "Because I went up the stairs ahead of Lady Georgiana."

"The victim was lying in one of the side alcoves where the lighting was very poor," Chief Inspector Burnall went on. "So I wonder how you happened to discover the body so soon after you went upstairs. You did say that you came upon it almost immediately, didn't you?"

"She discovered it because the knife was left lying on the floor. The princess kicked it, wondered what it was, and picked it up. Then she looked beyond and saw something lying there that proved to be the body."

"I'd prefer that the princess answer her own questions," the inspector said.

"I came right behind her," I said.

"And saw what?"

"I found her holding the knife, looking utterly shocked."

"Which brings us to an interesting question," Burnall said, looking hard at me. "Why did the killer drop the knife on the floor?"

"I suppose he had to leave in a hurry," I said. "I gather that Mr. Solomon only left the shop for a minute to deliver a book across the alleyway. If the killer had been in the shop, hiding, he would have seen this as an opportunity, rushed upstairs to catch Mr. Roberts unaware, then run out again before Mr. Solomon returned. Obviously he couldn't be seen running down a street with a bloody knife."

"Another interesting point," Burnall said. "The beggar who sat on the corner saw nobody running away just before you ladies arrived."

"Then the killer must have fled by another route."

"As far as we can tell, there is no other route," Burnall said. "It is a blind alley, of course. There is an attic, with a small window through which an athletic person could squeeze onto the roof tiles . . ."

"There you are, then," I said.

Burnall shook his head. "An athletic and daring person could then negotiate the steep pitch of the roof but would have to leap six feet across to a similar rooftop."

"So escape across the rooftops would have been possible," I said.

"Yes, but not probable. From the amount of dust in the attic, it would appear that the window has not been opened recently."

"Well, we saw nobody," I said. "And we

saw and heard nothing when we came into the shop."

"And yet Mr. Solomon stated that the murder could have only taken place moments before."

"That's right," I said. "The stain on his white shirt was still spreading, and he was still warm."

"Which brings me to the next interesting question," Burnall said. "Exactly what you two young ladies were doing at the shop in the first place."

"We've already been through this once," I said, fighting to control my irritation. A lady never shows her emotions, as my governess chanted to me many times, but I'd already gone through enough today that they were horribly near the surface. "Her Highness ran into an acquaintance at the British Museum yesterday. He invited her to come and see the place where he worked."

"You had met him previously where?" Burnall asked.

"In the park and then at a party," Hanni said.

"How long have you been in England, Your Highness?"

Hanni wrinkled her delicate little nose. "One week."

"So in one week you've certainly seen plenty of action. You've been at a party where a man falls off a balcony. You've met a young man in the park, and again at the British Museum, and gone to his place of employment only to find him dying on the floor." He crossed his legs as he leaned closer to her. "I don't know about your country, but things in England usually tend to be a lot tamer than that."

"What means tamer?" Hanni asked.

"I mean that life goes on here at a sedate pace, with little violence or excitement. Is that not true, your ladyship?"

"Usually, yes."

"So how do you explain that this current outbreak of apparent gangsterism has coincided with the arrival of Her Highness?"

Oh, dear. I wish he hadn't said that. Until that moment it had never occurred to me to link together Hanni's love of American gangster films with any of the strange things that had happened to us. I ran through the various events of the week quickly in my mind. The fall from the balcony—Hanni had been nowhere in sight. And as for stabbing somebody—well, that was plain ridiculous. For one thing she wouldn't have had time. I came up the stairs right after her. And for another, she had looked absolutely shocked. And for a third, why would she want to stab a harmless young man she thought was attractive?

"You're not suggesting that Her Highness is a gangster in disguise, are you, Chief Inspector?" I asked.

He gave a nervous half laugh, half cough. "Good Lord, no. But you must admit it does seem a rum coincidence."

"I agree that it does, but a coincidence it is, I assure you. You can't for a moment think that either of us had anything to do with Mr. Roberts's murder."

"I have to pursue the facts, your ladyship," he said.

"Then I suggest you extract fingerprints from the weapon and go after the criminal whose fingerprints they match, rather than upsetting us."

"Ah," he said. "Now that is an interesting fact. There are only two sets of fingerprints on the weapon, and they are yours."

"That doesn't completely surprise me," I said. "If someone can slip in unnoticed, kill quickly and silently, then he is obviously a professional and as such would have worn gloves."

Burnall nodded. "Not a bad observation, because we do rather suspect that it was the work of a trained assassin. One quick thrust between the third and fourth ribs up into the heart, then the weapon is instantly withdrawn to allow the blood to flow freely. The poor chap probably didn't know what had hit him. Death would have been instantaneous."

Hanni gave a little gasp of horror. "Please don't," she said. "It is too awful. I can't stop thinking about it. Poor Sidney, lying on the floor, and all that blood."

"Do you need to go on with this?" I demanded. "You're upsetting the princess and I'm feeling a little queasy myself."

"Just a few more questions, and then I'll leave you in peace," he said. "I'm interested to know just why you were keen to visit this young man at the bookshop."

"It was Her Highness's wish to do this."

"And is Her Highness keen on books then?" His smile was close to a smirk. I

found myself wondering whether policemen are hired for their annoying expressions or whether they develop them during
the course of their employment.

"Her Highness was rather keen on the
young man, I believe," I said, giving Hanni
a reassuring smile. "He was very present-
able and a thoroughly nice chap too."

"That being the case, why not meet him
somewhere more suitable? A tearoom, or
lunch in a more respectable part of the
city."

"Had we known exactly where the
bookstore was, I think we might have not
chosen to visit him there," I said. "But I am
not yet familiar with the various neighbor-
hoods of the city."

"I ask the question," Burnall said slowly,
"because of the nature of the bookshop. It
may sell old books, but it is also an unoffi-
cial meeting place of those with strong
leftist leanings. You might have seen the
leaflets and the posters on the walls."

"We did," I said.

"And this Mr. Sidney Roberts. You say
he was a thoroughly nice chap and yet it
may surprise you to know that he was a
card-carrying, fully paid up member of the

Communist Party. An active member at that. He spent the last year organizing labor unions, strikes and marches as well as writing a regular column for the *Daily Worker*."

"We did know he was a communist," I said. "The first time we met him was at Speakers' Corner in Hyde Park. He was passing out communist leaflets."

"And you thought this was a noble cause? You were about to hand over your castle and go to live among the masses, were you?"

"Absolutely not," I said, giving him my best Queen Victoria stare. I was not her great-granddaughter for nothing. "As I said, it was Princess Hannelore who wanted to meet him again and her motives were based more on his appearance than his political beliefs."

"There will be an inquest, of course," Burnall said. "Which presents a tricky problem." He paused, staring at the princess. "Your Highness probably doesn't realize what a mess you have plunged us into. It can't have occurred to you that back at your home in Germany the communists and the fascists are deadly rivals. The fascists have won the power for now, but it could possibly still go either way. The communists are working hard to create an upheaval so that they can seize power."

"It's not as if we were planning to join the Communist Party, Chief Inspector," I said. "And anyway, I always understood that one of the benefits of living in England was that it was a free country, where one can express one's opinion, however silly and extreme, with no worries about recourse from the authorities. Is that no longer true?"

"Of course," he said. "But we are not concerned with England here. We are concerned with Germany. You must know that there is a delicate balance at the moment between the fascist far right and the communists. There is also a strong movement afoot in Bavaria to restore Her Highness's father to his throne, thus making him a force against the Nazis. When the news reaches Germany that the princess has been in cahoots with communists, I'm afraid the German regime will see this as a confrontation—an attempt to undermine the government. World wars have been started on less."

I laughed uneasily. "You're trying to tell us that Germany might declare war because the princess went to a communist bookshop to meet a young man?"

"Who was found dead. She may be implicated in the crime."

"Of course she's not implicated in the crime. This is ridiculous," I snapped.

"Georgie, does this man think that I was the one who killed Sidney?" Hanni asked in a frightened voice. "I do not know how to stab somebody, and I liked Sidney. I wanted a chance to talk with a young man, away from court, away from baroness, who always says no. At home there is always someone to tell me what I must do and what I must say. Here I thought I was free."

"There you have your answer, Chief Inspector," I said. "Her Highness has just emerged from an education in the convent. She is eighteen years old. Speaking to young men is a novelty to her. As for Mr. Roberts's killer, you said yourself that the fascists and communists are at each other's throats. We witnessed that in Hyde Park the other day. A horrid clash with the blackshirts. Maybe you should be looking for your murderer among their ranks."

"Trust me, we shall be leaving no stone unturned in our investigation, your ladyship," Burnall said. He stood up. "Thank you for your time. As I said, you will probably be required to give evidence at the inquest. Please do not think of leaving London. You will be notified when it will take place."

With that he gave a curt nod and rose to leave.

Chapter 21

"This is not good, Georgie," Hanni said. "My father will get his knickers in a twist when he hears of it."

"His knickers in a twist? Where did you hear that?"

"Your cook. Mrs. Huggins. She said, 'Don't get your knickers in a twist' to your butler when he was upset. I like this expression. What means it exactly?"

"Something you don't want to know. One does not mention underwear in public, especially not in royal circles."

A flicker of enjoyment crossed Hanni's face. "Okeydokey," she said. "But my dad will still be angry. He will tell me to come straight home."

"I am going to see the queen," I said. "She'll decide what we should do next."

"Oh, swell. I like visits to palace. I will come with you."

"I rather think not, this time. It might be awkward as we discuss your future. You should go to Baroness Rottenmeister for now. I'll take you there myself."

"Everything has gone wrong," Hanni said.

"Now perhaps you see that your gangsters did not live such glamorous lives," I couldn't resist saying.

"I wish I had machine gun, then I'd shoot head off those horrible policemen," Hanni said.

"Hanni, for heaven's sake never let anyone hear you talking like that, even in fun," I said. "You are currently their only suspect in a murder."

"They can't pin the rap on me," she said.

"No more gangster talk. I absolutely forbid it," I said. "From now on you must act and sound like a princess at all times. You heard what the chief inspector said—wars have been started over less than this."

"I just make joke, Georgie," Hanni said, "because I am frightened."

"I'm a little frightened myself," I said. "But the police have gone now. We're home and we're safe and nothing else can go wrong tonight."

My grandfather tapped on the door before opening it. "Baroness Rottenmeister, my lady," he said in regal tones.

The baroness swept into the room like an avenging black angel, her cape streaming out behind her. If looks could kill, we'd have been sprawled on the carpet.

"What have you done, you silly girls?" she demanded in a booming voice. "The queen's private secretary telephoned me. He wanted to discuss this morning's tragedy. Naturally I knew no details because I wasn't there. And then I find out that a man has been killed and the police suspect Her Highness."

She glared at Hanni. "I leave you alone for two days. You beg me that you want to stay with Lady Georgiana. You tell me that she is responsible person and will take good care of you. And I believe you and think of my own comfort. Now I am deeply ashamed. My duty was at your side, even with the great inconveniences of living in this house. I should never have left you for one instant. I should have come to the party with you. I should have gone with you this morning and then none of this would have happened."

"The young man would still be lying dead, whether we had found him or not," I said. "And whether you had accompanied us or not."

"What do I care if this young man is dead or not?" The baroness was purple with rage by now. Obviously her governess had never told her that a lady is always in control of her emotions. "I care for the honor of your family. I care for the honor of Germany." Dramatic pause. "There is only one thing to do. I shall write to her father, asking for instructions, and I move back instantly to this house. I am willing to sacrifice my own comfort and happiness for the good of my royal family and my country."

Anyone would have thought she was being asked to undertake an expedition to the North Pole and live on seal blubber. Rannoch House really isn't that bad in summer.

"I am going to see Her Majesty as soon

as she summons me," I said. "She will decide the best course of action. It may be wiser if the princess goes home immediately."

"No way," Hanni said angrily.

"Hannelore, this has gone on long enough," the baroness said. "You must remember you are a princess and speak and act like one from now on. Go up to your room immediately and write a letter to your father, apologizing for your thoughtless actions." She lapsed into German at the end of this sentence, but I think that was the gist of it. Then she turned to me. "And you, Lady Georgiana, will be good enough to ask your cook to prepare a dinner that is kind to my digestion. Although with all this worry, I am sure I will not be able to swallow one mouthful."

I went down to Mrs. Huggins in the kitchen.

"Kind to her digestion?" she asked, hands on her broad hips. "I didn't notice much wrong with her digestion before. Knocked back everything she could lay her hands on, that one. A right pig, if you ask me. And in more ways than one. Ordering me and your granddad around as if she was the bleedin' Queen of England. 'You will do this and then you will do that.' I felt like telling her she was the foreigner here and London is my town and I don't let nobody speak to me like I'm dirt."

"Quite right, Mrs. Huggins," I said. "I know it's awful and I'm terribly grateful for everything. You've been an absolute brick. And your cooking has been splendid."

She blushed modestly. "Well, thank you kindly, your ladyship. Happy to do it, I'm sure. But can you tell me how much longer we're going to be expected to keep this up? Yer granddad is getting restless for his garden and his routine at home. He don't say nothing because he'd do anything in the world for you, but I can tell it's all getting his goat."

"Let's hope it's coming to an end, Mrs. Huggins," I said.

"It's not the housework and the cooking I mind," she went on. "I've never minded hard work in my life. Used to it, you see. But it's these people. Herself with the face like the back end of a bus, and that maid person, Fireguard or whatever her name is, creeping around, never saying a word, just staring at us when we speak good

English to her. And then there's that Mildred what you hired. Right stuck up, she
is. Coming down here and telling us how
much better everything was in the posh
houses she's been in. 'You can't get much
posher than her ladyship,' I told her.
'Related to the royals. If there was another
of them flu epidemics and the lot of them
died off, she might find herself queen one
day, and don't you forget it.'"

I smiled at her fondly. "Don't wish that
on me," I said. "Besides, it would have to
be an awfully large flu epidemic. I'm only
thirty-forth in line to the throne."

"Anyway, what I'm saying is, we'll stick
it out for you, but it better not be for much
longer."

"I do understand, Mrs. Huggins," I said.
"I feel rather the same way myself. The
princess is a delightful person in many
ways, but it's like looking after a naughty
puppy. You never know what she's going
to do next. And she doesn't have a clue
about what is proper and what isn't."

I looked up guiltily as I heard footsteps
but it was only my grandfather.

"So we've got the old dragon back here
again, I see," he muttered. "I've just had to

carry up her great pile of baggage. What on earth does she want all that stuff for? I've only ever seen her in black. And was she in a bad temper! Do this, and not like that. It was all I could do to hold my tongue. I tell you this, Georgie love, I'm not cut out to be nobody's servant. Never was."

"It really won't be for long now, Grand-dad. I've spoken with the palace and I've an audience with Her Majesty tomorrow."

"The sooner that lot is shipped back to Germany, the better, that's what I say," Mrs. Huggins muttered. "And good riddance to 'em."

"I have to confess I'll be relieved to see them go," I said. "But about dinner tonight. Could you possibly cook something that's kind to the baroness's digestion?"

"What about a nice set of pig's trotters?" she asked. I couldn't tell whether she was being funny or not, having never eaten the said part of the pig.

Before I could answer, my grandfather dug her in the ribs. "Give over, 'ettie," he said and Mrs. Huggins broke into wheezy chuckles. "Or a nice plate of jellied eels?" she went on.

"If she wants something nourishing, then

how about liver and bacon?" Granddad said when her laughter had died down. "Nobody can complain about liver and bacon. About as nourishing as you can get, that is. And a milk pudding to follow?"

"Right you are," Mrs. Huggins said. "All right with you, me lady?"

"Perfect," I said.

As I went to walk upstairs to our part of the house, my grandfather followed me. "So what did the inspector want?" he asked quietly. "Just routine, was it?"

"Anything but routine." I sighed. "He seems to think we may have caused a major international incident. If the princess is linked to a communist plot of some kind and the German government is anti-communist and pro-fascist, they may see this as an affront. Trying to convert their princess to the opposition, so to speak."

"Bloody stupid," Granddad muttered, then looked up at me with a guilty expression on his face. "Pardon the swearing. It just slipped out. So they think this man's death is somehow linked to communist activities, do they?"

"He was an active member of the Communist Party."

"Well, I never. Your German princess certainly picks 'em, don't she? Where on earth did you meet a communist?"

"In Hyde Park, at Speakers' Corner, and then again at that party."

"The party where the bloke fell off the balcony?"

"That's the one."

"Dear me," he said. "Makes you wonder if there's a link between the two deaths, don't it?"

"There can't possibly be. I was standing there, Granddad. I saw Tubby stagger backward, very drunk, and fall through the railings. I saw it."

"And this Tubby bloke. Was he also a communist?"

I laughed. "Good Lord, no. His family owns half of Shropshire."

"If you say so, love. But I can tell you this. When I was on the force, I'd have had a good look at that party, who was there and what was going on. You'll probably find out that this killing has nothing to do with communism. Probably something much more everyday than that—the young man got himself mixed up with the wrong crowd, that's what I'd guess."

"Then let's hope the police find that out quickly," I said. "It would be a huge relief to me." I paused, then a thought struck me. "Is there anything you can do, Granddad? I know you've been off the force for a while, but you must still know people. And you used to work that part of London, didn't you? Couldn't you ask some questions and find out if there are any gang rumors going around?"

"I don't know about that," Granddad said. "It's been a long while, ducks, and I'm pretty much tied down waiting on those Deutschy ladies of yours."

"Yes, I know you are. But all may be well by tomorrow. The queen may decide to send them home straight away, or she may bring them to the palace and we can all breathe again."

"Let's hope so, love," he said. "Let us hope so."

I went upstairs to change for dinner. I stood in my room listening to the sounds of the square outside my open windows. There were children playing in the central garden. I could hear their high little voices mingling with birdsong and the muted sounds of traffic. It all sounded so happy and normal and safe. And yet those newspaper reporters were still lingering by the railings, reminding me that nothing was normal and safe at all. Why did we have to time our visit to the bookstore so unluckily as to arrive at that critical moment? Moments earlier and perhaps we could have prevented Sidney from being killed. Moments later and someone else would have found the body.

I paused and considered this. Had the murderer timed his killing to coincide with our arrival, thus putting suspicion on us? What if he were a friend or acquaintance of Sidney Roberts and Sidney had confided to him that a foreign princess was going to be visiting him that morning? It would be the sort of thing one might brag about. Maybe Sidney had even mentioned it at the café and someone had overheard.

The beggar at the end of the alley hadn't seen anyone, either entering or leaving that street before us. What if the killer was already there, working in one of the adjacent buildings, maybe? All he'd have to do is to come into the bookshop when no one was looking, which would have been easy enough, then wait until he spotted us turning into the street before doing the deed and slipping out again and into the building next door. Nobody would have noticed, especially if he worked on the street and was habitually seen coming and going. We wouldn't have seen him because we were reading the signs on the various shops as we came. And if we had glimpsed him, we were looking for a bookshop, not a person. He would have still gone unnoticed.

That's what the police should be doing—questioning those who worked in the buildings around the bookshop. I should also suggest maybe that Granddad ask his own questions there. I could even go and ferret around myself if I could get rid of the princess and—wait a minute. What business was this of mine? It was up to the police to solve the crime. I had been an innocent bystander. I had absolutely nothing to worry about.

Then why was my stomach twisting itself into knots? I had the police hounding me, the baroness bullying me, and an imminent interview with the queen during which she'd probably tell me how extremely displeased with me she was. If

I were sensible, I'd catch the next train to Scotland and leave them all to sort it out without me. But then a Rannoch never runs. This was another of the words of wisdom instilled in me at an early age by my nanny and then my governess. It went along with tales of Rannochs past who stood their ground when hordes of English charged at them, or hordes of Turks, French or Germans, depending on the battlefield. All the stories ended with the particular Rannoch being hacked to pieces, so were not exactly uplifting in their moral.

What would a Rannoch do now, I wondered. Allow herself to be bullied by a German baroness, a smirking policeman, or the Queen of England? If I had my trusty claymore, I'd dispatch the whole lot of them with a single stroke, I thought, and smiled to myself. It was about time I learned to stand up for myself and let these people know that a Rannoch cannot be bullied.

I jumped as there was a tap on my bedroom door.

"You're wanted on the telephone," my grandfather said in a low voice, because Mildred was hovering somewhere close by. "The palace."

Chapter 22

Rannoch House,
Saturday, June 18, 1932

Diary,
Weather: gloomy. Overcast with the promise of rain.
Mood: equally gloomy. Due at palace immediately after breakfast.

I searched through the *Times* when Mildred brought it up to me. There was only a small paragraph. Police investigate Thames-side killing. The body of a young bookstore clerk was found stabbed in Haslett's Bookshop, off Wapping High Street, yesterday. Police are anxious to speak with anyone who was in the area about ten thirty.

No mention of us, thank heavens. Of course this was the *Times.* Who knows what the *Daily Mirror* might have said?

Breakfast was a somber affair. I found it hard to swallow anything. Even the baroness didn't go back for a second helping of bacon and eggs. We were all feeling the cloud of doom hanging over us. I couldn't wait to go to the palace and get it over with. I even let Mildred choose my outfit to wear to see the queen. She was very excited and proud to be doing so. "The palace—of course you'll want to look smart, but understated. This would definitely be an occasion for the pearls, my lady."

The fact that I let her put the pearls around my neck shows the height of tension. I've never voluntarily worn pearls in the daytime in my life. At ten past nine off I went, after obtaining reassurances from the baroness that she would not allow Princess Hannelore out of the house under any pretext, and from my grandfather the butler that he would not admit anybody. I tied a scarf around my head, hoping that nobody would recognize me, and hurried in the direction of Buckingham Palace.

I was tempted to make use of the

secret entrance in the side wall and thus gain access through that lower corridor past the kitchens, but I decided that this was one occasion when I should do every-thing by the book, and give Her Majesty no reason to find fault. So I mustered my courage, crossed the Ambassadors' Court and rang the bell at the normal visitors' entrance. It was opened by the same distinguished old gentleman who had accosted me once before when I was sneaking along a hallway. I never did find out who he was or his official title, and I could hardly ask him now. For all I knew he was the official royal door opener, no more than a glorified page. But he cer-tainly adopted the airs and graces of a higher position.

"Ah, Lady Georgiana, is it not?" He bowed a little. "Her Majesty is expecting you. May I escort you to her?" Without waiting for an answer he led me up a flight of stairs to the *piano nobile.* On this floor everything was on a grander scale: the carpet was lush, the walls were hung with tapestries and dotted with marble columns and statues, and the corridor went on for-ever. So did the old man's chatter.

"Unseasonably cold for June, so I understand, although I have not been outside myself today. Her Majesty always takes her turn about the gardens in the morning and did vouchsafe to her maid that it was 'a little nippy.'"

"Yes, it is somewhat chilly," I replied, wishing that the interminable walk down the corridor would soon come to an end.

At last, mercifully, because we had run out of talk about the weather and the English prospects for Wimbledon, he paused in front of a door, turned to me to make sure I was ready and then knocked.

"Lady Georgiana to see you, ma'am," he said.

We both stepped inside and bowed in unison.

Her Majesty was standing at the window, looking out onto the gardens. With one elegant hand resting on the tasseled velvet drapes, she looked as if she were posing for the next royal portrait. She turned to us and nodded gravely.

"Ah, Georgiana," she said. "Thank you, Reginald, you may leave us."

The old man backed out and closed the doors silently behind him.

"Come and sit down, Georgiana," Her Majesty said as she came across the room, indicating a straight-backed chair facing a brocade sofa. She chose the chair, so I perched on the edge of the sofa, facing her. She studied me for a long moment while I waited for the ax of doom to fall and for her to say, "We've decided to send you as lady-in-waiting to a distant relative in the Falkland Islands." Instead she sighed, then spoke.

"A bad business, this, Georgiana."

"It is, ma'am, and I'm sorry to have caused you embarrassment because of it. But I assure you that I had no idea that we were doing anything stupid or out of the ordinary when I took the princess to visit a bookshop. Had I known that it was in a less-than-desirable part of London or that it had any links to the Communist Party, I would not have agreed to it."

"This young man," the queen went on, "the one who was murdered. How exactly did you meet him?"

"We met him in Hyde Park, ma'am."

"In Hyde Park?" she said with exactly the same intonation with which Lady Bracknell delivered the famous line "A handbag?" in *The Importance of Being Earnest.* "Do you make it a habit of speaking to strange young men in parks?"

"Of course not, ma'am. Her Highness wanted to see Speakers' Corner and she fell into conversation with this young man who was handing out leaflets."

"Communist leaflets?"

"Yes, ma'am. But it was all perfectly harmless. He was well-spoken and seemed pleasant enough. Then we were surprised to meet him again at a friend's party."

"So he was one of your set, then?"

"I don't actually have a set. But as to whether he was of our class, he wasn't. I understood that he was from lowly origins and had gone to Cambridge on a scholarship, where he became friendly with some of the chaps at the party."

"So he frequented Mayfair parties but yet we are given to understand that he was involved with the communists?"

"Yes, I gather he was a keen socialist, very idealistic about improving the lot of the working people."

"A strange mixture, wouldn't you say?" she asked. "One wouldn't have thought that someone who felt so strongly about the lot of the working people would indulge in the extravagances of the rich."

"Very true, ma'am. In fact the host was surprised to see him at the party."

"The host being . . . ?"

"Augustus Gormsley, ma'am. And I believe Edward Fotheringay was also giving the party."

"Gormsley. That's the publishing family, isn't it?"

"That's right."

"Nothing communist about them." She chuckled. "The old man built himself the biggest monstrosity in Victorian England. Made Sandringham look like a peasant's cottage in comparison."

I smiled. "The champagne and cocktails were certainly flowing at the party," I said. I didn't mention the cocaine. I had no idea whether that flowed or not, or whether Gussie knew what was going on in his kitchen and was simply turning a blind eye to it.

"The question is, what are we going to do about it, Georgiana?" Her Majesty said. "We have sent word to the newspaper owners asking them to keep your names out of any reports for the moment and I am sure they will comply with this— except for the *Daily Worker,* of course. We have no influence over them whatsoever, but then nobody of consequence reads that paper, anyway. Unfortunately, as soon as there is an inquest, your names will be on the public record and there is not much we can do then. All highly embarrassing, of course. Especially when relations with Germany are always so fragile, and Germany itself is in such an unsettled state at the moment."

"Baroness Rottenmeister has already ordered Her Highness to write to her father, explaining that we had accepted what seemed like a polite invitation to see some rare books and we knew nothing of the place's communist connections. Also that we hardly knew the young man in question and it was pure chance that we timed our arrival so poorly."

The queen nodded. "I wonder whether I should telephone the King of Bavaria? I rather think the best approach, given the location that this awful thing took place, would be to say that you were doing charitable works among the poor."

"That might indeed be a wise approach," I said. "But I've already told the police that we went to the bookshop at the invitation of the young man."

"What was so intriguing about a bookshop, pray?"

"It wasn't the bookshop, ma'am. It was the young man in question. The princess was rather smitten with him, I believe."

"Oh, dear. Straight from the convent. Desperate to meet boys. So what do you think we should do now, Georgiana?"

I was taken aback by this. I had expected to be told what would happen, not to have my opinion sought.

"I was wondering whether we should not send the princess home right away, so that she doesn't have to endure the newspaper reporters and the inquest. Her father would surely not want to put her through those."

The queen gave a little sigh. "But then we would have no chance of achieving our objective, would we? We still haven't come up with a suitable occasion for David to have a chance to see her and chat with her informally. That boy is hopeless. I had planned to place him beside her at our little dinner the other evening, but then he ran out on us."

"We may have to give this up as a lost cause, ma'am. The Prince of Wales showed no flicker of interest in her during our brief conversation."

"The boy is a fool," she said. "How can any young man be more interested in a desiccated and vicious middle-aged American woman than in a sweet and lovely young girl?"

"I don't know how men's minds work, ma'am."

"I don't think this has anything to do with David's mind. I don't even think it has anything to do with lust. She has some uncanny hold over him. Maybe he'll grow tired of her before long, but I'd really like to nip it in the bud, while she still has a husband to return to. You'd think her husband would do something about it, wouldn't you? Give her a damned good hiding and take her home—that's what any red-blooded young Englishman would do."

I listened, nodding politely.

"No, I'd really like to give this one more chance, Georgiana," Her Majesty continued. "I have discussed the matter with the king and it occurs to me that I may have the solution as to how we could kill two birds with one stone, so to speak. I know that the Cromer-Strodes are currently entertaining people—do you know the Cromer-Strodes?"

"I have met their daughter, Fiona, but I've never been to their house."

"Dippings. A lovely house with some fine antiques, and a mere stone's throw from Sandringham in Norfolk."

I wondered how the Cromer-Strodes had managed to hang on to those fine antiques if they were but a stone's throw from a royal palace.

"The king and I are motoring up to Sandringham today. He has been working too hard recently and he's not at all well, Georgiana. So I have persuaded him to take a few days off and he does so love Sandringham. It's the only place where he's truly comfortable, I believe. We'll have to come back to London for the garden party next week, of course, but the journey is not too long and arduous."

"Garden party?"

"One of those ghastly invite-the-masses

events. Well, not exactly the masses, but dreary people like the head of the dock board and the railways and various members of parliament. People who feel entitled to shake hands with us once a year. You must bring Princess Hannelore. It will be good for her to see a traditional aspect of English life. You could motor up from Sandringham with us."

"Thank you, ma'am. I'm sure she'd enjoy it."

"Let's hope the weather is favorable this time. Last year it was most unpleasant, standing with that hot sun on one's back."

She paused. I waited for her to continue. Her eyes were focused on the far wall. "Those Worcester pieces," she said, indicating some royal blue china that was displayed in a Chinese cabinet, "so lovely, aren't they? We have the rest of that collection at Sandringham. I believe there is a bowl in the same pattern but I haven't managed to unearth one yet. If you ever see one during your travels, do let me know. . . ."

So that you can swoop down and relieve them of it, I thought. Her Majesty was notorious for pursuing antiques with such a passion that she had absolutely no scruples about acquiring them through fair means or foul.

"You were talking about Sandringham, ma'am. Do I understand that you'd want us to accompany you?"

"No, no, I don't think that would be the best idea. You see, David has given us to understand that he'll be coming to Sandringham with us and we don't want him to think that he's being thrown together with the princess. That would have quite the wrong effect. But my spies tell me that the dreadful American woman has managed to have herself included in the house party at Dippings—Lord Cromer-Strode married an American, you know, which is obviously why David is suddenly so interested in Sandringham."

I nodded with understanding.

"So my thought was this: if Princess Hannelore and you join the house party at Dippings, then David will be able to make the comparison—the young beauty and the old hag."

I laughed. "She may be old, but she's certainly not a hag, ma'am. She has exquisite taste in clothes and she's quite vivacious."

"So you like her, do you?"

"I absolutely loathe her, but I am just trying to be fair."

The queen smiled. "So what do you say, Georgiana? Does this seem like the best solution? We remove the princess from the public eye in London, whisk her to the safety of Dippings, and let things take their course from there."

"It does seem like a good plan, ma'am," I said, relieved that once we reached Dippings, the Cromer-Strodes would be responsible for her, not I. "But the police did indicate that we were not to leave London before the inquest."

"Not leave London? Blessed cheek. Do they expect you to flee the coop like the criminal classes? I'll have my secretary let them know that the king and I have invited you both to be with us in the country, after your unfortunate experience. We will personally guarantee that you will be motored back to London for the inquest."

"Thank you, ma'am."

"I just hope they manage to get to the bottom of this sordid business as quickly as possible. If the whole thing is brought to a satisfactory conclusion before the date of the inquest, then you might not even have to appear in public. And the newspapers would certainly have nothing to write about."

"Let us hope so, ma'am."

She was looking at me with that steely, unwavering stare of hers again. "You could help, Georgiana."

"Help with what?"

"To solve this murder. You have a good sharp mind. And you did so splendidly when your brother was wrongly accused."

"I solved that case mainly by accident, ma'am, and because my own life was threatened."

"Nonsense, you're being too modest," the queen said. "I was most impressed; so was the king. I think you could get to the bottom of this sordid little matter more swiftly than the police."

"I really don't think the police would take kindly to my interfering. I don't see how I could poke around and ask questions without incurring their suspicions."

"Your grandfather was a member of the police force, was he not?"

"Yes, ma'am, but several years ago, and he was only an ordinary bobby."

"Nevertheless, he'll know where to ask questions and whom to ask. I can't believe it can be that difficult, but policemen seem to be so dense. And they are like terriers— once they get one idea into their heads, they shake it and shake it and can't let it go."

Another thought struck me. "Ma'am, how can I look into a murder in London if I'm stuck at a house in Norfolk?" I blurted out, not thinking that this was probably an impolite way to address a queen.

"Ask your grandfather to do the spade-work for you. Then, when you have settled Princess Hannelore at Dippings, you can slip back to London. We'll make sure the Cromer-Strodes have a car at your disposal to take you to the station."

"You're most kind," I said, although I was thinking the opposite. How on earth did she expect me to solve a murder? Even with Granddad's help, it seemed impossible. I had no idea where to start. Did she really expect me to go snooping around the docklands, asking questions? But I reminded myself that she was the queen, and one did not say no.

Chapter 23

All the occupants of Rannoch House were waiting for me as I came in through the front door.

"Well?" Baroness Rottenmeister demanded.

"Am I to be sent home?" Hanni asked.

I saw my grandfather lurking near the baize door. I expect that Mrs. Huggins was listening on the other side of it.

"The queen has come up with an admirable solution. We are to go to a country estate called Dippings, owned by Lord and Lady Cromer-Strode. They are having some people to stay for a house party and it should be quite lively for the princess."

I saw Hanni's face fall and the baroness look disapproving.

"But the policeman said we must not leave London," Hanni reminded me. "I do not wish to leave London."

"And who are these people, the Cromer-Strodes? They are royalty?"

"Nobility," I said.

The baroness frowned. "It is insult to Her Highness that she does not stay with royal peoples. I will write to her father and say is insult."

"The queen thinks highly of them," I said. "And their estate is close to Sandringham, one of the royal palaces, where Their Majesties will also be staying next week."

Hanni looked brighter for some reason. "I like to see royal palaces. The queen does not yet show me around Buckingham Palace and she promised."

"You're invited to a royal garden party next week," I said. "You'll like that. Strawberries and cream on the lawn."

Hanni nodded. "Yes," she said emphatically. "This I shall like."

"When do we leave for this country house?" the baroness demanded.

"The queen is sending a car for us in an hour."

"An hour? We are expected to be ready in one hour?"

"The queen thinks it would be a good idea if we got away from London as quickly as possible."

"Hannelore, go and tell Irmgardt to pack immediately," the baroness said. "If the queen wishes it, we cannot refuse. I hope it is not damp and cold at Deepings, and that the food is not too English."

"I understand that it is a very fine house, and Lady Cromer-Strode is American."

"American?" Hanni perked up again, probably hoping to meet some gangsters in residence.

The baroness, however, was not convinced. "English. American. All the same. No idea how to cook good food."

They went upstairs to instruct Irmgardt to pack. I followed them to impart this news to Mildred, who seemed positively thrilled by it. "We're going to the country, my lady? And to Dippings, too. I've heard so many wonderful things about it. It is supposed to be quait, quait lovely."

Until that moment I hadn't quite realized that she'd expect to come along on this jaunt. How thick could I be? Of course I'd be expected to take my maid with me. I'd become too used to doing without servants.

"When do we leave, my lady?"

"Immediately, Mildred. The queen is sending a car for us."

At this she became quite flustered. "Then I must pack immediately. Where are your trunks kept? You will need all your dinner gowns, of course. It would never do to wear the same gown at dinner more than once."

"I don't think I have more than a couple of dinner gowns," I said.

But she went on, still in raptures, "And there is bound to be a formal occasion or a ball, and then there's your tennis outfit and is there possibly yachting nearby?"

I laughed. "I don't possess a yachting outfit, if that's what you mean. There may be boating on the Norfolk Broads."

"A wonderful opportunity for you, my lady." Mildred beamed at me. "There will no doubt be a good selection of suitable young men at the house party."

Oh no. Now even she was trying to marry me off. She hummed to herself as she started going through my wardrobe. She was obviously going to be in her element, probably the senior ranking maid, thanks to being attached to me, and she was going to relish every moment. Well, she was going to be disappointed when I had to return to London on the queen's business—unless I could sneak away without letting her know!

I left her humming and packing and went to find my grandfather below stairs.

"So it looks like Mrs. Huggins and me can scarper off home, don't it?" he said.

"I'm not sure when we'll be back in London. I'm sure it would be fine for you to spend the next few days at home, but could you possibly be ready to come back if we have to return to London?"

"I expect we can, although Mrs. 'uggins is getting a bit cheesed off."

"How can I contact you in a hurry?" I asked.

"You can always telephone the pub on the corner. The Queen's 'ead. They'll let me know, and we can be back in London in a jiffy if you needs us."

"I really appreciate this, Granddad. You've been wonderful."

"Get on with you." He grinned and ruffled my hair. "I can't say I'll be sorry to leave. Not that I don't enjoy your company, my love, but them other lot, I don't know how you put up with them."

"One does what one has to," I said. "And I couldn't have done it without you and Mrs. Huggins. You've been real bricks."

"So what happens now with the police investigation?" he asked. "Is it okay for you to go running off before the inquest?"

"The queen is vouching for us." I paused and took a deep breath. "There's one other thing. She'd like me to solve the case before the inquest."

"She'd what?" he boomed.

I smiled. "I know, it's ridiculous. I don't see how I can do anything without annoying the police and casting more suspicion upon myself."

"Added to which you'd be poking around some pretty nasty people. Someone wanted that young man dead badly enough to take a large risk."

"Her Majesty suggested that you could help me, Granddad."

"Me? I really don't see what I could do."

"You used to be a policeman in that area. You know people."

"I might still know a few old geezers around the docklands," Granddad conceded. "If anyone's going to ask the questions, I'd rather it was me than you. Ruddy cheek that queen of yours has got— wanting to send you into harm's way, just to avoid a royal scandal."

"Rather more than a scandal, the way they put it. More like a diplomatic crisis."

"Ruddy Germans. Nothing but trouble, they are. You'd have thought they'd learned their lesson in the war, wouldn't you? But no, this Hitler bloke comes along with his blasted Nazis and starts upsetting everything again."

"So will you find out what you can for me?" I asked. "When the princess is settled I'm supposed to come back to London to snoop around and solve this murder."

"You stay put in the country, ducks," he said. "I'll do my bit for you, but there's no way I'm letting you poke around communist haunts. I'm your grandfather and I'm telling you straight."

I looked at him and grinned. "Yes, Granddad," I said.

∽∾

Everyone was cheerful as the car arrived for us. It was a large Rolls with a well-attired chauffeur.

"Now this is as it should be," Baroness Rottenmeister commented. "Suitable transportation for Her Highness."

We left Mildred and Irmgardt standing on the pavement beside a Matterhorn of luggage, awaiting a taxi. No royal car for them. They were going to have to shepherd that pile of cases by train. I found myself feeling sorry for them and realized, with some shame, that such things had never crossed my mind before. Servants and luggage arrived where they were supposed to be and if they had inconveniences, they were no concern of ours. I think we truly believed that their one purpose in life was to make sure our lives ran smoothly.

Our car made its way through the faceless northern suburbs until the city sprawl melted into glorious countryside. Having been confined to London for most of the spring I was unprepared for the riot of summer green—spreading oak trees, rich pastures, wheat and barley already tall and feathery in the fields. There is nothing as lush as the English countryside in summer.

The baroness dozed in the heat. Princess Hanni looked out of the window.

"England is very flat," she commented. "No mountains."

"You're looking at the flat part of England," I said. "In the north and west we have many mountains, although not as high as the Alps in Bavaria."

"In Bavaria we have high mountains with snow," she said. "The highest mountains in the world."

"Not exactly," I said. "The Himalayas are the highest mountains in the world. The Alps are only the highest mountains in Europe."

"In Bavaria we have the highest peaks," she said. "The Zugspitze and the Jungfrau."

"Mont Blanc in France is higher, I regret to tell you," I said with a smile.

"Ah, Mont Blanc," she said dismissively.

Then she turned to me. "This place Dippings. Is it nice?"

"I expect so."

"Will there be young men there? We will
dance?"

"I have no idea, Hanni."

"Do you think that Darcy will be there?"

I kept my face completely composed. "I
shouldn't think so."

"Gee, that's too bad. I want to see him
more. I think he likes me."

There was silence in the car while I
tried not to think of Darcy, and especially
Hanni with Darcy.

"This is strange name," she said at last.
"What means Dippings?"

"I expect it means little dips in the flat
countryside."

"It is crummy name. Shall we visit the
king and queen at their house?"

"If they invite us."

"I am princess. They should invite me. It
is not right that I do not stay at palace."

"The queen was thinking of you. She
felt you would have more fun with people
your own age."

"But I do not meet people my own age.
Only you. I have not yet had date with fun

and sexy guy." I had been thinking that I had cured the princess of speaking American gangster slang. Obviously I hadn't.

"One week, Hanni. You can't expect too much in one week."

"But you do not understand. Soon I go home and then I will not be permitted to speak with men. Only guys my family want me to marry. Nobody hot and sexy. And someone like the baroness will always be with me. How will I learn what sex is all about?"

"I'm sure you'll pick it up rather quickly," I said. "You already seem to have the main idea."

"What main idea?"

"Hanni, we went to a party. You danced. You flirted. I saw you."

"What means flirt?"

"You know. Flutter your eyelashes. Tease. Act as if you are interested in a boy."

"This I can do. This I like to do, yes," she said. "But you do not. This is not good, I think. It means boy does not know you like him."

Well, that was a definite slap in the face. Maybe what she said was true. Maybe Darcy had moved on because I hadn't shown that I liked him enough. But flirting does not come easily to someone brought up in a remote castle with tartan wallpaper in the bathrooms, bagpipes at dawn and men who wear kilts.

"I'll try harder in future," I reassured her.

"I have not yet kissed a boy," she went on. "Is this very pleasurable?"

"Oh yes, very, with the right boy."

"You have found right boy?" she asked. "You know a hot and sexy guy?"

I stared out of the window, watching a stream meander through a meadow while cattle stood in dappled shade. "Obviously not yet, or I'd be married."

"You want to be married?" she asked.

"Yes, I suppose so. It's what every woman wants. Don't you?"

"Not before I have known what it is to live my own life," she said, seriously for her. "I have things I want to do. Things that married women cannot do, especially not married queens and princesses. I have dreams."

"Such as what?" I asked, intrigued.

"Silly things. Go to the shops. Eat in a café." She turned abruptly away and stared out of the window.

Only the baroness's rhythmic rumblings broke our silence. I found myself thinking things over. Everything had been so confused for the past few days. First Tubby plunging to his death and then the horrible episode in the bookshop with poor Sidney Roberts lying there, blood spreading across his white shirt. Granddad seemed to think there had to be a connection. Personally I couldn't think what it was, unless it had something to with the cocaine I saw in Gussie's kitchen. I knew little about drugs but I had heard that they were bought and sold by ruthless people. If Tubby and Sidney had been involved with them, and perhaps had not paid their bills, then maybe they had been taught the ultimate lesson. But by whom?

The flatlands of East Anglia opened up before us—a landscape that seemed nearly all sky. White clouds hung like cotton wool, sending patches of shadow over the fields. In the distance a church spire betrayed the presence of a village among trees. We passed through Little Dippings, and then Much Dippings, a similar village with a cluster of thatched pink and white cottages around a church and pub (the

Cromer-Strode Arms), before driving along a high brick wall and turning in at an impressive gateway. The first part of the estate was wild parkland, with lots of trees and what looked like rhododendrons, although they had already finished blooming. A pheasant took off with a clatter of wings. A small herd of ornamental deer moved away as they heard the car approaching. Then Hanni said, "Look. What kind of animal is that over there in those bushes? It is pink, but I do not think it is a pig."

I stared hard at the pink thing among the foliage. It seemed to have an awful lot of limbs. "I really don't know," I said, but then suddenly I did. It seemed to me that it was two people, without clothes, wrapped around each other in the grass and doing what I could only guess at. Our driver, on the other side of his glass partition, coughed discreetly and put his foot down on the accelerator. As the couple heard the approaching car, a head was raised in surprise. I caught a glimpse of a shocked face before we passed.

Chapter 24

Then we came around a bend and there was Dippings before us in all its glory. Like most houses in the area, it was built of red brick, which had mellowed over hundreds of years into a lovely muted rose pink. The Elizabethan chimneys were striped in white and red brick and a classical portico and flight of marble steps had been added to the front of the house in Georgian times. There was an ornamental pond with fountain playing in the forecourt. A flight of white doves wheeled overhead. All in all a most pleasing aspect. We drove between well-kept lawns and shaded drives until we came to a halt at those front steps.

The baroness stirred.

"We have arrived," Hanni said. The baroness hastily adjusted her hat as the door was opened by footmen.

"Welcome to Dippings, my lady," one of them said as he helped me out.

We had barely set foot on the gravel forecourt than a figure came flying down the steps to greet us. She was tall, angular and almost painfully thin. Her face was a perfect mask of makeup, from the plucked eyebrows to the startling red lips (though not executed quite as perfectly as my mother's). Her mauve dress had panels that flew out around her as she hurtled toward us, arms outstretched.

"Welcome, welcome to Dippings," she called in a southern American drawl. "You must be Lady Georgiana, and this is the princess. Welcome, Your Highness." She attempted a jerky bob of curtsy. "How lovely to have you here with us. I can't tell you how excited I was when the queen called and suggested you join our little gathering. I know you'll just love it here. Everyone does. My husband is such a wonderful host. He always takes care of everyone so well and makes sure they have a good time. Come on in. Come on in."

Hanni and I glanced at each other, feeling somewhat breathless, as she went ahead back up the steps, still talking away. "We've quite a jolly little group here. Some young people your age. You probably know most of them, I'm sure, but my nieces are here from America. Such dear girls. You're going to love them, I just know it."

We entered a wood-paneled foyer, hung with family portraits and the occasional, obligatory pair of crossed swords and frayed standard from some long-ago battle.

"I'm afraid you're too late for lunch," she went on, "and tea won't be for another hour. But I expect you're starving. How about some sandwiches and lemonade out on the back lawn? Or do you want to see your rooms first? We've sent someone to meet the train with your luggage so you should be able to change as soon as it arrives."

She paused for breath. I realized she had asked about a dozen questions and hadn't waited for a single answer. I tried to remember what the choices had been.

"There's not much point in going up to our rooms before our maids and our luggage arrive," I said, "so some lemonade on the lawn would be lovely."

"I don't know where everyone else has got to," she said. "They may be playing tennis, although it's rather hot for it today, wouldn't you say? I expect Fiona is with her American cousins. You remember my daughter, Fiona, don't you? I know you two girls were at that fearfully expensive school together."

It's funny how outsiders always give themselves away as being "not one of us." People I knew would never consider whether a school was expensive or not. If it was the right school and the rest of the family had been there, one bit the bullet and paid for it somehow.

Lady Cromer-Strode (I presume it was she although there had never been proper introductions) now led us through a series of dark paneled rooms and galleries until we came to a charming drawing room with lots of low, comfortable armchairs and French doors opening onto lawns. Chairs and tables had been set up in the shade of an enormous copper beech in the middle of the lawn and several people were sitting there. They looked up as we came out onto the terrace and down the steps to the lawn.

"Here they are. They have arrived," Lady Cromer-Strode announced to the world.

The young men rose awkwardly from their deck chairs. It is never easy to get out of a deck chair gracefully. "Everybody, this is Lady Georgiana and Princess Hannelore. They're going to be joining our jolly little gathering. Won't that be fun?"

"And may I present Baroness Rottenmeister, who is accompanying the princess," I said, since she had been ignored by our hostess until now and was hovering behind us, looking decidedly out of sorts.

"What-ho, Georgie. Good to see you again." One of the young men revealed himself to be Gussie Gormsley. "And you, Your Highness."

"Please, call me Hanni. We are among friends," she said.

Fiona Cromer-Strode, large and pink, came to embrace me. She was carrying a tennis racquet and looked revoltingly hearty. "How absolutely lovely to see you again, Georgie. Doesn't it seem simply ages since we were at Les Oiseaux? Wasn't it simply ripping fun?"

"Yes, it was." Fiona and I had scarcely known each other at Les Oiseaux, but now I remembered she had always been annoying.

"This my cousin Jensen Hedley," she said. "She's visiting from Baltimore. Her two sisters are away for the day, visiting Cambridge, but you'll meet them at dinner tonight."

The pale, elegant young American, wearing a dress that could only have come from Paris, smiled charmingly. "Gee, I've always wanted to meet a real princess," she said and shook Hanni's hand.

"I thought you were more interested in meeting a prince," Fiona teased.

"All the princes around here seem to be otherwise occupied," Jensen said and gave a quick glance over her shoulder.

Mrs. Simpson was lounging in the shade behind us, wearing white shorts and a bright red halter top and apparently reading a magazine. She hadn't bothered to move when we arrived. Now she felt eyes on her and looked up.

"Why, it's the actress's daughter," she said, in feigned surprise. "Fancy seeing you here."

"The queen suggested it so that she could keep an eye on us from Sandringham," I said. "We are apparently close to Sandringham, as you probably know." I smiled sweetly.

Her eyes narrowed, then focused on Hanni. "And who is the pretty little blond girl?"

"Her Royal Highness Princess Hannelore of Bavaria," I said, stiffly. "Highness, this lady is Mrs. Simpson, also visiting from America."

"I love America." Hanni was beaming. "Do you have gangsters in your town?"

"I sincerely hope not," Mrs. Simpson said. "Baltimore is a refined and old city. Our hostess and I went to the ladies' seminary together there. The very same school that the Misses Hedley also attended. Isn't that right, Jensen honey?"

"Reagan and I attended the seminary," Jensen said. "Danika was educated at home, on account of her delicate health."

Reagan, Jensen, Danika, Wallis—was nobody in America called plain Jane or Mary?

"Such interesting names," I commented.

"We also have a brother, Homer," Jensen said.

"Ah, so you have a parent interested in the classics?" I asked.

She wrinkled that button of a nose, frowning. "No. Daddy likes baseball."

"So how is your dear mother?" Mrs. Simpson asked me. "Still keeping herself busy in Germany?"

"She comes and goes," I said. "I saw her recently in good health, thank you."

"She has staying power, I'll say that for her. Still, I suppose that tough upbringing on the streets has given her resilience."

"Surviving Castle Rannoch would have given her more resilience," I said, not willing to be drawn into a spat. "The rooms there are much colder and bleaker than my grandparents' house." I went to move away, then couldn't resist asking, "Are you here with Mr. Simpson?"

A frown crossed the perfectly made up face. "Regrettably, he has been called back to America on business."

"Dear me. What a pity." I gave her a sweet smile and realized that she no longer intimidated me. At least adversity does have some advantages.

Lemonade and sandwiches arrived. Jensen Hedley dragged off Gussie to play tennis. The baroness parked herself in one of the deck chairs and promptly tucked into the sandwiches. They looked so tempting—egg and cress, crab and cucumber and even smoked salmon, my favorite—that I was about to join her when a man in wrinkled cricket whites came sauntering across the lawns. He had a red, weathered face surrounded by a halo of wispy white hair and childishly innocent eyes. What's more, I recognized him. His was the face that had peered over the bush when we arrived.

Chapter 25

The elderly man gave no indication of having recognized us, however, and came toward us with a big smile on his face. "Well, well. Here they are. Spendid. Splendid. Cromer-Strode." He shook our hands heartily. "And I met you when you were a little girl," he added to me. "At Hubert Anstruther's. I believe your mother was—"

"Married to him at the time," I finished for him, still not quite able to look him in the eye. I couldn't stop wondering who had provided those other pink arms and legs in the bushes and whether Lady Cromer-Strode knew anything about it.

"And this delightful young person is our visiting princess." Lord Cromer-Strode turned his attention to Hanni. "Is this your first experience of an English country house, Highness?" He took her hand, pressing it between his.

"Yes, it is my first visit to England," she said.

"Then you must let me give you a tour of the grounds," he went on. "Give you a feel for the place. Dippings is noted for its sublime landscapes and the rose garden is in all the guide books. We have trippers clamoring to take a look almost daily. Come along, drink up that lemonade and we'll have time for a turn before tea."

A turn at what? I wondered. A feel for which place? Did he make a habit of such behavior? I wondered if I was being invited along as chaperone.

"We'll leave my daughter and Lady Georgiana to catch up on news, shall we?" he went on, making it perfectly clear that I wasn't. "They have hardly seen each other since schooldays. Off we go then."

He put an arm around her waist and shepherded her away. I stood there in an agony of indecision. Could I come up with an excuse to go after them? Surely even the most randy of old men would not try anything with a visiting princess, would he? I could already hear the queen's voice ringing in my ears; *And you just sat there and allowed her to be deflowered in broad daylight? Germany will declare war and it will all be your fault.*

If I see them heading toward the rhododendron shrubbery, I'll go after them, I decided.

"Isn't it spiffing fun that we're together again, Georgie?" Fiona came to stand beside me. I remembered she always was on the hearty side.

"I'm not sure whether I should be letting the princess go off unchaperoned," I said as the two figures disappeared around the side of the house.

"Don't be silly, she's with Daddy. He'll take really, really good care of her," Fiona said. Like other members of our class, she didn't say her *r*s properly. The words came out as "weely, weely." With her I suspected it was affectation. She slipped her arm through mine. "Why don't we go for a little walk too? We have some darling, darling little woolly lambs at the home farm. Well, they're rather fat and jolly now but they were absolutely darling a month or so ago."

Since the home farm was in the same general direction that the princess had taken I agreed to this.

"Isn't it too, too lovely to be together again?" Fiona said. "I know we're going to have such a jolly time. Mummy has invited lots of absolutely topping people and it's going to be splendid fun."

I managed a happy smile.

"Have you heard my news?" Fiona said. "Did you know I am engaged to be married?"

"No, I didn't. Congratulations. Who is the lucky man?"

"Why, it's dear Edward."

"Edward?"

"Surely you know him. Everybody does. Edward Fotheringay."

"Lunghi Fungy, you mean?" I blurted the words out.

"I don't like that silly nickname. I have forbidden Gussie to address him in that way. But I'm so glad you know him. Isn't he wonderful? Everybody adores him."

Including my mother, I thought. And

from what I saw, he reciprocated the sentiments.

"And is Edward here at the moment?" I asked casually.

"Of course he is. We couldn't have a house party and not invite Edward, could we? He has driven my American cousins into Cambridge today, seeing that he was a student there and can show them around properly."

Given his behavior with my mother and his flirtation with Hanni, I wondered just what else he might be showing them during the course of the day.

"But they'll all be back in time for dinner," Fiona continued merrily. "Ah, here we are. This is the home farm. Isn't it absolutely sweet? Almost like a toy farm. I've always adored it. And Daddy loves it so much. He spends most of his time here, just talking to the pigs."

I snorted. I couldn't help it. I know a lady never snorts but it just came out. The pink image from the shrubbery was simply too strong. So his family thought that he spent all his time at the home farm, did they?

By the time we returned to the house our luggage and maids were installed in our bedrooms. I found that Hanni had come back, apparently unscathed, before me and was talking with the baroness in her room, while the silent, scowling Irmgardt scurried around, unpacking trunks.

"And how was your walk?" I asked cautiously.

"I enjoy very much," Hanni said. "He is very kind man. Very friendly. We had to climb over stool, is it called?"

"Stool?"

"Between fields."

"Stile," I said. "You mean steps over a wall?"

"Yes. We climb over stile and he was kind enough to lift me up and down."

And do a little incidental groping, I thought.

"The princess's room is most satisfactory," the baroness said. "I understand your room is next door. My room is not so pleasant, I regret to say. At the back of the house, facing north, up flights of very steep stairs."

"I'm sorry," I said. "Should we speak to Lady Cromer-Strode about it?"

The baroness sighed. "I am prepared to suffer," she said. "Obviously a German title means nothing to these people. I am treated like a maid."

"Perhaps they are not aware of your rank," I said. "The queen arranged this and she may not even have been aware that you would be accompanying us."

"That could be true," she said, "especially if you did not remind Her Majesty that I was staying with you."

So I was to be the guilty one. "I'll try and have your room changed for you."

"Please do not derange yourself. I shall suffer. The extra stairs shall be good for my fitness."

"I haven't even seen my own room yet," I said. "It may not be as pleasant as this one. I'll call for you when it's teatime, shall I?"

"Teatime? I thought we just ate on the lawn."

"That was a snack to keep us going until tea," I said.

"At least we are to be fed properly here," the baroness commented as I left Hanni's room. Mildred had already unpacked everything was busy pressing out every crease. Truly she was a marvel. I couldn't think why I'd be so relieved to get rid of her again.

"What a delightful view from your window, my lady," she said excitedly. "I'm sure you are going to have such a happy time here. And I see there are some attractive young men. I passed one of them in the hall just now. Very handsome and quite flirtatious too. He actually winked at me." And she blushed.

At four o'clock we made our way down for tea, which was held in the long gallery. Lady Cromer-Strode was wafting around gushing and officiating. "Do try the Victoria sponge. It is Cook's specialty. And those little crunchy things. Divine. I don't know where my husband can have gotten to. Up at the farm again, I suspect. He puts in far too many hours on that farm. Absolutely dedicated, isn't he, Fiona, honey?"

Fiona agreed. I rather fancied I saw meaningful glances pass between some of the guests and wondered which ones of them had been taken on visits to the farm. We tucked in well even though it was only an hour since we'd eaten sandwiches. Isn't it remarkable what fresh air will do for the appetite? There were the most delicious scones with thick cream and homemade strawberry jam as well as brandy snaps and cream puffs that were so light they melted in the mouth. Obviously the baroness was going to be very happy here. One by one the other guests drifted in. Jensen and some other tennis players. A young man I thought I recognized came to sit beside me.

"Hello, I'm Felix," he said. "I don't think we've met."

"Georgiana," I replied. "And I think I saw you at Gussie's party the other night."

"The fateful one when poor old Tubby toppled?"

I nodded.

"That was a rum do, wasn't it? Who'd have thought poor old Tubby?"

"Does Gussie give a lot of these parties?"

"Oh, all the time, old bean. The host with the most is our Gussie."

"He must have a good allowance. The champagne and cocktails were positively flowing," I said awkwardly. One of the rules of our set was not to discuss money, but in my role as sleuth, I rather needed to know where Gussie acquired his.

"Well, I don't know about allowance, but he does all right by himself, old Gussie,"

Felix said guardedly. "One way and another." There was something in the way he said it that made me wonder about that cocaine. I had thought of Gussie as the genial host, but what if he supplemented his income by supplying his friends with drugs?

"You were at Cambridge with him, were you?" I asked.

His face lit up. "Oh, absolutely. All Trinity men. We rowed in those days. Not any-more. Gone to seed rather."

"So what do you do now?" I asked.

"Not much, really—to the despair of the pater. Haven't found my niche in life yet. Wasn't cut out for the army or the law or the church and there's not much else left, is there?"

I agreed that there wasn't.

"So how about you? Are you one of those fearsome bright girls who went to university?"

"I'm afraid not. Although I'd quite like to have gone, but it wasn't offered."

Felix nodded in sympathy. "Hard times, I know. Everybody penny pinching. So I suppose you were forced to go out and earn your own living?"

"I wasn't allowed to, actually. It was frowned upon."

"What do you mean?"

"Not considered suitable."

At this moment Gussie sauntered over. "So you've met Georgie, have you? Jolly good. So I hear the relatives have also arrived for a few days. Shall you be visiting?"

"Relatives?" Felix asked.

"King and queen, old chap. Don't be so dense. She's Binky's sister."

Felix turned bright pink. "Oh, I say. I've put my foot in it rather, haven't I? Talking about penny pinching and having to work for a living?"

I laughed. "We're penny pinching like everyone else, and I'd love to work for a living."

"There's a splendid girl staying here who's doing frightfully well in her own business. I'm terribly admiring," Felix said. "Oh, here she is now."

Belinda entered the room, deep in conversation with his lordship. From the chatty way that they parted, I found my suspicions running riot. She saw me and came straight over.

"Darling, what a lovely surprise. I had no idea you'd be part of this bun fight."

"Belinda, what are you doing here?" I asked.

"Darling, have you ever known me to turn down a free meal? I told you I was going to the country. One simply can't stay in London when the weather turns warm."

"How is it that you know absolutely everybody?" I asked.

"One works at it, darling. It's a matter of survival. With the amount I'm making from my fashion business at the moment, I'd starve, so it's a question of going where the food and wine are good. And after all, we were at school with Fiona."

"We loathed her," I said under my breath. "Remember when she first arrived and would follow us everywhere? You told her awful stories about the upstairs lavatory being haunted so that we could have some peace and quiet there."

Belinda laughed. "I remember." She looked around the room. "I say, it's rather a jolly party, isn't it? Quite a few people you know, including Lunghi Fungy."

"I've just heard he's engaged to Fiona."

"Been promised to each other since

birth, darling. Nothing will come of it. Who could be married to someone who gushes about little woolly lambs?"

"She seems to think something will come of it. She even asked me to be a bridesmaid."

"Then perhaps Lunghi is doing the sensible thing. After all, Fiona is an only child and she'll inherit all this someday. Lunghi's own family situation is precarious."

"Aren't the Fotheringays an old family?"

"But flat broke, darling. Old man lost everything in America in the crash of '29, just like your father. Lunghi's been out in India working for some trading company like a common clerk, so one understands."

"I see." I wondered if my mother knew this. Usually her instincts were spot on. Maybe his youth and extreme good looks were too much of a temptation.

With tea over we went upstairs to change for dinner. It's funny how life at country houses is centered around one meal after another. And yet those who live such lives don't seem to become overly fat. Maybe it's all that tramping around the home farm, not to mention other energetic forms of activity around the estate. I let Mildred select a dress and jewelry for me and even attempt to make my hair look fashionable. The result was not displeasing. I came down again to find that the French doors in the drawing room were still open and Pimm's and cocktails were being served on the terrace. It was a balmy evening. Swallows were swooping wildly overhead. A peacock was calling from the copse nearby—that unearthly shriek that sounds like a soprano being killed with a saw. Groups of guests were already standing together, chatting. The three Misses Hedley were now talking with their cousin Fiona, all wearing almost identical green flowered dresses, which made them look like a living herbaceous border. Another group of younger guests, including Gussie and Belinda, were standing to one side, smoking and drinking cocktails, while the older set was clustered around Lord Cromer-Strode. I picked out Mrs. Simpson standing apart, hands on painfully thin hips, staring out across the park and looking displeased. Maybe she had expected a dinner partner who had been detained at Sandringham!

"Ah, here is the delightful young Lady Georgiana." Lord Cromer-Strode came to meet me and put an arm around my waist as he steered me toward the company. "I'm sure you know the young folk, but you may not have met Colonel and Mrs. Horsmonden, just back from India, and Sir William and Lady Stoke-Podges, also old friends from colonial days." He kept his arm firmly around my waist as he said this and, to my shock, his fingers strayed upward until they were definitely making contact with the underside of my breast. I didn't quite know how to react, so I stepped forward to shake hands, thus freeing myself. A glass of Pimm's was pressed upon me. We made pleasantries about the seasonably fine weather and the possibility of rain before the first Test match. Lord Cromer-Strode talked of getting together an eleven to play the village cricket team and there was heated discussion on who should be opening bat.

"Young Edward has a good eye and a straight bat," his lordship said. "Ah, here he is now. Wondered where you had got to, young man."

Edward Fotheringay came onto the

terrace with Princess Hanni. He had a slightly guilty look on his face. She was looking pleased with herself. Baroness Rottenmeister was nowhere to be seen.

"So you've found our visiting princess, have you, my boy? Splendid. Splendid. Come along, everybody, drink up."

Fiona broke away from her cousins and rushed to greet him. "Edward, my sweet, sweet pet. You don't know how I have been pining for you all day. How was Cambridge? Terribly, terribly hot and nasty?"

"Quite pleasant, thank you, Fiona. It's finals week. The place is like a morgue. Everyone studying, you know."

Guests continued to arrive, most of them older people I didn't know. Baroness Rottenmeister appeared, head to toe in black as usual and with a face like thunder.

"I called for the princess, but she had already gone ahead without me," she said to me. "You have taught her bad habits."

After a while the first dinner gong sounded.

"Everyone know who they are escorting in to dinner?" Lady Cromer-Strode fluttered around us, ushering us toward the French doors like a persistent sheepdog.

Mrs. Simpson appeared at her shoulder. "It appears that my dinner partner isn't here, Cordelia. Do I take it that your husband will escort me to table?"

"My husband?" Lady Cromer-Strode looked flustered. "Why no, Wallis. That wouldn't be proper. Lord Cromer-Strode escorts the highest-ranking lady. And that would be Lady Georgiana, surely?"

"Her mother was a common tart," Mrs. Simpson said loudly enough for her voice to carry.

"A well-known actress, Wallis. Be fair," Lady Cromer-Strode muttered in answer. "And her father was first cousin to the king. You can't argue with that."

"I also happen to have royal connections," Mrs. Simpson said in a miffed voice.

"Yes, but not official ones, Wallis. You know very well that everything in England is done by the book. There are protocols to be followed. I'm sure that Sir William Stoke-Podges will be happy to escort you, won't you, William?"

She thrust them together before she fluttered over to me. "Lady Georgiana, I think that maybe you should go in to dinner with my husband."

"Oh no, Lady Cromer-Strode." I gave her an innocent smile. Mrs. Simpson paused, waiting for me to concede that she was indeed the ranking female. "Her Highness the princess outranks me. She should go in with your husband."

"Of course. How silly of me. Princess Hannelore, honey, over here." And she was off to grab Hanni while I was paired up with Colonel Horsmonden.

"And what about me?" The baroness appeared at my side, still looking seriously out of sorts. "I appear to have no escort."

"Oh, dear." Lady Cromer-Strode clearly hadn't put her into the starting lineup. "You see, nobody told us that the princess would be bringing a companion. I'm so sorry. Now let's see. Reverend Withers, can I ask you to do me a favor and escort this lady into dinner? What was your name again, honey?"

The baroness flushed almost purple. "I am Baroness Rottenmeister," she said.

"And this is Reverend Withers. Your wife isn't here, is she, vicar?"

"No, she is visiting her family in Skegness."

"Then you'll be kind enough to take this lady in to dinner, will you?"

"Delighted, my dear." He offered her his arm.

The baroness stared at him as if he was something a little higher up the evolutionary scale than a worm. "You have a wife? And you are priest?"

"Church of England clergyman, my dear. We're allowed to marry, y'know."

"A Protestant!"

"We are all children of God," he said, and steered her into the line. I went to take my own place beside the colonel.

"Now we seem to be one man short." Lady Cromer-Strode glanced down the line of couples. "Who could that be? Who is not here?"

As if on cue, Darcy O'Mara came up the steps onto the terrace. He looked dashing in his dinner jacket, his dark hair slightly tousled and his eyes flashing. My heart did a flip-flop as he fell into place with Belinda. What on earth was he doing here?

Before I could see if he was going to look my way there was a stir among the guests and the butler stepped out to announce, "His Royal Highness the Prince of Wales, my lady."

My cousin David, looking dapper as only he could look, came striding out with that jaunty air of his.

"So sorry I'm late, Lady C-S." He kissed her on the cheek, making her flutter all the more. "Got held up at Sandringham, you know. Hope I haven't put you out at all. Ah, Wallis, there you are." He made a bee-line for her. Wallis Simpson shot me a triumphant smile as she slipped her arm through his and she pushed past me to the front of the line.

I hardly noticed the insult because David's speech had triggered some sort of memory. Those two big initials lying on a sheet of paper in Hanni's room at Rannoch House. C.P., wasn't it? Who had sent her a sheet of paper with only two letters on it, and what did they mean? And why did they have a big red *X* slashed through them the second time I saw them?

Chapter 26

The banqueting room was aglitter with chandeliers dangling from a ceiling painted with cherubs. Many-branched candelabras were set along a mahogany table that extended the full length of the room. Light sparkled from silver cutlery and reflected in the highly polished surface. I was seated near the head of the table, between Colonel Horsmonden and Edward Fotheringay. The Prince of Wales sat on one side of Lord Cromer-Strode and Hanni on the other. Mrs. Simpson was directly opposite me.

"Still no escort of your own, I see," she

said. "Time is marching on, you know. You won't have that youthful bloom forever."

"I'm waiting for one who doesn't officially belong to someone else," I said, and gave her a sweet smile.

"You have a sharp tongue, young woman," she said and promptly turned her attention to the prince and Lord Cromer-Strode. On one side of me, I overheard Lord Cromer-Strode telling what was obviously a really bawdy anecdote. "So the farmer said, 'That's the biggest bloody great pair of . . .'" The end of this sentence was drowned out with Mrs. Simpson's shrill laughter and the prince's chuckle. Hanni looked bemused. I suspect she didn't get the double entendre, although Lord C-S's gesture had been plain enough to me. But then, as I watched, I saw that Hanni's attention was not directed to those directly around her. She was busy casting come-hither glances at first Edward and then Darcy.

I thought again about those strange letters. Had they been some kind of threat? If so, why hadn't she shared her fears with me? Who knew she was in London and where she was staying?

The meal began with lobster bisque and went from strength to strength from there. Colonel Horsmonden launched into accounts of his life in India—tiger shoots, maharajas' palaces, mutinies in the bazaars, each tale made boring as only an old colonel can make it, peppering them with names of people I had never heard of.

In the spirit of self-preservation I mentioned to him that Edward had also just come back from India and suddenly they were talking across me.

"I'm surprised we've never met, my boy," the colonel said. "I thought I prided myself in knowing everyone in the service over there."

"Ah, but I wasn't in the service," Edward said. "I was in trade, sir. Import-export."

"Stationed where?"

"All over the place. Never in one place for long, you know. And I also did a bit of mountain climbing in the Himalayas."

"Did you, by Jove. Then you must know old Beagle Bailey. Ever climbed with old Beagle Bailey?"

"I can't say that I have, sir."

"Don't know old Beagle? Institution in the Himalayas, is old Beagle. Mad as a hatter, of course. So who did you climb with?"

"Oh, just some chaps from Cambridge."

"And where did you pick up your sherpas?"

"We didn't use sherpas."

"Didn't use sherpas? How did you manage? Nobody climbs without sherpas. Dashed foolish. They know the country like the back of their hands."

"They were only small climbs that we undertook," Edward said quickly. "Just weekend stuff. A bit of fun, you know."

"Not much fun if a storm comes down in the Himalayas," Colonel Horsmonden said. "I remember once we were in Kashmir. Going up a glacier on Nanga Parbat. Do you know Nanga Parbat? Damned fine mountain. And within ten minutes the storm had come down and we almost got blown off the dashed mountain."

They talked on. I was conscious of Hanni's eyes moving from Edward to Darcy, and of Darcy eating unconcernedly. The Prince of Wales chatted with Lord Cromer-Strode but his eyes never left Wallis Simpson. So much for being captivated by Hanni, who looked as innocently voluptuous as anybody could possibly look. Certainly Lord Cromer-Strode was aware of her charms. He kept turning to pat her hand, stroke her arm, and, I suspect, grab her knee under the table, judging by the amount of time only one hand was visible. Hanni didn't seem to be objecting, whatever he was doing.

Gussie was also chatting away easily as he ate, regaling the American girls with tales of English boarding schools and making them shriek with laughter.

"A fag master? What on earth is a fag master?" one of them demanded. "It sounds just terrible."

And I found my thoughts straying to the events of the past week. If Gussie was indeed supplying his friends with cocaine, and if Tubby and Sidney Roberts had somehow fallen foul of him, how could he sit there behaving as if nothing had happened? Surely that was a stupid idea on my part. Gussie was one of those affable, not too bright young men I had danced with during my season. I could picture him trying drugs, even selling drugs to his friends, but not killing anyone. It just didn't make sense.

Dinner ended and Lady Cromer-Strode led the women into the drawing room while the men lit up cigars and passed around the port. Mrs. Simpson hogged the best armchair, and Belinda started chatting with the American girls. The baroness and Hanni had obviously had words. I heard the baroness say in English, "It is unpardonable insult. Tomorrow morning I shall telephone your father." Then she stalked to the far side of the room and sat down, away from the rest of the company.

I wandered across to the open French doors. The scent of roses and honeysuckle wafted in from the gardens. A full moon was reflected in the pond. A perfect night for romance and the man with whom I wanted to stroll in the moonlight was in the next room, only he was showing no interest in me. Maybe Mrs. Simpson was not wrong. Some of us just didn't flirt naturally. Perhaps my mother could give me some pointers, but I doubted it. She oozed sexuality. It came naturally from her pores. I had inherited the blood of Queen Victoria, who was not amused by much and, in spite of producing umpteen children, could never have been dubbed as sexy.

Hanni came to stand beside me. "It is real swell, *ja*?" she said. "Darcy is here. And Edward too. I can't decide which one I like better. They are both hot and sexy, don't you think?"

"They are both good looking," I said, "but one of them happens to be engaged to Fiona."

Hanni grinned. "I do not think he loves her very much. During dinner he looked at me and he winked. That must mean that he likes me, yes?"

"Hanni, you are to behave yourself. We are guests of Fiona's family."

"Too bad." She paused. "Her father is a real friendly guy too. But he pinched my bottom on the way in to dinner. Is that old English custom?"

"Certainly not," I said.

"And on our walk he asked me if I liked to roll in the hay. Hay is what you feed to animals, no? Why should I want to roll in it?"

"Lord Cromer-Strode is a little too friendly, I believe. Please watch out when you are alone with him. And especially if he suggests a roll in the hay."

"Why? Is this bad thing?"

"It is not the sort of thing that visiting princesses do." Again I found myself staring around the room, wondering just who had been with him in the rhododendrons earlier. Belinda saw me looking at her and beckoned me over. "So I see Darcy O'Mara is here," she said. "Do you think he was officially invited or is he party-crashing again?"

"Lady Cromer-Strode seemed to be expecting him." I tried to sound disinterested.

"I wonder what he is doing here. These people certainly aren't his usual crowd. I didn't even realize he knew the Cromer-Strodes. Which can only mean one thing." She gave me a knowing smile. "You see, he is still interested in you."

"I don't think I'm the one he's come for," I said as I watched the men drift into the room amid lingering clouds of smoke. Hanni looked up expectantly and then turned and walked deliberately out onto the terrace. Edward went to follow her, then thought better of it. Darcy gave me a look that I couldn't quite interpret, then did follow her. I stood watching them go, trying not to let my face betray any emotion.

"Maybe I should go after them," I said to Belinda.

"You shouldn't run after him," Belinda replied. "Not a wise move."

"Not for myself," I said. "For Hanni. I'm supposed to be keeping an eye on her and she is awfully eager for sexual experiences. I'm sure Darcy will be only too willing to oblige."

"He probably will," Belinda agreed. "No man would refuse what that innocent little miss is offering so obviously and freely, and Darcy is certainly more hot-blooded than most men."

I sighed. "I've wrecked my chances with him, haven't I? If I hadn't been so stupidly moral and correct, he wouldn't have looked elsewhere."

"You can't change the person you are," Belinda said. "All that history of family honor instilled into you—you'd have felt wretched if you'd gone to bed with Darcy and then he'd still dumped you."

"I feel pretty wretched now," I said. "I know he's completely unsuitable, but I can't help the way I feel about him."

"Nobody can choose when and where to fall in love. It just happens. You see somebody and . . ." She stopped, looking across the room. Edward Fotheringay was surrounded by Fiona and her American cousins, who were giggling at his every word, and he was staring straight at Belinda.

"It's a little hot in here, don't you think?" she said casually, putting one hand up to the back of her neck in a remarkably suggestive gesture. "I think I might also stroll on the terrace." And she moved gracefully toward the French doors. After a minute or so Edward followed her. So that was how it was done. She made it seem so easy. If I tried it, I'd probably trip over the door frame or fall off the terrace.

Chapter 27

I stood alone, observing the Prince of Wales now making a beeline for Mrs. Simpson, who was patting the arm of her chair as if he were a pet dog. The older men clustered around the brandy decanter and murmured something about playing billiards. The older women sat together on the sofa and gossiped among themselves.

"You're awfully pensive tonight." A voice at my elbow made me jump. Gussie smiled at me. "Penny for your thoughts?"

"I'm rather impoverished at the moment," I said. "I'll share them for half a crown."

He laughed. "So you drive a hard bargain."

"Sheer desperation, I assure you. It's hard to live in London with absolutely no funds."

"Yes, I suppose it must be."

It had just struck me that I had an ideal opportunity to pump him for information. "It must be lovely to be you and to be able to give all those jolly parties and live in that beautiful flat," I said.

I thought he gave just a momentary frown. "I don't know if I like the flat quite so much anymore. Not since old Tubby fell off my balcony. I still can't get over it. I keep wondering if there was anything I could have done to save him—apart from stronger railings, of course."

"I feel the same way," I said. "It was like watching a film, wasn't it? Not quite real."

"My feelings exactly. Almost in slow motion."

I nodded.

"I say," he said after a pause, "do you fancy a turn about the garden? It's a lovely night. Full moon and all that."

"Thank you," I said. "That would be lovely."

He took my arm and steered me out onto the terrace. I was conscious of Darcy and Hanni standing close together, only a few feet beyond the French doors. She was looking up at him adoringly. Inside, somebody had started playing the piano—"Clair de Lune." There was no sign of either Belinda or Edward.

"It's a lovely night, isn't it?" Gussie said. "Quite balmy, still."

"It's a beautiful night." I slipped my hand into Gussie's and directed him down the steps from the terrace. My heart was beating very fast. We were stepping into unknown territory here. I wasn't sure where flirting ended and seduction began. I turned to Gussie and gave him an encouraging little smile. "I was waiting for someone to take me for a stroll in the moonlight," I said. "It's very romantic, isn't it?"

"Well, I suppose it is. I didn't think you'd be interested, you know."

"Why?"

"Well, because, I mean to say, you're Binky's sister. But you're a grand girl, Georgie. Not at all bad looking either. In fact I can't think why some fellow hasn't snapped you up before now. You'd make a splendid wife. Good breeding. Reliable."

"You make me sound like a spaniel," I said. "Safe, reliable. How about warm and sexy?"

He laughed nervously. "Dash it all, Georgie, you are Binky's sister."

"I'm also a woman." I nearly laughed as I said it. What a stupid line.

"Yes, you are." He fell for it. He was looking at me in a strange, speculative way.

We were now alone on the dark, moonlit lawn. I could hear the fountain splashing and the distant tones of the music. I turned to face him.

"Well, aren't you going to kiss me?"

"I say. Rather."

He brought his lips toward mine. They were surprisingly cold and moist. A little like kissing a cod. When I had kissed Darcy, I wasn't conscious of lips or tongues or anything. Just that wonderful sensation of tingling, surging desire, melting into him. Now I was horribly conscious of everything Gussie was doing or trying to do: his large, flabby tongue, for one thing. And his hands, which were reaching down inside the back of my dress to unhook my brassiere. But I kept my eyes closed and pretended that I was in rapture, making little moans of pleasure from time to time.

This seemed to egg him on. His breathing became louder. He tried to reach under my arm and grab my breasts. Then he half dragged me to a nearby stone bench. We sank down together. One hand slid down the low neck of my dress and fondled my right breast as if he were testing a ripe orange. Then a hand started sliding up my skirt until it made its way between my legs.

By now I was a little alarmed, and confused. Just how far did I want this to go? Wouldn't now be a good time to stop? Gussie was panting like a steam engine and wrestling with my knickers. It suddenly came to me that I didn't want to lose my virginity to Gussie Gormsley. If I had resisted Darcy when I had wanted him with all my being, then it was surely rather hypocritical to give in so easily to someone I didn't want.

Gussie was now inching down my panties.

Other thoughts tumbled into my consciousness: it was rumored that one bled the first time. In fact bloody sheets were carried out of the bedchamber as proof that the deed had been done. What on earth would people think if I staggered back into the drawing room bloody and disheveled? My cousin the prince and Mrs. Simpson were sitting there. Word might even get back to Her Majesty.

Gussie was now fumbling to undo his belt. He reached into his trousers and produced something I couldn't quite see, but he took my hand and placed it upon the thing. I recoiled in horror. The thing was twitching with a life of its own. It reminded me of a newt we'd once kept as children.

"I'm sorry," I said, trying to draw away, "but I should go back inside. They'll wonder where I've got to."

Gussie was still panting. "You can't leave me like this, Georgie," he said, pushing up my skirt with frantic gestures. "You can't egg a chap on and then want to stop. I've got to have a bit of the old rumpy-pumpy, you know. Now do be a good girl and give it to me."

He pushed me back quite roughly until I

was lying on the cold stone of the bench. I hadn't realized until then how strong he was or how far we were from the house. He started kissing me again, lying on me with his full weight. I couldn't help thinking of one of Belinda's favorite maxims: If rape is inevitable, lie back and enjoy it.

Suddenly that didn't seem so amusing anymore. I didn't want to be another Belinda. I didn't want to turn into my mother. I shook my mouth free of him. "I said no, Gussie." I tried to force him off me. He was having trouble lifting my skirt high enough. Thank heavens there was rather a lot of material in the skirt, and a couple of layers of underskirt too. I tried to bring up my knee, but he was very persistent.

"I said let go of me." I pushed, wriggled and turned at the same time and we both rolled off the bench onto the damp grass. I tried to get up. Gussie tried to pull me back down.

"What's going on here?" a man's voice demanded. "Some damned animal in the bushes. Go and get my gun!"

Gussie scrambled to his feet and took off without waiting for me. I stood up, and was brushing myself down when I realized that the voice belonged to Darcy.

"He took off like a greyhound out of the gate, wouldn't you say?" Darcy said in an amused voice.

"What are you doing here?" I demanded.

"Just stretching my legs. Nice night for a walk. More to the point, what were you doing?"

"None of your business."

"Don't tell me you were enjoying it."

"Again, it's none of your business what I do."

"It's just that a month or so ago you gave me a long lecture about not wanting to turn out like your mother and saving yourself for the right man and the right time. Please don't tell me that you find Gussie Gormsley more irresistibly attractive than me. If you do, I really shall go and get my gun and shoot myself."

"I wasn't intending to let Gussie . . ."

"I see. That was not how it appeared to the outside observer."

He started to walk beside me back to the house.

"Anyway, I can take perfectly good care of myself," I said. "You always seem to be showing up and acting as if you have come to rescue me. But you really don't need to."

"My pleasure, your ladyship."

"Please don't let me keep you another second from the enchanting Princess Hanni. Who knows, maybe you'll end up in a fairy-tale castle and have to learn the goose step."

He actually smiled at this. "It's hard to resist when a woman literally throws herself at one," he said.

"I'm sure it is. She's just out of the convent. She is determined to find out what she's been missing."

"I'll say." He smiled again.

"And no doubt you'll be delighted to show her."

"I'm only human, after all. We chaps find it hard to say no to a warm body."

"I believe she's still waiting for you." I started to walk ahead of him.

He caught up with me and grabbed my arm. For a moment I thought he was going to embrace me, but then he said, "You can't go inside like that."

"Like what?"

"Well, for one thing you have grass

stains on your back, and for another, you have bits of underwear sticking out from your dress. Ah yes, I see. Your brassiere has mysteriously become unlatched. Allow me to—"

"Absolutely not," I said. "I'll manage."

"You can't go back in there with bits sticking out. Stand still." I shivered involuntarily at the touch of his warm hands on my back. "There. Reasonably respectable again." His hand lingered on my bare shoulder.

"Thank you." I started to move away from him.

"Georgie," he said quietly, his hand still on my shoulder. "When I disappeared from London—I had to go away in a hurry."

"Evading the law?" I asked.

"I had to go home to Ireland. I got word that my father was selling the estate to Americans. I rushed home to try and make him change his mind. I was too late. The deed was done."

"I'm awfully sorry."

"I suppose it was inevitable. He was strapped for cash. They made him an offer he couldn't refuse. And the only good thing is that they want to resurrect the racing stable. They're keeping my father on as trainer / adviser / general dog's body. He's going to live in the gatehouse." I saw him wince as if in pain. "Lucky he couldn't sell the title along with it, or I'd be plain Mr. O'Mara for the rest of my life."

"I really am sorry, Darcy," I said.

"Well, there's nothing I can do, but now I really am homeless. I'm certainly not going to stay at the gatehouse and watch some millionaire from Texas living in my family home."

"Darcy, where did you go?" Hanni's voice floated toward us.

"Your lady love is waiting," I said as Hanni appeared from the darkness.

"Georgie—that woman you saw me with at the Savoy—"

"You really don't have to explain your women friends to me, Darcy." For some reason I felt that I might cry. I only wanted to escape to the safety of my own room.

"She wasn't a woman friend. She was my sister, Bridget. She felt the same way I did about losing the house. We were commiserating together."

Before I could say anything, Hanni

spotted Darcy and came running toward us. "Darcy, where did you go? I lost you," she complained.

"Just doing a good deed," Darcy said. "I was a boy scout, you know. My lady." He gave a slight bow and then turned back to Hanni, and allowed himself to be led away by the hand, leaving me alone in the moonlight.

⚜

I tried to slip back into the drawing room without anybody noticing. I had no idea if Gussie had returned before me, and in what state he had been. I expected all eyes to be on me, but the scene in the room was exactly as I had left it: the prince sitting obediently on the arm of Mrs. Simpson's chair, looking down at her as if she were the only woman in the room; the other women still chattering, heads together. I heard one of them say, "That can't possibly be true. Where did you hear that?"

"Anyone feel like a game of billiards?" Lord Cromer-Strode asked. "Colonel? What about Edward? Where has the damned boy got to now?"

Fiona was staring at the French doors,

stony-faced. "He's taking a walk. It is rather hot in here," she said.

"How about whist?" Lady Cromer-Strode sensed tension in the atmosphere. "Anybody for whist, bridge if you'd rather, or what about pontoon?"

While tables were being set up, I took the opportunity to creep up to my room. Once there I stood staring out of the open window into the night, trying to come to terms with what had just happened. How could I have been so stupid to have encouraged Gussie? And why did Darcy take the trouble to explain his actions to me, only to run off after Hanni again? Nothing about men made sense. Why had we wasted time at school on deportment and French and piano when what they should have done was to give us lessons on understanding male behavior. Perhaps it was beyond comprehension.

A woman's laugh floated across the lawns, setting my imagination running riot again. How long did the queen expect me to stay here? I wondered. Could I now conclude that Hanni was well settled and flee back to London? At this moment I longed to be sitting in my grandfather's little kitchen while he made me a cup of tea so strong that the spoon almost stood up in it.

"Forget the lot of 'em, my love," he'd say. "They ain't worth tuppence."

"My lady, I am so sorry," said a voice behind me. I leaped a mile. It was Mildred of course. I had completely forgotten about her again. What was it about her that made her so unmemorable? Maybe that I was wishing she didn't exist? Now she came scuttling into the room, looking flustered and embarrassed. "I had no idea that you would wish to retire so early, my lady," she twittered. "I thought the young folk were still downstairs. I gathered there was a gramophone and dancing, so naturally I assumed—"

"It's quite all right, Mildred," I said. "I can't expect you to stand to attention waiting for me at all hours."

"Oh, but you can, my lady, and you should. What use is a lady's maid if she is not available and ready for service at all times? I was having a nice chat with Lady Cromer-Strode's personal maid. We knew so many people in common, you see, and then a footman came into the servants' hall and said that he'd seen you going upstairs. My heart nearly stopped, my lady." She put her hand to her chest in impressive fashion. "I ran upstairs as fast as my legs could carry me. Please say you'll forgive me."

"I do forgive you, Mildred. Now if you like, you can go back to the servants' hall and your nice little chat."

"Are you not feeling well, my lady? May I have some hot milk sent up? Some hot Bovril? Some iced lemonade?"

"I am perfectly well, thank you. Just tired, and I wish to be alone."

"Then let me help you out of your garments and you'll be ready for bed."

"No—thank you." I blurted out the words more fiercely than I intended, remembering the unhooked brassiere and those grass stains. Mildred wouldn't comment. Maids didn't, but she'd notice and she'd gossip. "I'd rather be alone tonight, thank you, Mildred. Please leave me."

It was the closest to my great-grandmother, Empress of all she surveyed, that I had ever come. It produced an immediate effect. Mildred actually curtsied and backed out of the room. Most satisfying, in fact the one satisfying thing in a long and annoying day. I undressed, feeling hot with shame as I wrestled off the remains of my brassiere and noted my crumpled dress. What would Mildred think?

I lay in bed, feeling very alone and empty. Darcy was now with another woman. He had come to my aid, but only because he pitied me. I lay for a long time, watching the moonlight stream in through the long windows. It shone full onto a painting on the far wall. It was a painting of the Alps and reminded me of my happy schooldays in Switzerland. What's more, I recognized the mountains. "Jungfrau, Mönch, Eiger," I murmured to myself and felt comforted having a familiar sight looking down on me. Then something nagged at my brain. I heard Hanni's voice saying something about her beloved Bavarian mountains. "The Zugspitze and the Jungfrau," she had said. But the Jungfrau was in Switzerland.

Chapter 28

I woke with early morning sun streaming in through my window and a dawn chorus of birds that was almost deafening. A cool, fresh breeze was blowing in through my open windows. I no longer felt sleepy so I got up. It would be hours before breakfast was served and even an hour or so before I could expect Mildred with the tea tray. I decided to go for a walk. I tip-toed down the main staircase and let myself out through the front door without encountering anybody. The lawns were heavy with dew. The rosebushes were strung with spiderwebs on which the dewdrops glistened like diamonds. A low strand of mist hung over the ornamental pond. As I started walking I began to feel better. I had been cooped up in London for too long. I was a country girl at heart. My ancestors had tramped those Scottish Highlands. I strode out, arms swinging, and started to hum a tune. Soon this whole Hanni business would be just a bad dream. She'd be back in Germany, breaking a succession of hearts. I would be back at Rannoch House. I might even go home to Scotland until I was summoned to Balmoral. I'd ride my horse every day, avoid Fig and visit Nanny.

I had crossed the lawn and moved into the shade of a stand of trees. Suddenly I froze. Someone was moving through the rhododendron bushes. My mind went instantly to his lordship's antics but surely even someone as lusty as he couldn't be at it at six in the morning. Then I caught a glimpse of a figure all in black. So at least he or she was fully clothed, whoever it was. That should have been a relief, but the way that figure was skulking immediately made me suspicious. A poacher, maybe? Perhaps it would be wise to reveal my presence and thus not startle the person.

I coughed loudly. The effect was instant. The figure spun around and I was amazed to see that it was Irmgardt, Hanni's maid.

"Irmgardt, what on earth are you doing?" I asked, before I remembered that she spoke no English.

"Die Prinzessin," she said, *"macht Spaziergang."*

This much German I could understand. So the princess was out walking early.

"Where is she?" I asked. *"Wo?"*

Before she could answer there was a tramping through the bracken and Hanni appeared, looking red cheeked and ridiculously healthy.

"Oh, Georgie, you are awake too. It is lovely day, is it not? The birds made so much noise that I could not sleep, so I go for walk. At home we walk much, up mountains. Here there are no mountains," she added regretfully then glanced at Irmgardt, who was still following us. "But my maid does not allow me to go alone. Go back, Irmgardt. I do not need you." She repeated this in German, shooing her away like a duck or a chicken. Irmgardt retreated reluctantly. "Old broad make her follow me," Hanni muttered to me. "She does not trust me to go out alone no more. Now I've got two pain in necks."

At that moment we heard the thud of hoofbeats and Edward Fotheringay came riding toward us on a fine bay.

"Morning, ladies," he called, reining in his mount. "Lovely day, isn't it? I've just been for a good gallop. Old Cromer-Strode keeps a fine stable. Where are you two off to?"

"We both woke early and are taking a stroll," I said.

"Why don't you come for a ride with me?" Edward said. "I'll go and see about some mounts while you go and change."

Actually I was dying to get on a horse again but Hanni said, "I do not like to ride horses. I do not like my clothes to smell of horse sweat. But I would like to go for a ride in your new car, like the American girls. That would be real swell. I never went out alone in a motorcar with a man."

"Oh, right-o," Edward said. "Always happy to put my new machine through its paces for a pretty girl. Give me a few minutes to take the horse back and change my clothes and then we'll be off."

He urged his horse to a canter, leaving us to walk back to the house together.

"Your baroness is not going to be happy about this, Hanni," I said. "She won't allow you to go out unchaperoned in a young man's car."

"I do not care what she thinks or says." Hanni tossed her head defiantly. "She is here as my companion, not as my mother. Besides, I do not wish to be with the baroness. She is in bad mood."

"Why is that?"

"She says she is treated like servant here. Her rank is higher than theirs but they make her stand at back of line and they seat her with not important people like a bad married priest."

"I expect they didn't realize who she is," I said. "They probably think of her as just your companion."

"She says I must tell them and demand that she is treated with respect," Hanni said. "But I do not wish to do this. It is rude, don't you think? It is not my fault that she is old and ugly."

"Hanni, you really mustn't talk like that,

even when we are alone. You are a royal person. Whatever you say will be made public, you know."

"I know you won't tell anyone because you're my pal."

"But I really can't let you go out alone with a young man," I said.

"You can come with us. You can watch me."

Did I really want to watch Hanni and Edward making cow eyes at each other, and more to the point, would they want me sitting there in the backseat watching them? But then a thought struck me. I was supposed to be doing a spot of sleuthing. In fact it was rather important that I begin sleuthing as soon as possible. Sometime within the next week there would be an inquest into the death of Sidney Roberts. Our involvement in that death would be made public. A royal scandal would ensue, Germany would react with horror, diplomatic messages would fly across the Channel and if we were really unlucky, a new world war would break out. I couldn't turn down such a perfect opportunity to question Edward, away from the bustle of Dippings.

"All right," I agreed, "I'll come along and play gooseberry."

"Play gooseberry?"

"Another silly English term," I said.

"English is very silly language," Hanni said.

I had to agree with her.

⚭

Edward didn't seem to mind too much that I was being brought along. "The more the merrier," he said. "So where do you want to go? Anywhere in particular? We could make a day of it."

A brilliant idea came to me. Cambridge—it seemed to be the one link between Edward and Gussie and Sidney Roberts. I couldn't see how I'd find any clues there—no dropped note in the cloisters saying, *Meet me by the river. Drug shipment due at dawn,* but it would be interesting to observe Edward in his old habitat.

"I think the princess might enjoy seeing Cambridge," I suggested. "If it's not too far to drive."

"Not at all. Always glad to show off the old college," Edward said, smiling at Hanni.

We made our getaway from Dippings

before the general populace had stirred. The butler kindly arranged for some tea and toast so that we didn't depart on an empty stomach, and the cook hastily made a hamper for the journey. It was all very civilized and a jolly day seemed to be ahead of us—if one didn't count poor Sidney Roberts. Hanni seemed to have completely forgotten about him. He hadn't come up once in conversation. Nor did she seem to have any worries about an upcoming inquest and the public attention that it would generate. Perhaps she wanted to be in the spotlight. It certainly went with her personality. She sat in the front seat of Edward's natty little sports car, occasionally glancing up at him with obvious delight that she was finally (almost) alone in a car with a boy.

"I bet your baroness wasn't too pleased about this." Edward turned to her with a wicked grin.

"I did not wake her," Hanni said. "She does not like to be awoken too early. Irmgardt will tell her where I have gone."

"You'll probably be sent straight back to the convent when you get home," Edward teased.

"I have proper English lady, relative of king, in the backseat," Hanni said. "She will make sure you behave well."

"Ah, but what about you?" Again Edward's grin was flirtatious. "Can she succeed in keeping tabs on you? Not an easy task, I fear." He glanced back at me and winked.

I smiled back. "I'm really looking forward to seeing Cambridge," I said. "I've never been there."

"Never seen Cambridge? Then you haven't lived. It's quite the most beautiful city in England. Far superior to Oxford, of course, which is nothing but a bustling country town."

"I detect prejudice."

He laughed. He had a most appealing laugh. I could see why the girls were drawn to him. I was a little drawn myself, but since I was clearly fourth in line after Fiona, Belinda and Hanni, not to mention my mother, there was no point in pursuing this. I wondered about Edward and Fiona. Did he know he was engaged to her, or was it one of those things that families arrange on the birth of their children? I could see the way he was looking at Hanni, and I had also seen him follow Belinda into the garden last night. Men who followed Belinda had only one thing on their minds.

The fifty-mile drive through leafy byways was delightful. Dappled sunlight, the cooing of pigeons, the sound of a cuckoo and the wind in my hair in the backseat of the open car. Hanni and Edward chatted from time to time but as we gathered speed I couldn't join in their conversation from the backseat, which gave me time to think. What had Sidney Roberts been doing at that party? He was clearly out of place, from the point of view of both class and views. Dedicated communists surely do not habitually frequent parties at which the sons and daughters of the decadent upper crust indulge in cocktails and cocaine—not unless he had come to convert us, which he didn't seem to be doing. Instead he seemed remote and ill at ease, lurking on the balcony.

I replayed that balcony scene in my mind, but Sidney had given no indication of why he was there—unless, like many of the lower classes, he was flattered to have been invited. Or, like Darcy, he simply wanted some good food and drink. But he didn't seem the type.

I remembered that Gussie had seemed surprised to see him at the party. He'd asked Edward what Roberts was doing there and Edward had implied that he had to invite him and he was a good enough chap in his way. What did he mean by "had to" invite him? Were they somehow beholden to him? Another suspicion came into my mind. Was Sidney the one who supplied their drugs? Was the earnest communist character merely a façade?

"So you were at Trinity College, were you, Edward?" I leaned forward from my backseat.

"That's right. Good old Trinity. One of the younger colleges, I'm afraid. Founded by Henry the Eighth. Those American girls yesterday laughed themselves silly when they heard that something founded in fifteen hundred and something was considered young. But it's definitely one of the loveliest colleges. I'm going to give you a tour and you'll have to agree."

We were entering the city of Cambridge. The view as we crossed the Cam and saw those golden stone buildings across spacious lawns almost took the breath away. On the river itself was a merry scene with students punting and sitting on the lawns, enjoying the sunshine. The occasional student cycled past, books under his arm and black gown flapping out behind him in the wind. A pair of female students, deep in heated discussion, strolled under the trees. I looked at them with interest, as one examines a new species in the zoo. I hadn't really considered that women would also attend the university and felt a pang of regret that I would never have that kind of opportunity.

We abandoned the car under the shade of a huge chestnut tree and started to walk. The glorious sound of boys' voices floated out from King's College Chapel, where it must have been time for matins. Edward played at dutiful tour guide, identifying each building that we passed until we came to an impressive arched gateway in a high wall.

"You see," he said, ushering us through the arch. "Quite the loveliest, don't you think?"

I followed them through the gate and

into a vast courtyard bordered by richly carved yellow stone buildings. A lush green lawn covered most of the area and in the middle was an ornate roofed fountain.

"This is the great court, the largest of any at Oxford or Cambridge," Edward said. "They say the students used to wash in that fountain before there were proper bathrooms and of course this is the site of the famous great court run. The object is to run around the perimeter of the court before the clock finishes chiming noon. It's only been done a couple of times, I understand. Come on. Follow me."

I fancied I could still hear those sublime voices from King's College, until I realized that Trinity possessed a similar chapel, with its own choir. Sweet notes hung in the air. I almost began to believe that angels inhabited Cambridge.

"It's so peaceful here," I said as we crossed the court.

Edward laughed. "They're all holed up studying for final exams," he said. "You should see it on a normal Saturday night." He opened a door for us to step into the darkness of a building. "This is the hall, where we take our meals," he said, indicating a dark-paneled, high-ceilinged room to our left. "I probably shouldn't take you inside. The chaps wouldn't take kindly to visitors during exam time. And through here is another court, and you have to see the Wren library."

"Sir Christopher Wren?" I asked.

"The very same."

Just as we were about to leave the building a young man in a far more impressive gown than I had seen so far came sweeping in through the door. He went to pass us with a cursory nod then stopped. "I say, I know you, don't I?" he said to Edward. "Fotheringay, wasn't it? You were an apostle, if I'm not mistaken."

"And you are Saunders," Edward said. "So you've become a fellow, have you?"

"For my sins. Too lazy to move out, I suppose, and the food's good. What have you been doing with yourself?"

"Been abroad mostly," Edward said.

"Have you, by Jove. Good for you." He gave Edward a strange look that I couldn't quite interpret. "Wish I weren't so dashed lazy. Where did you go?"

"Oh, here and there. All over the place." Edward shifted from one foot to the other, clearly uncomfortable in the other man's presence.

"And who are these delectable creatures?" the gowned man asked, suddenly turning to us.

"Guests at a house party in Norfolk," Edward said. "Lady Georgiana Rannoch and Princess Hannelore of Bavaria."

The other man threw back his head and laughed. "Good one, Fotheringay."

Obviously he thought his leg was being pulled. But Edward did not attempt to assure him. "Well, we'd better be getting along," he said. "Good seeing you, Saunders."

"You'll probably run into a few other angels if you keep your eyes open," Saunders said, then nodded to us and went on his way.

We stepped out into bright sunlight and continued across a second court, not as large as the first, but just as charming.

"What are apostles?" I asked.

"Oh, just some undergraduate club we belonged to," Edward said carelessly.

"Was Gussie a member too?"

"Gussie? Good Lord, no." He laughed. "Not Gussie's cup of tea at all."

"How about Sidney Roberts?"

"Sidney Roberts?" He sounded surprised. "He may have been. Can't really remember. He was an unremarkable kind of chap, poor devil. Now that's the Wren library over here."

He strode out ahead of us to a truly beautiful building with delicate columns and large arched windows, then opened the door for us to step inside. That distinctive smell of old books, furniture polish and pipe tobacco permeated the air. It reminded me of some other place. I tried to identify the room at Castle Rannoch before I remembered the bookshop. Which gave me an idea. I waited until Edward led us upstairs, then I turned back and slipped into the library proper. An elderly man sitting at a desk looked up in horror as I came in.

"Young lady, what are you doing here?" he hissed at me, sotto voce. "Visitors are not permitted during finals week."

"I'm so sorry," I said, "but we were being shown around and I do so love old books that I had to get a glimpse of the place for myself."

His expression softened. "You are fond of old books then?"

"Passionately," I said. "I collect them."

"Most unusual for a young lady."

"I often visit a wonderful old bookshop in London. It's called Haslett's, in the East End, down by the river. Do you know it?"

He nodded. "A most eclectic collection. Have you made any major finds there?"

"One or two." I looked directly at him. "By the way, who are the apostles?"

"I take it you don't mean Matthew, Mark, Luke and John?"

"I heard some undergraduates discussing them."

"It's a sort of secret society, one gathers. Highly socialist in its leanings—rights for the workers and down with the old order. All that kind of bosh. Did you hear about them at the bookshop?"

"No, I overheard a couple of chaps saying something just now. And angels?"

"Ex-members become angels, so I'm told. I think it's all perfectly harmless. Young men become so passionate, don't they? Then they settle down, get married and turn out to be perfectly normal." He chuckled. "I would love to show you some of our rarest editions, but as I said, no visitors are allowed during finals week, so I regret . . ."

"That's quite all right. Thank you for your time," I replied and made a hurried exit.

"We thought we'd lost you," Edward said as I caught them coming down the stairs.

"Sorry, I was daydreaming and wandered off in the wrong direction." I gave him a winning smile. So Edward and Sidney Roberts had both been members of the same secret society—a society with strong leftist leanings. But how could that be significant?

Chapter 29

Clouds were gathering in the western sky as we drove home. The air had become muggy, with annoying little midges flying around and the promise of a thunder-storm brewing. Hanni dozed in the front seat beside Edward. I stared speculatively at the back of his well-cut hair. Edward Fotheringay, alias Lunghi Fungy, enigma. He studied modern languages yet chose to go to India, where he drifted around, not doing much of anything apart from a spot of disorganized climbing, from what one gathered. He had been a member of a secret society with socialist leanings and yet he dressed expensively and enjoyed a life of luxury. He was supposedly engaged to one girl but openly and shamelessly flirted with others. God knows what he did with Belinda—and I'd almost forgotten his involvement with my mother!

"So Edward," I said, leaning forward in my seat, "which modern languages did you study?"

"German and Russian."

"Interesting. Why those?"

"I'm a lazy bugger, actually. My mother was of Russian ancestry so I didn't have to work too hard."

"What did Gussie study?"

"Classics, stupid idiot. I mean to say, what use are classics? He had a hard time of it too. He wouldn't have got through Greek if that swat Roberts hadn't coached him and done his translations for him."

I gave a merry laugh. "So that's why he was beholden to Sidney Roberts. I wondered why he was invited to your party."

Did I detect a certain stiffening in his demeanor?

"And what made you go to India?" I

went on, chatting away merrily. "Did you have some family connection there too?"

"Grandfather had been there in the police force in the Punjab, but that wasn't the reason. I just had the desire to travel and India is an easy place to move around if one is English. Those nice free bungalows to stay at, and dinners at the officers' mess and dances."

"It sounds like a fascinating place," I said.

"Oh, rather. Elephants and tigers and things. And primitive customs—burning their dead on the steps of the Ganges. Disgusting habit."

"So what will you do now, do you think?"

"Haven't decided yet."

"I understand that marriage is on the horizon, or so Fiona says."

"Fiona would." He glanced down at Hanni, who was now blissfully asleep. "It's one of those dashed annoying things—both sets of parents decided it would be a good idea when we were infants. Oh, don't get me wrong. Fiona's a nice enough girl, but . . ." He let the end of the sentence die away.

"She will inherit Dippings one day," I pointed out.

"That's true. And there's no shortage of cash there. Sorely tempting, but unfortunately not my cup of tea."

The first fat raindrops pattered onto the car.

"Blast and damn," Edward muttered. "Now we're going to get wet. I took off the hood. I'll just have to put my foot down and make a run for it."

The engine roared as the motor car positively flew down the lane, wheels screeching at each corner. For a while it was exhilarating, but suddenly I became scared. He was driving so fast that he'd have no chance if we met a vehicle like a hay cart coming in the other direction. I was flung from side to side as he took the sharp bends. And I caught a glimpse of his face. It was alight with a strange, fierce exhilaration.

The storm broke in earnest when we were about ten miles from our destination. Thunder rumbled overhead. We were soaked through by the time we pulled up in front of Dippings. Servants rushed out with big umbrellas. There was a flash followed by a great clap of thunder as we went up the steps. Lady Cromer-Strode came out of the long gallery to greet us. "We were just finishing tea," she said. "Oh, you poor dears, just look at you! You're soaked. I'll have the servants run baths for you immediately or you'll come down with a chill. Edward what on earth were you doing driving with the top down in such weather?" Then her gaze fell to Hanni and her expression changed. "Your Highness," she said, "I am so sorry. We had no idea how to contact you, you see, or we'd have brought you back at once. Such a tragedy."

"What is such a tragedy?" I asked.

"Her Highness's companion, the baroness. I'm afraid she's dead."

"Dead?" Hanni's voice trembled. "You tell me that Baroness Rottenmeister is dead? Was there an accident?"

"No, my dear. It was natural causes. The doctor says it was a heart attack, sometime this morning. It was after the maid brought in her morning tea. She was of advancing years, wasn't she?"

"But—but I had no idea." Hanni's bottom lip trembled like a child's. "And I was rude to her last night. I quarreled with her. Maybe I made her upset and this caused the heart attack."

I put an arm around Hanni's shoulder. "I'm sure it was nothing you did, Hanni. People have little arguments all the time."

"Yes, but now she has died and I can't ask her to forgive me. I shall go to hell." Hanni was trying hard not to cry.

"Come on," I said, my arm still around her shoulders. "We need to get you out of these wet clothes. Irmgardt will run you a nice hot bath and perhaps Lady Cromer-Strode will be good enough to have some hot chocolate sent up to your room. Then you can have a good rest."

"I do not wish to rest. I should have dreams. Old broad will come back to haunt me," she said.

I tried not to smile as I led her upstairs.

"Georgie, what will happen now?" she asked. "They will want me to come home immediately."

Oh, good Lord. I hadn't thought of that complication. Of course her parents wouldn't want her to stay on with no chaperone. I remembered that the queen was nearby at Sandringham House.

"I will visit Her Majesty," I said.

"Must we do this today?"

"I'm afraid we must. Her Majesty would want to know about it and she'll certainly need to contact your parents."

"Then I will come with you. I will talk to them myself."

"Oh no, I think it would be wiser if you stayed here. They would not wish to discuss your future in front of you."

"You treat me as if I was a pet dog." Hanni pouted. "I do not wish to go home." She sneezed suddenly.

"Your parents will be even more angry if you catch a chill."

I opened Hanni's bedroom door and firmly escorted her inside. Irmgardt was sitting mending in the window. She jumped up with a look of horror on her face when she saw the princess. "Hot bath, Irmgardt," I said. "*Heiss Bad*. Right away."

She scuttled out of the room, while I helped Hanni out of her wet things and put her into her bathrobe as if she were a small child. She gave me a watery smile. "You are kind person, Georgie." She was looking at me almost as if she felt sorry for me. She probably was sorry for me—the hopeless old maid at twenty-one!

"So did you know that the baroness had a weak heart?" I asked her.

She shook her head. "She always seems so healthy. She takes long walks. She has good appetite."

That was certainly true. It did cross my mind that too much rich food at Dippings, after rather lean offerings at Rannoch House, might have contributed to her demise. I was glad that her death had been ruled a heart attack. Because if it hadn't, it would have been the third suspicious death in a week.

Chapter 30

Mildred fussed over me when she saw the state I was in. By now I was feeling miserable and a little shaken and didn't mind being fussed over. Neither did I mind being tucked up in bed with a glass of hot chocolate and some nice biscuits. Mildred had instructed me to stay there until she came to dress me for dinner, but after half an hour I was restored and ready to tackle my next unpleasant task. I asked the butler to make a telephone call on my behalf to Sandringham. He did so and I was summoned to the royal presence right away. Lady Cromer-Strode was happy to provide a car, luckily with a roof on it, as it was still coming down in buckets. The drive was only ten miles but it seemed like an eternity as I rehearsed what I was going to tell the queen. Of course it wasn't my fault that the baroness had died, but I rather felt that she might see it that way. Too many unfortunate things had happened to the princess since she had been entrusted to my care.

Even under rainy skies the ornamental gardens of Sandringham at the height of summer are incredibly beautiful. The beds, laid out in their formal designs, were absolutely perfect. Not a bloom was out of place. The house was less perfect, in my opinion. It was one of those sprawling Victorian country homes that are a horrible mixture of styles, bits jutting out here and there, towers, turrets, cupolas, and a mixture of red brick, gray stone, white and brown decorative trim and seaside boardinghouse windows. But I knew that the king was particularly fond of the place, and that was all that mattered.

A footman bearing a large black umbrella whisked me inside. I was led through to a small sitting room and announced. I found the royal couple behaving like any other household on a Sunday afternoon. The king had his stamp collection spread out in front of him on a small table. The queen was in the middle of writing letters. She looked up and extended her hand to me.

"Georgiana, what a pleasant surprise," she said. "I'm afraid you're a little late for tea. Do sit down." I attempted the usual kiss and curtsy with the usual clumsy nose-bumping results.

"I'm just replying to a letter from my granddaughter Elizabeth. Her penmanship is very pleasing for her age, don't you think?" She held up a letter for me, written on lined paper in a neat, round childish hand.

"And what brings you here, my dear?" the king asked. "Surely not just to keep a couple of old fogies company?"

"I am so sorry to disturb you, ma'am, sir," I said, "but I felt I should let you know right away. A rather unfortunate thing has happened." And I related the news about the baroness.

"Good gracious. This is unfortunate," the queen replied, glancing across at her husband. "A heart attack, you say? I sup-pose they are sure of that?"

I stared at her in surprise. "What do you mean, ma'am?"

"It did just cross my mind that she might have taken her own life, out of guilt for letting the young person under her protec-tion become involved in a murder investi-gation. These foreigners are known to have an exaggerated sense of duty."

"Oh, I don't think so, ma'am," I said hastily. "The baroness did not strike me as that kind of person. She thought a lot of herself, for one thing, and also she was a Catholic. Don't they consider suicide a mortal sin?"

"We all do," the queen said. "But in cer-tain cases it is understandable. We must notify the girl's parents immediately. We haven't yet received a reply to the letter we wrote a few days ago. We could per-haps use the telephone, of course. Do you think a telephone call would be the right thing to do, my dear?"

The king frowned then shook his head. "It's not as if it's a national emergency, is it? Never did like telephones. Damned annoying things. All the shrill ringing and then you can't hear a blasted thing that's being said on the other end and you end up shouting. No, I think a letter should suffice, May."

"Then I will compose one immediately."

"And what should happen to Princess Hanni, ma'am? She probably shouldn't be sent home before the inquest, should she?"

The queen frowned. "No, that wouldn't be the right thing to do. And as to that, have you made any progress?"

"I have learned a few interesting facts, ma'am, but I wouldn't call it progress yet. I shall begin my investigation in earnest tomorrow."

"What are you having the girl do now, May?" The king looked up from his stamps.

"Just keep her eyes and ears open. We are trying to avoid any embarrassment, you know, and Georgiana has a good head on her shoulders."

The king snorted. "If we lived in a different sort of country, you'd be head of the secret police."

"What rubbish. I merely find our own solidly loyal police force a little on the plodding side, that's all. I don't see that asking Georgiana to assist them in their investigation is so wrong."

"They'll certainly think it is. Leave the investigating to professionals and let the young girl enjoy herself the way young girls are supposed to."

"If you think so, my dear." The queen gave me a knowing look that indicated I was to take no notice of the king.

"So what should be done with the princess?" I asked.

"We could bring her here, of course," the queen said, "although it's remarkably dull for a young person and I don't think I could prevail upon my son to entertain her. He's being extremely perverse these days."

"These days. He's been perverse since he was born," the king muttered.

"He was at Dippings last night, I take it?"

"Yes, ma'am."

"I thought so. And he had a chance to talk to the princess?"

"I don't think he noticed her, ma'am, even though he was seated at dinner opposite her."

"I take it the American woman was there."

"She was."

"With husband?"

"Minus husband this time. On business in America, so we are told."

"You see, it is becoming serious, just as I told you." The queen glanced over at her husband, then turned back to me. "And do you think my son is still smitten with her?"

"Like a puppy dog, rushing to her beck and call," I replied. "She bosses him around shamelessly. She even calls him by his first name in public."

The queen sighed. "Dear me. How utterly vexing. I had such hopes that the Prince of Wales might behave like any normal healthy male and show interest in such a charming young thing as Princess Hannelore. Tell me, Georgiana, is the princess happy at Dippings?"

"Very. There are lots of young people and she is having a good time."

"Then let us leave her safely where she is until we receive word from Germany. We'll give my little scheme one last chance before she has to go home."

I thought of Lord Cromer-Strode and his rolls in the hay and his pinching of bottoms and wondered just how safe Hanni would be. But I couldn't find a way to express this particular fear to someone as starchy as my austere relatives. Besides, the queen was still talking and one does not interrupt. "The Cromer-Strodes will be motoring up to London for our garden party on Wednesday so I will request that they bring Hannelore with them. She'll enjoy that. And Lady Cromer-Strode is a good sort. She'll make sure the girl is well looked after. Which will leave you free to pursue other things." And again she gave me that knowing, frank stare.

On the way back to Dippings I wondered if I should catch a train to London that night. I certainly had no wish to face Gussie or Darcy again, if they were still there. Actually I didn't want to endure another jolly evening in company. Then I realized that, of course, it would not be a jolly evening. There had been a death in the house, so presumably no dancing, cards or gramophone would be allowed. Oh, golly, would one be expected to wear black? I had only brought light colors with me. But then I suspected that was true of all the guests. It was midsummer, after all, and the only person wearing black had been the now deceased baroness.

The rain looked as if it might be easing up as we drove through Little Dippings. There was a definite brightening to the western sky, as if the setting sun were trying to break through.

"Do the trains run on Sunday evenings?" I asked the chauffeur.

"Oh no, your ladyship," he replied. "No trains at all on a Sunday from Dippings Halt. Tomorrow morning at eight is the first one."

So I was trapped whether I liked it or not. I shifted uneasily on the leather seat of the Rolls. I had felt as if I had been walking on eggshells ever since Hanni arrived, and now I felt that I might snap like an overwound watch spring any moment. I suppose the news of the baroness's death had been a final straw. Three deaths in one week—my grandfather would say that was too much of a coincidence. And yet the baroness's death had been ruled a heart attack—I presumed by a competent doctor. And anyway, who would want the baroness dead, apart from Hanni?

I almost smiled as I remembered Hanni's

gangster talk of "taking out the old broad," then remembered how distraught she had been on receiving the news. She had found the baroness annoying, that much was obvious, but that didn't mean she wished her dead. And besides, she had been in a car with me when the baroness had died. Of course Irmgardt had still been in the house. . . . Ridiculous, I said to myself as we swung through the gates into Dippings.

The butler himself came out with a large umbrella to meet me.

"You are just in time for supper, my lady," he said. "Lady Cromer-Strode thought just a simple meal, given the distressing circumstances."

"The baroness's death, you mean?"

"Precisely, my lady."

"Very sad," I said. "I understand she was dead when the maid took her tea in this morning?"

"Oh no, my lady. She was alive and well when the maid delivered her morning tea."

"That would be Irmgardt, the princess's maid?"

"No, my lady. It was your own lady's maid, Mildred, who kindly volunteered to take up her tea, seeing that you had already left for the day. It was when the baroness did not appear for breakfast that our parlor maid, Mary Ann, went to summon her and found her dead. The poor child has been quite distraught all day. A very sensitive little thing."

"I take it a doctor was called?"

"Oh, indeed. Her ladyship's own physician, Doctor Harrison. But he was too late to do anything, of course. He said it was a massive heart attack and there was nothing anybody could have done, even if they had been with her. Very sad for the princess, to have lost her companion."

"Very sad indeed," I agreed as we stepped into the entrance hall and heard the sound of voices coming from the dining room. Among them I detected Hanni's light chatter. She sounded as if she'd recovered from her shock quite well. "Are we changing tonight for dinner, do you know?" I asked.

"Only if you have brought a more somber color with you, my lady."

I didn't think I had but I went up to my room to see what miracle Mildred could produce. Knowing her she had probably managed to dye one of my outfits black in time to wear. Then I froze, halfway up the stairs. Mildred! I had forgotten all about her. What on earth was I going to do with her if I went back to London? I couldn't bring her to an empty London house from which the cook and butler had mysteriously disappeared. Suddenly she felt like yet another millstone around my neck. Why on earth had I hired her in the first place? Trying to do the right thing, as usual. I wished I had been born more like my mother, whose one thought in life was to please herself and the rest of the world be damned.

She wasn't in my bedroom when I went in, but the butler must have alerted her because she came flying in breathlessly a minute after me.

"I'm sorry, my lady. I didn't know when you'd be returning or whether Their Majesties would ask you to dine with them."

"It was just a brief visit to inform them of the baroness's death," I said. "I understand that you were the last person to see her alive."

"I was, my lady. And I feel terrible now. Perhaps there was something I should have noticed, something I should have done."

"The doctor said it was a massive heart attack and nobody could have done anything," I said, "so please don't distress yourself."

"She was snoring, you see. I tapped her quietly and told her that her tea tray was on the bedside table. She muttered something in German, but I don't speak the language so I have no idea what she said, and given her temperament, I thought it wise not to startle her, so I tiptoed out again."

I nodded.

"But now I'm asking myself whether she was trying to tell me that she felt unwell or I should fetch a doctor, and of course I didn't understand."

"She was probably telling you to go away and let her sleep," I said. "There was nothing you could have done, Mildred. Honestly."

"You're too kind, my lady." She managed a watery smile. "I think maybe the blue dress for dinner, as it is the plainest."

"Mildred," I said carefully, as she took the dress from the wardrobe, "I'm going up to London in the morning. If my business takes too long I may have to stay overnight at Rannoch House, but there is no need for you to accompany me. I'll inform Lady Cromer-Strode that you'll be staying on here, awaiting my return."

"Very good, my lady," she said and gave a secret smirk. Obviously she was having a good time and being well fed at Dippings.

Chapter 31

Dippings, Norfolk
Monday, June 20, 1932

Diary,
Two days in a row that I've been up at crack of dawn. I hope it isn't becoming a habit. Luckily rain has stopped. Looks like lovely fine day. Unfortunately I won't be enjoying it. I have places to go and people to see. I wish the queen didn't have such faith in me. I haven't a clue what I'm supposed to do!

I had the chauffeur drive me to Little Dippings Halt, the nearest railway station, to catch the eight o'clock train to London. Then I had to change twice before I caught the express from Peterborough to King's Cross. Frankly it was a blessed relief to be away from people and it gave me time to do some serious thinking. I went through the various events—Tubby tumbling from the balcony, Hanni standing in front of Sidney Roberts's body with a bloody knife in her hand and now this news that the baroness had died of a heart attack. The three tragedies seemed completely unrelated—an accident, a brutal, daring murder and a death by natural causes. Maybe they were just that but three deaths within a week were a little over the norm, even for the most violent of societies. And they had all happened since Hanni came into my life.

Which made me wonder whether the incidents were somehow actually directed at her: was there some kind of plot against her? I knew her father was no longer a reigning monarch, but he was no longer in favor with that funny little man Hitler, who seemed to be the rising star in German politics. And there was a move to restore him to his throne. Could this be some plan to discredit her father? I had heard that the German Nazi Party was ruthless and would stop at nothing to further its cause. . . . But if someone wanted to do away with Hanni, why not just stab her instead of a harmless young man like Sidney? Or was he so harmless? Why had he been invited to that party? Why had he come? They weren't his crowd at all. He was clearly ill at ease there.

I tossed these thoughts around but still had come to no great revelations as we puffed into King's Cross Station. I had intended to go to Rannoch House first, but then I remembered that my grandfather and Mrs. Huggins would probably not be there. So instead I caught the train east, out to the Essex suburbs. Granddad came to the front door, wearing an old apron, and looked astonished to see me.

"Well, blow me down with a feather," he said. "What are you doing here, my love? I thought you was living it up on a country estate."

"I told you the queen wanted me to try and solve this murder before the inquest, so I've left Hanni and come to see what you and I can do."

"And I thought I told you, in no uncertain terms, that you was to stay well away," he said with a frown, as he ushered me into his spotless little house.

"I can't. Queen's orders."

"Then let her come and ruddy well solve it herself," he said angrily. "Putting a young girl like you in harm's way."

He led me through into the kitchen, where he was obviously in the process of preparing his lunch. Runner beans, fresh from the garden, were being sliced on the kitchen table. He lit the gas under the kettle without waiting to see whether I wanted tea at this hour of the day.

"I won't do anything silly, I promise." I took a chair at his kitchen table. "Have you managed to find out anything yet?"

"Give us a chance, ducks. It's been the weekend, hasn't it? Mrs. Huggins and me, we had to pack up our stuff and scarper out of your posh house and get ourselves settled in at home. But I did ask a couple of questions of a bloke I know who's still on the force in the city. I see him sometimes down the Queen's 'ead. He couldn't help much, mind you, but he did say these communists—most of them are harmless enough. They want a world that can never exist—equality for everyone, money shared around equally, jobs for all. Sounds wonderful, but won't ever happen, will it? People are greedy, see. They don't want to share. And my pal did say that the communists over on the Continent aren't quite as idealistic and harmless. Russia's sending out agitators, trained to whip up crowds, stir up hatred for the ruling classes, and get the people mobilized in action. There's going to be civil war in Spain, he says. And that's Russia's aim. Topple governments one by one."

"That's obviously why there was so much fuss when Princess Hanni appeared to be involved in an incident at a communist meeting place, even though I'm sure Sidney was one of the harmless sort."

"There are some nasty pieces of work among them," Granddad said. "Look what they did when they took over Russia. Killed their own grandmothers without a second thought. Murdered your poor relatives, didn't they? Down to the smallest nipper. Lot of savages, if you ask me. Of course, you'd never get the British people to rise up like that. We're too sensible. We know when we're well off."

"I hope so," I said. "But I really don't

think that this murder had anything to do with communism. It just happened in the wrong location. I suspect it was something quite different—someone with a grudge against Sidney Roberts, or it may be to do with drugs. Perhaps Sidney owed money for drugs and hadn't paid up."

Granddad smiled. "They wouldn't kill him for that, love. You don't kill the goose that lays the golden egg, do you? Threaten him, break his kneecaps, but keep him alive to find ways to get the money. That's what the drug peddlers would do."

I shuddered. "I was wondering whether Gussie Gormsley was peddling drugs. He lives awfully well and there were some hints that his money is ill gotten. But I can't see Gussie breaking anybody's kneecaps."

"Can you see him stabbing anybody?"

"Frankly, no. I don't think he'd have the skill, for one thing. And if the murderer could only have escaped through an attic window and across the rooftops—well, Gussie's a little heavy for that sort of acrobatics."

The kettle let out a shrill whistle and Granddad poured the boiling water into the teapot. "So what had you planned to do, now that you're here?"

"I've no real idea. Go and interview Sidney's parents, maybe have a chat with Chief Inspector Burnall and see what he has found out."

"You think he'd welcome that, do you? Poking your nose into his investigations?"

"I'll be subtle, I assure you. I'll visit on the pretense of asking whether a date for the inquest is set and letting him know that Hanni needs to return to Germany soon—oh, and I think I should attend one of the communist meetings—incognito, of course. Sidney did invite Hanni and me to come to one, so I'm sure they're quite safe. I could look around and see who is there and what is said."

Granddad shook his head and made a tutting sound.

"It will be all right, Granddad."

"Just as long as them blackshirts don't bust in on it and turn it into a right old punch-up. They like doing that sort of thing, you know. Another bunch of hooligans, if you ask me. And that Oswald Mosley—calls himself a gentleman? Well, no English gentleman I know behaves like that.

Wants people to go around saluting him, like that Hitler!"

"What would you do?" I asked him. "You've helped to solve real cases, haven't you?"

"I was mostly just on the beat," he said. "But I did work with some good men, and I did learn a thing or two. I remember old Inspector Parks. He had some fine old sayings. For instance, he used to say, 'Start with what you know. Start with the obvious.'"

I frowned, thinking. "Well, the obvious is that three people have died in a remarkably short space of time, but only one of them was a murder, so that's the one we should be looking at."

"Another of his old sayings was 'If anything seems to be a coincidence, there's probably more to it.' So was anyone present at all three of these suspicious deaths?"

"Only Hanni and I. Oh, but wait, we were away when the baroness died, on a trip to Cambridge with Edward Fotheringay. Gussie was present when Tubby fell off the balcony and was in the house when the baroness died."

"And you say you suspect he might be making some money from supplying drugs to his friends?"

"It did cross my mind."

He nodded. "That's something I could look into for you. I know a couple of blokes who might know a thing or two about the drug trade. Go on, don't let your tea get cold."

I took a sip.

"So going back to the obvious—what exactly did you see with your own eyes?"

"Tubby falling. Not being pushed. Hanni standing with a knife in her hand . . ."

"So we have to consider the possibility that she was the one what stabbed him."

I laughed. "Oh no. That's impossible."

"Why is it?"

"She's a princess, Granddad. A young girl. Just out of the convent. Innocent and naïve."

"Not too naïve to try to swipe something from Harrods," he pointed out.

"But taking a handbag is one thing. Killing someone—I can't believe that. For one thing, she looked absolutely stunned, and I really don't see how she would have had time to do it, since I was only a few steps behind her, and for another, how did she come by the knife? It was quite long, you know. She couldn't have hidden it inside her little handbag. And then comes the question of why. Why would a German princess want to kill a harmless lower-class young man she'd only just met and whom she rather fancied?"

Granddad took a slurp of his own tea. "Another of old Inspector Parks's sayings was, 'In a murder case the first question should always be, Who benefits?'"

I thought about this. "In Tubby's case, we'd have to see who inherits the estate with him gone. In Sidney's case, nobody. I don't think he had anything to leave."

"Not just monetarily. Who would benefit from his being out of the way?"

I thought again. "Well, I did hear that he worked with labor unions, to help them organize strikes. Maybe one of the big factory owners wanted him out of the way because he was a nuisance. That might make sense because the police think the efficiency of the stabbing indicated a trained killer."

"And just how do you propose to find out who might have hired a trained killer?"

I put down my teacup. "I have absolutely no idea, Granddad. Frankly I don't know what I'm doing, but I have to give it a try, don't I? I really don't want to start a new world war."

Granddad put down his teacup and burst out laughing. "Oh, that's a good one, that is. You—starting a new world war because a young bloke gets himself stabbed?"

"Look how the last one started! With one silly archduke being assassinated in a little unimportant country. People seem to think an incident involving Hanni and the communists might be enough to unsettle things in Europe. I don't see how, personally, but . . ." My voice trailed off.

"You worry too much, love," Granddad said. "You take yourself too seriously. You're young. You should be enjoying yourself, not feeling responsible for other people."

"I can't help it. I was brought up with duty rammed down my throat."

He nodded. "Well, I'll see what I can do."

"And I wondered if you might come back to Rannoch House with me. Just for a day or so. I don't like the thought of being alone there."

"Of course I will, my love. As long as you don't expect me to dress up in that ridiculous butler's outfit. But I don't think you'll get Mrs. Huggins to join us this time. Had enough of that kitchen of yours, she has. Said it gave her the willies working underground like a mole."

"I quite understand. Of course she needn't come. It's just me. I've left my new maid at Dippings and Hanni's staying there until things are decided for her."

"So you and I best get working then." He picked up the beans. "But first we need a good lunch. I was going to do lamb chops and new potatoes, with beans from my garden. How does that sound?"

I smiled at him. "Perfect."

Chapter 32

After lunch we caught the train up to the Smoke, as my grandfather called it. Then we went our separate ways, he to Scotland Yard and I out to the western suburbs this time and to the address I had found for Mr. and Mrs. Roberts, Sidney's parents.

The Robertses lived in a humble semi-detached house in Slough. Its red brick façade was coated with the grime of end-less coal fires and its pocket handker-chief–sized front garden sported one brave little rosebush. On the journey there, I had thought out how I should approach

Sidney's parents. I knocked and the door was opened by a thin little woman in a flowery pinny.

"Yes?" she said, eyes darting suspiciously.

"Mrs. Roberts, I'm here about your son," I said.

"You're not another of those reporters, are you?" She went to close the door again.

"No, I was a friend of his from Cambridge" (all right, so it was a small lie, but detectives are allowed a certain degree of subterfuge, aren't they?) "and I wanted just to pay my respects and tell you how very sorry I was."

I saw the wariness soften and crinkle into pure grief. "You're welcome to come inside, miss," she said. "What did you say your name was?"

I hadn't, of course. "It's Maggie," I said, reverting to my maid's name as I had done once before. Maggie MacDonald."

"Pleased to meet you, Miss MacDonald." She held out her hand. "The hubby's in the back parlor. He'd like to meet one of our Sidney's friends."

She led me down a dark hallway into a little room with the obligatory three-piece suite and piano, its top littered with Goss china pieces, little souvenirs from past day trips to Brighton or Margate. A man had been sitting in one of the armchairs, reading the paper. He jumped to his feet as I was ushered in. He was painfully thin and balding, wearing braces over his shirt. His face looked completely haggard.

"We've got a visitor, Father," Mrs. Roberts said. "This young lady used to know our Sidney at the university and she's come to pay her respects. Isn't that kind of her?"

"Much appreciated," he said and immediately I felt rotten about deceiving them. "Take a seat, please. And how about a cup of tea, Mother?"

"Oh no, please. I don't want to put you to any bother," I said.

"No bother, I'm sure." She scuttled out into the kitchen, leaving me to face Mr. Roberts.

"So you knew our Sidney at the university, did you?"

"Yes, but I lost touch with him when we graduated, so you can imagine what a shock it was to read about him in the newspaper. I couldn't believe it was the same Sidney Roberts that I had known. I just had to come to London and find out for myself what had happened."

"It happened, all right," he said. "Our bright, wonderful boy, his life snuffed out just like that. Doesn't seem fair, does it? I went through the whole Battle of the Somme and I came out without a scratch, but I tell you this, miss, I'd willingly have sacrificed my life in a second in exchange for his. He had so much to live for, so much promise."

Mrs. Roberts had come back in with a teapot under a crocheted cozy and three cups on a tray. Obviously this was one of those households where there is always tea ready. "Here we are then," she said with forced brightness. "Do you take milk and sugar?"

"Just milk, please," I said. She poured me a cup and the cup rattled against the saucer as she passed it to me with an unsteady hand.

"I was telling her how I wished I could have traded my life for his," Mr. Roberts said.

"Don't get yourself worked up again, Father," Mrs. Roberts said. "This has really been hard on him, miss. First losing his job and now this. I don't know how much more we can take."

I looked longingly at the door, fervently wishing that I hadn't come. I also wished I could help them with money, although I rather suspected that they wouldn't take it.

"I understand that Sidney still lived at home?" I asked.

"That's right. He came back to us after the university," Mr. Roberts said. "We were worried that he'd get a job far away and his mother was delighted when he said he'd be stopping in London, weren't you, old dear?"

She nodded, but put her hand to her mouth.

"The newspaper said that Sidney was killed in the docklands area of London? What was he doing there?"

Mr. Roberts glanced at his wife. "He worked in a bookshop. All that education and he ended up working behind a counter like any of the other young men from around here. I'll tell you, miss. We had such high hopes for our Sidney. He was such a bright boy, see. We scrimped and saved to send him to the grammar school and then he goes and gets a scholarship to Cambridge as well. He had the world at his feet, our Sidney did."

His voice cracked and he looked away from me.

"We thought he'd go into the law," his wife continued for him. "He had always talked about becoming a solicitor so we expected him to become articled to a good firm when he came down from the university. But no. He announces to us that he wants nothing to do with the bourgeois establishment, whatever that is."

"It seems he got in with a funny lot at his college," Mr. Roberts said confidentially. "You probably knew about them, if you was one of his friends there."

"The apostles? The secret society? Is that who you mean?"

"That would be the ones. You've heard of them then?"

"I did hear something about them. And I know that Sidney was—well, rather idealistic about things."

"Idealistic? Ruddy stupid, if you'll pardon the language, miss," Mr. Roberts said. "All this talk about power for the people and down with the ruling classes and everyone should govern themselves. It can never happen, I told him. The ruling classes are born to rule. They know how to do it. You take a person like you or me and you put us up there to run a country and we'd make a ruddy mess of it."

Mrs. Roberts hadn't taken her eyes off her husband's face. Now she looked at me as if willing me to understand. "His father tried to make him see sense, but it was no use. He started writing for that *Daily Worker* newspaper and hanging around with those communists."

"Bunch of layabouts the lot of them. Don't even shave properly," Mr. Roberts intervened.

"No good can come of this, we told him. When you want to get a proper job, this will come back to haunt you."

"His mother wanted to humor him to start with," Mr. Roberts said. "You know how mothers are, and he was her only boy, of course." He paused and cleared his throat. "She thought he'd grow out of it. Young people often do go to extremes, don't they? But then they find a nice girl, settle down and see sense. Only—only he never got a chance to grow out of it, did he?"

"Do you have any idea at all who might have done this awful thing?" I asked.

They stared at me blankly. "We think it had to be a mistake. The person who stabbed him mistook him for someone else. It was dark in that place, so we hear. Maybe the killer stabbed our poor Sidney by mistake. I can't think of any other explanation for it."

"Had anyone threatened him?" I asked.

Again they stared blankly. "We never heard he was in any kind of trouble," Mr. Roberts said. "Of course he would go to them communist rallies and sometimes there was a bit of a scuffle there. His mother didn't want him to go. But apart from that, we've no idea. It couldn't have been anybody trying to rob the till, because he was upstairs when they stabbed him."

"Have the police given you any idea at all of what they might suspect?" I asked.

"If they have any ideas, they certainly haven't shared them with us," Mr. Roberts said bitterly. "Asked a lot of stupid questions about whether Sidney was connected to any criminal activity. They thought it was done by a professional because of the way he was stabbed, I gather."

Mrs. Roberts shifted forward to the edge of her chair. "But we told them he'd always been a good boy. Never done a thing to make us ashamed of him. And if he was up to anything shady, we'd have known, wouldn't we, Father?"

"Was Sidney worried about anything recently?" I asked.

They glanced at each other.

"Funny you should say that, miss. I think something was upsetting him. He had a nightmare and we heard him moaning in his sleep and he said, 'No, it's wrong. You can't do it.' In the morning we asked him about it but he'd completely forgotten. So maybe he was in some kind of trouble and hadn't told us. They do have gangs working in that part of London, wouldn't you say? Perhaps they wanted to pressure our Sidney to take part in a robbery or something and he'd refused. He would refuse, you know. Very upright, was our Sidney."

"Or we wondered whether he'd overheard something not meant for his ears, and he was killed because he wanted to go to the police."

"That sounds possible," I agreed, wondering why it had never occurred to me before. "What about Sidney's current friends? I know who his friends were at university. Did he keep up with the old crowd?"

"Not very much," his mother said. "There was that young man with the silly name. Sounded like a mushroom."

"Edward Fotheringay, pronounced 'Fungy'?" I asked her.

She smiled. "That's the one. He came to the house a couple of times and picked up Sidney in his little sports car. 'I thought you said you was against the upper classes,' we said to him. His dad liked to tease him from time to time. But he said that this Edward was all right and cared about the masses too. Apart from that, he didn't bring anybody home. No girlfriend, as far as I could see. He didn't go out much, apart from those communist meetings. He always was rather serious, wasn't he, Father?"

"No girlfriend he ever told us about anyway," Mr. Roberts said. He was looking at me strangely, with his head cocked to one side, like a bird, and it suddenly came to me that he thought I might be Sidney's girlfriend. "If you'll pardon my saying so, miss, but you seem very concerned about him. More than the average acquaintance from university would be."

I gave what I hoped was a nervous laugh. "It's true. We were close friends once. That's why I was so angry to hear about this. I want to get to the bottom of it. I want his killer to be brought to justice."

"We're very grateful for any help, miss." The Robertses exchanged a look.

I decided to plunge ahead. "I was wondering . . . Sidney wasn't drinking or smoking too much recently, was he?"

"He'd take the odd pint and the odd cigarette, but no more than the average person, not as much actually, because our Sidney was always careful with his money, as you probably remember. He left quite a bit in his savings account, didn't he, Father?"

My ears pricked up—so quiet, well-behaved Sidney had been squirreling away quite a bit of money, had he?

"He did. Over fifty pounds," Mr. Roberts said proudly.

So much for the theory that Sidney was selling drugs. Fifty pounds wouldn't have begun to cover one of Gussie's parties.

I finished my tea and took my leave of the Robertses.

I was feeling tired and depressed by the time I arrived at Rannoch House and was relieved to find my grandfather already in residence and yet another cup of tea on the stove. This one, however, was most welcome.

"So did you learn anything?" my grandfather asked.

"Only things that I can now rule out. Sidney Roberts was a good boy, according to his parents. He lived simply at home. He had fifty pounds in a savings account. They had high hopes for him and were disappointed when he became a communist sympathizer. So we can assume that he was not profiting from selling drugs, nor was he a drug user. There was a suggestion that maybe he had fallen foul of some kind of criminal element—that some gang wanted him to carry out some kind of robbery for them and he had refused, or that he'd overheard something not meant for his ears."

Granddad nodded. "A possibility in that part of town. He worked in a bookshop that sold old books, you say. Were there rare books among them—books that could be sold for a bob or two? Maybe someone had asked him to nick a few."

I hadn't thought of this. The simplest of solutions. "You could find out about that kind of thing, couldn't you? Your friends on the force could come up with gangs who might deal in stolen art, antiques, that kind of thing."

He nodded. "Yes, that would be easy enough. But it seems rather extreme to me. You don't stab a bloke through the heart because he won't nick a book for you. However, if he was going to rat on them to the coppers . . . you say he was an upstanding young man . . . now that's another business. I'll see what my old pals have got to say on that."

"And tomorrow I'm going to Inspector Burnall," I said. "Their investigation might have turned up a thing or two by now."

"I wouldn't count on it, love," Granddad said. "Now, about our supper tonight. There ain't much food in the larder, seeing as how we thought you was going to be away. What do you say I go and get us a nice bit of fish and chips?"

I started to laugh. "Granddad, I don't think you'd find fish and chips in Belgravia," I said.

Chapter 33

Rannoch House
Tuesday, June 21, 1932

Diary,
Going to be a hot day. Muggy and still, even at eight thirty. Not looking forward to what lies ahead. Not cut out to be sleuth.

The morning's post brought a letter from Buckingham Palace. I thought this was strange, given that the royal couple was in Norfolk, but when I opened it I found that it was merely an official invitation to the royal garden party the next day. It concluded, *Please present this invitation to gain admission to the palace grounds.* So I was to be facing Her Majesty the next day. She'd expect me to have something to tell her. I had better put in a good day's work today.

After breakfast Granddad set off for his old police station in the East End and I headed for Scotland Yard. I was in luck. Chief Inspector Burnall was in his office and I was ushered in. The chief inspector, dapperly dressed as always, looked surprised to see me.

"What brings you here, my lady? Come to give yourself up?"

I gave him my best imitation of my great-grandmother's steely stare. He wilted under it. "Just joking, my lady. Now, what can I do for you?"

"I came to find out if a date for the inquest has been set. It appears that Princess Hannelore may have to go home to Germany quite soon, so if you think her testimony may be helpful, you should probably schedule the inquest before she leaves."

"She's intending to do a bunk, is she?"

"Her companion, the Baroness Rottenmeister, has just died. Naturally protocol would demand that she not stay on in this country unchaperoned."

"Another death? They seem to be falling like flies around your princess. Are you sure her last name isn't Borgia?" Again he gave a tentative chuckle.

"The baroness died of a heart attack while the princess and I were being shown around Cambridge," I said coldly. "And you can't seriously believe that the princess or I had anything to do with the murder of Sidney Roberts, other than coming upon his body."

"She was found with the knife in her hand."

"But you said yourself that the blow was delivered by a trained assassin. Do you really think that the nuns trained her to kill at the Holy Names convent?"

"I suppose not," he agreed.

"And you can't possibly suspect me."

He hesitated for a second, making me continue, "Really, Chief Inspector—what possible motive would either of us have had to want Mr. Roberts dead? I had only met the man twice before—once in a park and then a brief conversation at a party."

"Three times," he said. "You met him three times, not twice. At the British Museum, remember?"

"Ah. Well, actually I didn't meet him at the British Museum. Princess Hannelore did."

"Oh?"

"We became separated and when I found her again she told me excitedly that she'd met Sidney doing research there, and he had invited us to his bookshop."

He paused then said, "So you only have Her Highness's word that she had met this man there?"

"Yes, I suppose so."

"So if Her Highness had wanted an excuse to go to the bookshop, she could have concocted this story."

"I suppose she could. But why?" Even as I said the words I saw one possibility. Hanni was smitten with Sidney. She wanted a chance to meet him again. She had proven herself not above subterfuge when it suited her.

"You've thought of a reason?" he asked.

"Yes. I'm afraid the princess was rather boy mad, Chief Inspector. And I believe she was setting her cap at Sidney Roberts. I can't see why, because she certainly wouldn't have been allowed to continue a friendship with a penniless, lower-class man. Perhaps he appealed to her because he was forbidden fruit in her eyes."

The chief inspector nodded. "And an unknown assassin chose that exact moment to stab Mr. Roberts and then vanish into thin air. Very convenient, don't you think?"

"Not vanish into thin air. Didn't the shop owner say that there was a window in the attic and a way across the rooftops?"

Chief Inspector Burnall shook his head. "We examined that window. The dust on the sill had not been disturbed."

"He could just as easily have hidden among the bookshelves and then slipped out after we left the shop to call the police. He could have taken refuge in a nearby building and we probably wouldn't have seen him. But the point is, Chief Inspector, that we didn't kill Sidney Roberts, we had no motive for killing Sidney Roberts and we certainly did not have the expertise to kill him."

"I suppose I have to accept that," he said. "But maybe you can help me out by suggesting someone who might have had a motive."

"Why would I know that?"

"You were all at the same party a few nights previously, when another young man died. A party at which I gather cocaine was in use?"

"I told you, I personally witnessed that death. It was a horrible accident. Tubby was reeling drunk. He fell against the railings and they gave way. Nobody was near him."

"Not entirely thanks to being drunk, as it turns out," Burnall said slowly, not taking his eyes off my face. "An autopsy revealed that he had a considerable level of alcohol in his system, that's true. He also had a lethal amount of phenobarbital. Someone had slipped him what the Americans call a Mickey Finn."

"Poisoned him, you mean?"

"Knocked him out. Someone wanted to make sure he fell off that balcony, and to doubly guarantee this, they had also removed some of the screws that held the bars in place."

"Good heavens." I couldn't think of anything else to say.

"So I want you to think carefully, my lady. Do you have any reason to suspect that someone at that party wanted your pal Tubby out of the way? Or did you possibly see someone tampering with a drink?"

I shook my head. "It was dark and people were mixing cocktails all the time. An awful lot of drinking was going on and Tubby had a glass in his hand every time I saw him. As to who wanted him out of the way, I should have thought you'd have examined the line of inheritance by now."

"We have, my lady. No brothers, so the estate would pass to a cousin. Several cousins, including the young man who gave the party."

"Gussie Gormsley?" I asked in a shocked voice.

"As you say. Augustus Gormsley. Granted he's only a second cousin, but maybe he has similar intentions on those ahead of him in the line."

I laughed. "Oh, surely this is madness, Inspector. Gussie is—" I was about to say harmless and then I remembered how he would have forced himself upon me if Darcy hadn't shown up. Not entirely harmless then. But I pictured that scene on the balcony and saw Gussie handing Tubby the drink. "That drink wasn't even intended for Tubby," I said. "Gussie was offering it around. Tubby took it."

"Who was it intended for then?"

I froze as I remembered. Gussie was trying to press the drink upon Sidney Roberts. After Sidney had refused, Tubby had taken the drink and downed it. But could I really bring myself to mention this fact? After all, these were members of my set. We didn't go around killing people. And I had only seen what happened after Gussie came out onto the balcony. He could have offered the drink to any number of people inside first.

"I've no idea," I said. "Gussie was just being a good host and making sure that everyone was drinking."

"I see." Again he looked at me long and hard.

"So may one ask whether you have made any progress in the murder of Sidney Roberts?" I asked, changing the subject. "He wasn't mixed up with any kind of criminals, was he?"

"Why do you ask that?"

"Because I went to see his parents to express my condolences and his mother said he had been worried lately and in his sleep he muttered something about it being wrong and that they shouldn't do it. So I thought that maybe he'd been coerced into something illegal."

"Interesting." He nodded his head. "As of yet we haven't heard that kind of rumor, but we'll look into it. We'll be looking into every angle, I can assure you—unless there is any other tidbit of information you'd like to share with me right now."

"Had I any information, I would share it willingly," I said. "I take it you have been notified that the princess is staying near Sandringham at the moment, and I shall be at Rannoch House for the next day or so, so you'll know where to contact us about the inquest."

I rose to my feet. He did the same. "You people, you stick together, no matter what, don't you?" he said.

"What do you mean?"

"I believe you know more than you're telling me, but one of your lot is to blame and it will come out. And when it does and I find you've been withholding evidence, I'll come after you. I don't care who you are."

"I'm sure you don't," I said coldly. "You

arrested my brother earlier this year when he was completely innocent. But I repeat what I just said: I know nothing about either of these strange events. I wish I could tell you more."

Then I made a grand exit.

Chapter 34

As I walked back to Rannoch House through St. James's Park, watching children playing, couples strolling hand in hand, office workers sitting on the grass enjoying the sunshine, it seemed to me that nobody had a care in the world but me. Of course this was fallacious thinking. At this very moment all over the city there were men lining up in the hopes of finding work, or getting a handout of soup or bread. But the depression couldn't spoil a summer day's fun in the park for these people. I, on the other hand, could not shake off my burden.

After my visit to Chief Inspector Burnall, I was more confused than ever. One of my lot. The words kept echoing through my head. One of my lot had definitely killed poor Tubby Tewkesbury and the person who had handed him the drink had been Gussie. But he had first tried to press the drink upon Sidney Roberts. Had Gussie known he was carrying a drink laced with phenobarbital? Had he intended to let Sidney fall through that railing? In which case why? Various possibilities went through my mind—upright Sidney had threatened to report the cocaine use to the police, or he had been some kind of go-between, ferrying drugs between the docklands and Mayfair, until his conscience got the better of him. But did one kill for what seemed so trivial a reason? And if Gussie hadn't known the drink was laced then who else at the party wanted Sidney dead and why? The partly unscrewed railings seemed to indicate Gussie—after all, it was his flat.

I glanced across at the simple white outline of the modern block, fronting the park. Maybe I should see for myself. Gussie was safely far away in the country.

I should be able to persuade the doorman to let me in. I changed course and made for the block of flats. The uniformed doorman saluted and let me into the glass and marble entrance hall where a hall porter sat. I explained to him that I had been at the party.

"Oh, that party," he said, nodding with understanding.

"And everything was rather chaotic and we left in rather a hurry," I said. "And I'm afraid I might have left my little evening bag in the flat."

"I'm sorry, miss, but Mr. Gormsley is not in residence," he said.

"I know that. I was staying with him in the country until yesterday," I said. "I'm sure he wouldn't mind my taking a look around for my bag. You must have a pass key and I am awfully fond of it, you know."

I saw him wrinkle his forehead, debating. Then he got to his feet. "I suppose I could take you up there for a moment." He shuffled into his cubicle to fetch a set of keys and then escorted me up in the lift.

Gussie's flat smelled of stale smoke, and the afternoon sun streaming in through those huge windows made it rather unpleasantly warm. The porter stood in the doorway. He obviously had no intention of leaving me alone.

"I'm not sure which room I might have left it in," I said. "It all looks terribly neat and tidy, doesn't it?" It did. Gussie's man had done a splendid job. I went into the drawing room with its low modern furniture and ghastly modern art. There was a desk in the corner but I could hardly make the porter believe that I had opened it to stash my evening bag inside. And of course I had no idea what I might be looking for. A blotter with the imprint of a letter telling Sidney he had better deliver the drugs or else? Probably not. Or a letter from Sidney saying that he felt compelled to go to the police? The wastepaperbasket was empty, the desk pristine.

"Maybe I left it in the bedroom," I said, making him raise an eyebrow. "We left our wraps on the bed, I remember. Perhaps it fell under the bed."

"I'll look for you, miss. I don't want you getting down on your hands and knees," he said. I waited until he went ahead into the bedroom, then I dashed back to that desk. It opened easily enough. It even contained a letter rack of unanswered mail. I flicked through it quickly, opened one drawer after another, then closed them as quietly as possible.

"Any luck?" I called.

"Nothing, miss."

"I'll just check the kitchen then." I moved away from the desk.

After ten minutes I had to admit that I had found nothing. Of course the police would probably have given the flat a thorough search by now and taken away anything incriminating. All I could surmise, as I rode the lift down with the hall porter, was that Gussie was living beyond his means. He had an awful lot of unpaid bills, some of them second and third demands, from his tailor, his wine merchant, from Fortnum's. So if he was peddling drugs, he wasn't getting rich from it.

"I'm sorry you didn't find what you were looking for," the porter said as he ushered me out.

It was now well after lunchtime and my stomach was growling in unladylike fashion. I continued through the park back to Rannoch House and found no sign of my grandfather. I grabbed some bread and cheese and changed my clothes before venturing out again. I was rather relieved that Granddad wasn't there, because my intention was to do a little snooping around in the area of the bookshop and possibly to attend a meeting at the communist headquarters. I didn't think he'd approve of either. I left him a note saying that I was meeting friends and probably wouldn't be home until after supper. I didn't want him to worry.

I found the bookshop with slightly less difficulty this time. The alleyway looked like a peaceful backwater, deep in late afternoon shadow while the sun painted the upper stories of the warehouses around it with a rosy glow. Even the Russian tearoom only contained two very old men, their heads sunk to their chests and half-drunk cups of tea in front of them. The beggar was no longer on the corner; in fact, nothing moved as I made my way toward the bookstore. A loud toot made me jump until I remembered that the river lay just beyond the bottom of the alleyway. A bell jangled as I let myself into the bookshop. I noticed that it hung at the top of the door on one of those little brackets. I had forgotten about the bell. We would have heard it jangling if anyone had tried to slip out of the bookshop behind us, wouldn't we?

Mr. Solomon appeared from the depths of the shop. "May I help you, miss?" He didn't seem to recognize me and I wondered if he had poor eyesight.

"I was one of the young ladies who found your assistant stabbed last week," I said. "I've felt awful about it ever since and I'm sure you have, too."

"Indeed I have, miss. Such a fine young man. So much promise."

"I just wondered whether the police are any closer to finding out who did this," I said.

"The police tell me nothing," he said. "I'm in the dark as much as you are, although my money is on those blackshirts."

"Blackshirts?"

"Yes, the thugs that that fascist Mosley surrounds himself with. You've heard about him and his New Party, have you? Now there's a troublemaker if ever there was one. Modeling himself on that horrible man Mussolini."

"I saw them in operation recently, causing a disruption at Speakers' Corner."

He sighed. "They came in here, you know, only a couple of weeks ago. They despise communists and of course they despise Jews. Nothing but thugs. They tipped over a tray of valuable rare books before they left."

"But why stab Mr. Roberts?"

"As a gesture of superiority, maybe, or they may have thought they were killing me, since I represent everything they hate."

"Have you suggested this to the police?"

"I rather get the impression that some policemen admire the fascist ideas and certainly despise socialism. They don't want to be equal. They like power."

I looked at his serious face with its sunken eyes and perpetual worried frown and wished I could do something useful.

"Sidney worked here and he also wrote for the *Daily Worker*, is that correct?"

"He did. He wrote very well. Had he lived, I believe he might have become a fine writer."

"And I also understand that he was

involved in helping unions to voice their grievances."

"He did that too. He was a fine orator as well. The party needed people like him—men who truly wanted to make lives better. There aren't many of them around, I fear."

"So you didn't ever get an idea that he was mixed up with anything—well, illegal?"

"Illegal?" He looked shocked. "What are you suggesting, young lady?"

"I don't know—burglaries, drugs?"

"Our Mr. Roberts? He would have refused. He had the highest moral standards."

There was nothing more I could think of asking and I couldn't find an excuse to let me investigate the shop for myself, but I was reluctant to leave.

"Sidney invited me to come to one of his meetings," I said. "I didn't have a chance to, but I feel that I should, to honor his memory if nothing else."

Mr. Solomon stared at me critically. "That is a fine sentiment, young lady. It just happens that there is to be a lecture tonight at the church hall around the corner. I think you may find it very informative. Eight o'clock it starts. I look forward to seeing you there."

I came out into the deep shadow of the alleyway and stood looking back at the dusty paned windows, wondering if I might have a chance to slip back inside should Mr. Solomon leave for a moment. And if I did gain access, what then? The police had thoroughly searched the place and found nothing. Or if they had found anything, they were not willing to share the information with me. I lingered for a while until Mr. Solomon finally emerged. He closed the door behind him and turned the key. I flattened myself into a doorway as he passed me, then went to try the door. It was, of course, hopelessly locked.

I heard a nearby church clock chiming the hour. Five. Crowds were streaming past the end of the alleyway, dockhands and typists going home for the day. I had three hours to kill before the lecture but it hardly made sense for me to go home on one of those packed tube trains. By the time I found my way back to the nearest tube station and arrived home, I would have to turn around and leave again, and my grandfather would probably try to stop me. So all in all it made sense to stay in this part of town. I came out of the alleyway and located the hall where the meeting was to be held, just around the corner as Mr. Solomon had said. It even had a sign on the notice board outside: *Tonight: Mr. Bill Strutt, of the British Workers League, will give a talk on Vision for a New Britain. Come and hear his inspiring talk.*

I wandered back along Wapping High Street, taking in the sounds and smells of the docklands—the dank, rotting smell of river water competing with fish and chips from an open shop front, the mournful tooting of tugboats echoing over the clattering of shoes on cobblestones. I went into the fish and chip shop and bought myself ninepenceworth of cod and chips, then ate them from the newspaper as I walked along. Very satisfying until I noticed the grease staining the glove I had stupidly forgotten to remove. I kept walking until I made my way back to the Tower of London, with Tower Bridge framing the Thames. The white stonework of the tower was glowing pink in the evening sunlight.

It presented a most attractive picture. I found a bench and sat taking in the busy river scene. A cargo boat came upriver, causing the bridge to open and backing up traffic on either side. The river flowed past, dark and oily, with flotsam twirling in the turbid waters. The sun sank lower and a chill breeze swept up the river, making it no longer pleasant to sit there.

I still had more than an hour to go and although Wapping High Street was busy enough at this time, it wasn't the sort of area where one should draw attention to oneself. I wished I had a male escort so that I could go into one of the many pubs that were doing good business, in spite of the depression. Finally I remembered the Russian tearoom. I went back to the alleyway and went inside, causing stares all around. It was only when I was seated that I noticed that all the other people sitting at the tables were men.

"I remember you," the elderly waiter said in a strong accent. "You and the other girl. You came here when the poor young man was stabbed."

"That's right," I said.

"Why do you come back here again?"

he demanded, in a voice heavy with a foreign accent.

"Sidney Roberts invited us to one of his meetings, so I felt I should attend in his memory."

He sniffed. "Not a good place for young girl after dark. You should go home."

As the sun sank, it had occurred to me that it probably wasn't a good place to be after dark and that I somehow had to find my way back to the nearest tube station when the meeting was over. But I had seen buses. I'd take a bus to a better part of town, where I could find a taxicab. I ordered a cup of tea. It came up in a glass in a silver holder, and was pale and sweet with lemon floating in it. I sipped gratefully and made it last, while I listened to the conversation going on around me. I guessed it to be mainly in Russian, but I thought I heard some German too.

At about seven thirty I left and went back to the hall. The doors were open and one or two people were already seated inside—workingmen in cloth caps, and a middle-aged woman in black. They nodded to me and I returned the nod. Gradually the benches were filled, and the air became heavy with smoke (and coughing). The smell of unwashed bodies in the lingering warmth of the summer evening was not too pleasant either. The bench was already feeling hard and uncomfortable and I could sense eyes upon me. I was sure I stood out as not belonging, even though I had dressed as simply as possible. Many of these people were in threadbare clothes, their elbows and knees well patched. I was too clean, too civilized, too well dressed. I was seriously wishing I had followed Granddad's advice and not come. What could I hope to achieve by being here? These people were Sidney's friends. They would have wanted to protect him, not kill him.

"I haven't seen you here before." A young man in a bright red waistcoat sat down beside me.

"No. It's my first time. I was a friend of Sidney Roberts—you know the one who was killed last week?"

"Oh yes. I heard about it. Poor fellow." He was well-spoken and I noticed that he wore a signet ring. One of us, then.

"Welcome," he said. "My name's Miles. I think you're in for a treat. Bill is a splendid speaker."

I wanted to ask this Miles if he was possibly at Cambridge with Sidney, but at that moment the door at the front of the hall opened and several men filed out onto the stage. The speaker was introduced. He was an unassuming little man, probably in his forties and not much better dressed than his audience. But when he started to speak, I could see what Miles had meant. He talked of a vision for a new society—wealth being shared, the workload being shared. "The empire has grown fat and strong on the backs of the workers," he said, thumping the table now as he warmed up. "And do we get any thanks? No, we get our pink slips instead when production drops. Who fought in the trenches in the war? The workers. We did. And where were the officers? Drinking Scotch behind the lines. And who is lining up for jobs or bread today while the bosses go home to a big roast dinner? You've got it, my friends. We have kept the empire running and nobody has ever thanked us.

"So what if we made it change? If we

were the bosses? If we elected our own to run the coal mines and the wool mills and the docks and the country? We'd know how backbreaking the work was, wouldn't we? We'd see that every man got fair pay for his labor. We'd improve safety conditions. No more mine cave-ins, no more fingers lost to faulty machines. And it can happen in our time. All we need is to make our cause known and the people will rise up behind us. Elect us to parliament and it will be like an ever-growing stream."

"There's already a Labor Party, in case you haven't noticed," a heckler called from the back.

"Labor Party?" Bill Strutt laughed. "And what do they care about the workers? No more than the Tories, do they? Have they stopped the layoffs or supported the strikes and hunger marches? No, they bloody well haven't. It's time for a change, comrade. It's time for true socialism. It's time for us to take over what is rightfully ours."

"And what makes you think we'd be better off?" another heckling voice demanded. "Look at Russia. Are they better off under Joe Stalin? They're starving, mate. One wrong move and they're sent to Siberia, so I've heard."

"Ah, but Russia's different," Strutt said. "The Russian peasants—well, they were almost like serfs, weren't they? Not educated like our British workers. Not used to having a say in the running of things like our British workers. So Russia's still got a long way to go, but as for us—we're ready to take over, comrades. . . ."

There were halfhearted cheers and stamping of feet. I began to feel it was all rather silly. I looked around me. Many of the faces were focused on the speaker, enraptured. Then I froze. The lighting in the hall was poor but in a far corner I thought I had spotted a face I knew. It looked remarkably like Edward Fotheringay.

Chapter 35

I pulled my cloche hat more firmly down over one eye so that Edward couldn't spot me and waited for the speech to end. It did, amid heckles and hurled insults. It seemed an element of the crowd had been planted merely to stir things up. Finally Bill Strutt had had enough.

"Comrades, I see we have some present who don't want to listen or learn. In every society there are closed minds that we will never reach, and so I'll call it a day right here, before things turn violent. I ask you to remain calm and controlled as you leave here. Let's show that we are the better people, that we don't need violence to promote our cause. Hang on to the vision, comrades. To a better future for us all—a communist future!"

There was loud applause, and a few boos, as he stepped down from the stage. The crowd was on its feet, making for the front doors. I glanced over at Edward and saw that he was inching forward through the crowd, like a salmon swimming upstream, rather than joining the exodus. I too was being swept toward the exits. I dodged and moved aside, gradually working my way to the side aisle where I was out of the stream. The men who had been on the stage had now disappeared through the small door to which Edward was also heading. I moved forward painfully slowly, jostled by burly laborers and dockworkers.

"Exit's this way, love," one of them said. "Come on, I'll buy you half a pint." He attempted to put an arm around me.

"No, thanks. I'm waiting for someone," I said, dodging out of reach. I looked around but Edward too had now disappeared. There was a door to one side marked *Lavatory.* I went inside and locked the door behind me. Finally the clatter of feet subsided. I came out to find the hall in darkness. There was still a modicum of daylight coming in through high windows, enough for me to see the layout of the hall and the fact that the big doors at the end were now shut. Everyone had gone home, except for those who had disappeared through the little door beside the stage. I made my way there, stumbling over a chair that had been left in a side aisle and then holding my breath in case anyone had heard. But nothing moved as I reached that doorway. I opened the door and went through.

Inside the narrow passage was complete darkness. I looked around for a light switch, then thought better of it. I shouldn't draw attention to my presence. I didn't know how safe I was—Edward, after all, had been the one who mixed the cocktails that evening. He had been the one with that strange, exhilarated look on his face as he drove very fast through the rain storm. There was definitely something about him that was not to be trusted.

I crept down the narrow passageway, inching along by feel. When I came to a half-open door on my right, I checked it out, only to find it was a broom cupboard. I counted paces from it, realizing that it would be a place to hide should the men return this way unexpectedly. The passage ended suddenly in what seemed to be a wall. My fingers searched over it but found no door or knob. Where could they have gone? And why hadn't I been sensible enough to carry a torch, as any good detective should?

At last my fingers located a crack in the wall, what felt like the side of a door, but I could still feel no knob, nor the top of the door. I put my ear to it and could hear faint voices beyond it.

"That girl was here this afternoon," I heard a man's voice say clearly. "She was planning to attend the meeting tonight."

"Yes, I thought I saw her in the hall." Was that Edward's voice? It was too muffled for me to be sure.

"Do you think she suspects anything?" The third voice appeared to be female, but deep and guttural, with a pronounced foreign accent.

"What does it matter? She'll be too late, won't she?" Edward's voice again?

"You still mean to go through with it, then?"

"I know what happened to Roberts— stupid little prig with his lower-class morals. If I were planning to back out, I'd be on my way to Australia as fast as my legs could carry me."

"I am still disturbed about Roberts. Was it really necessary to kill him?"

"He would have betrayed us." This was the foreign woman's guttural voice.

"And you still think this is a wise course of action? Given the situation?"

"What option do we have? The first attempts failed and time is definitely running out."

"It was stupid to kill the baroness."

"No choice, old boy. She was going to telephone the princess's father, and that would never have done, would it?"

So it seemed there were three speakers, two males, one female, all speaking softly as though they didn't want to be overheard.

"So everything's in place, then? Anything you need us to do?"

"Have the escape route ready, if either of us manages to get away."

"It's not the ideal situation. I've said that all along."

"It will have to do. Now or never, don't you agree?"

"I suppose I have to agree. I never thought this was a good idea in the beginning. What's it going to achieve, apart from turning half the population against us?"

"You're not going soft on us, are you, Solomon?"

"You know my views on violence. Only when absolutely necessary."

"Quite right. When absolutely necessary."

The voices were moving off. Something else was said but I couldn't catch it. I thought I heard some kind of thud. I felt my way back down the hall and into that broom cupboard in case they reappeared suddenly. But they didn't. I waited and waited until my legs were stiff and cramped from standing bent over among the mops and buckets. Finally I came out and listened. Nothing. There must have been another way out from the room in which they had been speaking.

I worked my way back to the main hall. It was dark outside by now with a street lamp twinkling in through one of the windows. The hall had become a place of danger—with flickering shadows and strange shapes. A raucous burst of singing from a pub made me fully aware that I was in an area where there was not likely to be safety. Slowly and carefully I made my way down the aisle, until I had reached the front doors. I pushed hard, but they refused to give. I searched for a handle. There was none. From what I could tell, they were padlocked from the outside. I was trapped in here.

There had to be another way out. Those speakers had gone through what appeared to be a solid wall and had not returned. I made my way back again, conscious now of every small sound, the echo of my feet on a stone floor and mysterious rustles and creaks which were probably no more than an old building settling in the night air but which sounded horribly ominous to me. I couldn't make myself believe that I was completely alone. I saw moving shadows in every corner and jumped at a passing motorcar's horn.

"Buck up, Georgie, this isn't like you." I gave myself a stiff talking-to. I, who had dared to stay up on the ramparts to spot my grandfather's ghost; I, who had been lowered down the castle well by my brother and his friends—now I was scared to be alone in the dark? Well, this was a little different. I had just heard several people confessing to killing the baroness and Sidney Roberts, from what I could gather. That meant my life wasn't worth much if they discovered me here.

I made my way slowly back down that narrow passage and found the crack in the wall again. I felt around but couldn't come up with a corresponding crack for the other side of a door, nor could I find any kind of handle. I pushed. I poked. Then in frustration I kicked at the floorboard. I felt something give and part of the wall swung silently inward. I hesitated only a second before stepping through. I knew where I was instantly, of course. That characteristic smell of old books and pipe tobacco. I was back in the bookshop. So there had been another way out that the police hadn't discovered. Not very bright of them.

I wondered which floor I was on. There

was almost no light. I wondered if I could find a light switch and if I dared to turn it on. I stood silently listening, just in case the speakers had not left but only moved to another part of the shop. I certainly didn't want to bump into anyone in the dark. To reassure myself, I reached back to touch the doorway through which I had come, and couldn't find it. I backed up, my heart beating faster now, and touched bookshelves on three sides of me. If it had been a secret entrance, it had swung back into place. I was now trapped in the bookshop.

After waiting what seemed like an eternity, listening for any sound or movement, I left the shelter of my side aisle, feeling my way along the bookshelf. Ahead of me I could see a faint glimmer of light, barely enough to outline the rows of bookshelves. Slowly I made my way forward, toward that light, until my foot stubbed against something soft. I bent down, then recoiled in horror. A person was lying there. Cautiously I reached out and touched, feeling down a sleeve until I located a hand. It was still warm. I held the wrist for a pulse, but I couldn't detect one. The faint glimmer of light outlined the glasses on a skeletal face. It had to be Mr. Solomon.

I should go for help. Maybe there was still a chance to save him. I inched around him and felt my way forward. The glimmer of light grew until I could see it was a street lamp, shining in through the dusty panes of the front windows. I let out a huge sigh of relief. I'd be able to find the nearest policeman and tell him everything I knew. Whatever these people had planned, I'd be able to stop them. I grabbed the front door handle. It moved but the door wouldn't open. I shook it, jiggled, pushed with all my might, but apart from making the bell jangle peevishly, nothing happened. They had locked the door behind them. I was trapped in here with Mr. Solomon's body.

I looked at the windows and wondered if I could find anything strong enough to break them with, but the panes were so small that I'd never be able to get out that way.

I sank to the floor beside the window and rested my arms on the wide window ledge. At this moment I didn't want to be grown up and independent and on my own in a big city. I wanted more than anything to be home. I wanted to be with Nanny, and Binky, and even Fig at this moment, in a safe place far from here. And I wanted someone to rescue me: I peered out of the window, hoping that my grandfather would come and break down the door and take me away. But I had told him I was going out with friends and he had no idea who my friends were or how to contact them. And Darcy was far away in the country, taking moonlight strolls with Hanni—since Edward had left the field entirely open for him.

I'd just have to sit here until morning, when people came to work and I could break a window and shout for help. And then . . . then the police would come and I'd have to explain how I was trapped alone with Mr. Solomon's body. And they'd only have my word that I wasn't one of those who killed him. I could picture Harry Sugg's annoying grin. "Oh yes?" he'd say. "Got locked in by mistake, did you? And this man just happened to die by mistake, did he? Well, I don't see anyone else inside this locked building, so do you mind telling me who killed him if you didn't?"

Thoughts buzzed angrily around inside my head. These communists were planning something awful, something that Sidney had refused to take part in and Mr. Solomon had objected to: a violent demonstration of some kind—taking over the Houses of Parliament or even killing the prime minister maybe. And if one of them came back to the shop in the morning, perhaps with a van to take away the body, they would find me and I'd be disposed of too. I sat there in the lamplight as it shone on the books piled on the floor around me. Really this was the untidiest shop I'd ever seen. Close to me was a stack of children's books. I started looking through them, hoping to find a familiar and comforting friend from my nursery days. But they turned out to be foreign, with illustrations of evil witches and savage ogres. Not at all comforting. At the bottom of the pile there was one called *Let's Learn Russian.* The cover had a picture of two happy, smiling communist children, carrying a hammer and sickle. How appropriate, I thought. Perhaps they handed out a copy to everyone who attended those stupid meetings. I flicked it open.

The Russian alphabet is different from ours, I read. You will need to master it before you can read Russian words. My eye scanned down the page. Russian uses the letter *C* when we would use the letter *S.* My gaze moved further. The Russian letter *R* is written like our *P.* I found myself thinking of the two letters someone had sent to Hanni, the first time with a question mark, the second time with a cross through them. *C.P.* not C.P. but S.R.— Sidney Roberts?

Which meant it had to be Edward Fotheringay and his stupid Cambridge leftist secret society. He had studied modern languages, German and Russian. His mother had been Russian. He claimed he had been in India but Colonel Horsmonden had never met him there and Edward had been evasive in answering the colonel's questions. Which now made me suspect that he had never been in India. He'd been in Russia, training for the moment when he was sent back here to overthrow the government by force, as the communists had done there. Or maybe to create chaos and perhaps a new world war, out of which world communism would emerge triumphant. I should have picked up the signs earlier. He was the one who mixed the cocktails at the party and tried to kill Sidney there. And he had tried to involve Hanni. I didn't see how or why, unless he wanted to stir up trouble between England and Germany, or use her somehow to put the German communists in power. But she was naïve enough and he was handsome enough that she'd believe anything he told her.

So the next question was: had Edward persuaded her to help him kill Sidney? But it didn't make sense. We had been at the bookshop together. She had gone up those stairs only moments before me and she certainly had no knife on her, and she certainly hadn't learned to kill at the convent.

I closed the book and put it back. This was absurd. The letters probably had nothing at all to do with Sidney Roberts or his death. The night dragged on. I must have dozed from time to time, because I sat up with a crick in my neck and noticed that the sky had taken on a grayish tinge. Daylight was coming. Poor Mr. Solomon was lying there, his mouth and eyes open, looking as if he was a wax dummy in Madame Tussauds.

I had to find a way out of here. I prowled as far from the light as I dared, examining side aisles and kicking walls for any sign of a hidden door. But by the time it was light, I had pushed and kicked at every bookshelf and still had found nothing. Of course, there was always the attic that Mr. Solomon had mentioned. It was certainly worth a try. I went upstairs and spotted a trapdoor in the ceiling. It had a cord attached. I pulled and a ladder hung down. I went up it cautiously because I am rather afraid of spiders and I hate cobwebs. It certainly was dusty up there. Piles of books were stacked next to old trunks and shapes hidden under dust sheets. In the half-light they looked ominous and I almost expected a sheet to fly off, revealing God knows what.

But I made it successfully to the small window at the far end. The sill was clean where the police had dusted for prints, and luckily they must have forced the window open because I didn't have to struggle too hard to do so. I dragged over a trunk, stood on it, and stuck my head out. The world outside was blanketed in thick mist so that it was impossible to see more than a few feet. What I could see was not encouraging. Oh, golly, the roof was steep and ended in a sheer drop. The slates were damp with the heavy mist. I didn't relish trying to climb out and if I started to slide, I'd have no way of stopping myself.

I climbed back down inside and piled books on top of the trunk until they were high enough for me to climb out of the window. I eased myself out, then pulled myself up until I was standing on the window ledge, holding on to the top of the window frame for support. The only way to go was up. I inched my way around the dormer window, clambering up the side of it until I could reach the top of the roof. I was thankful that I had worn my old lisle stockings and not my good silk ones, and my crepe-soled sandals rather than leather. Even so the slates were horribly slippery and I could hardly breathe because my heart was beating so fast. I straddled the roof apex, rather like riding a horse. In the direction I was facing I could make out that my roof ended against the blank wall of a taller building. No point in going that way, then. I couldn't see any drainpipe or way down at all.

So I turned around and moved in the other direction, inching forward with my heart hammering in my chest. It was an awfully long way down. I reached a cluster of chimney pots and managed to maneuver past them, then continued on as the roof turned at a right angle. I came to the end of the building and stopped, biting back tears of frustration. Between my roof and the next building was a gap. It wasn't particularly wide but there was no way I could lower myself down to the gutter and then turn to a position from which I could leap across, even if I had the nerve to leap across. And if I leaped, I had nothing to hold on to.

I had no idea what to do now. My muscles were trembling from the exertion and tension and I didn't want to go back to that attic window. If I shouted from up here, would anyone be able to hear me? Certainly not see me in this mist. Then the mist swirled and parted for a moment and

I heard the lapping of water. Somewhere below me was the Thames. I waited patiently for the mist to part again. The river was a good way down but directly below me, and I had jumped off a tall rock into the loch at home many times. The question was, would it be deep enough? This was answered almost immediately by the deep sound of a ship's siren sounding eerie and mournful through the mist. Big cargo ships docked here, and it appeared to be high tide. Of course it would be deep enough. Anyway, I couldn't come up with a better plan after a night with little sleep and a lot of terror.

The sky became lighter and the mist swirled and broke apart. Every now and then I was treated to a clear view of the gray waters below. I could do this. I was going to do it. I swung my leg over and moved, crablike, down the steep surface. A slate came loose and slithered down the roof to plop into the water. A pair of pigeons took off, fluttering, from the roof nearby, almost making my heart stop and making me lose my balance. Through the mist behind me came sounds: the city was waking up.

I don't know how long I would have perched there, trying to pluck up courage, but I realized that my foot was going to sleep. That wouldn't do. I had to act now. I took a deep breath, stood up on the gutter, then jumped outward. I hit the water with a mighty splash. The cold took my breath away. I went under and kicked to the surface, spluttering, the taste of oily water in my mouth. Mist curled around the surface of the water and hid the banks, making me unsure in which direction I was facing. My skirt clung around my legs like some horrible type of sea creature as I fought to stay calm. The distant moan of a foghorn reminded me that big ships sailed here. I had no wish to be run down by a passing cargo boat. To my left I could make out the dark outline of the building from which I had just jumped and I struck out for it.

Now the only problem would be finding a way up from the river. A blank wall presented itself to me. Then I heard a shout and saw men standing on a high dock that jutted out to my right. Suddenly one of them peeled off his jacket and jumped in, swimming to me with powerful strokes.

"It's all right, love, I've got you," he said.

He put an arm around my neck and dragged me back to the shore.

I wanted to tell him that I was perfectly capable of swimming to the steps by myself, but he was holding me so tightly I couldn't talk. We reached a ladder, extending up to a dock, and hands hauled me unceremoniously out of the water.

"Well done, Fred," voices said.

"You'll be all right now, love."

Then one said, "You shouldn't have done it. He's not worth it. There's always something to live for. You'll see." And I realized that they thought I'd been trying to kill myself. I didn't know whether to laugh or be indignant.

"No, you don't understand," I said. "I got locked in a building by some communists and the only way to escape was onto the roof, and the only way down from there was to jump."

"Of course it was, darling." They looked at each other, grinning knowingly. "Come on, we'll take you back to the hut and get you a cup of tea. No need to mention this to the police."

And I realized, of course, that suicide was a crime.

Chapter 36

An hour later I was safely back at Rannoch House, confronting an angry grandfather.

"Almost out of my mind with worry, I was," he was yelling. "I didn't know whether something had happened to you or you were just staying late at one of them fancy parties you go to."

"I'm so sorry," I said, and explained the whole thing to him.

"Ruddy silly thing to do," was all he could say afterward. "One of these days you'll go too far, my girl. If you was a cat, you'd have used up several of your nine lives already."

"I know," I said. "But it was really lucky that I took the chance because now I know. As soon as I've changed, I've got to see Chief Inspector Burnall and tell him what I've discovered," I said. "They are planning some kind of trouble, Granddad."

"You ain't going nowhere," he said firmly. "First of all I'm running you a hot bath, then you're going to eat a good breakfast and then we'll telephone Scotland Yard and Chief Inspector Burnall can come to you. He won't be in his office yet anyway, will he?"

One couldn't argue. It was like being with Nanny again. When she had that certain look, one just knew that all protests were futile. I allowed myself to be marched upstairs, then I lay luxuriating in hot water for a time before dressing and coming down to a boiled egg and fingers. Even this was like being in the nursery again and it gave me a lovely warm feeling of security.

Granddad made the call to Scotland Yard and Chief Inspector Burnall arrived in person about half an hour later.

"You have something important to tell me, my lady?" he asked.

I related the events of the previous evening. He listened attentively.

"And can you name any of these people?"

"There were two men and one woman, I think, although the woman's voice was deep and foreign, so it could have been another man. The dead man was Mr. Solomon. I'm sure of that, and I'm pretty sure that one of them was Edward Fotheringay."

"The same Edward Fotheringay who is currently sharing a London flat with Gormsley?"

I wanted to say "How many Edward Fotheringays can there be?" but I nodded politely instead. At this moment he was listening to me.

Then he smiled and broke the illusion. "This is all rather far-fetched, wouldn't you say, your ladyship? Are you sure you're not trying to lead me up the garden path, away from your pal Gormsley, for example?"

"I can prove it to you," I said. "You'll find Mr. Solomon's body in his bookshop. I believe they killed him because he wasn't willing to go along with their scheme, just as Sidney Roberts had objected to it."

Burnall was on his feet immediately and making for my front hall. I heard him barking orders into the telephone. He came back into the room.

"I have men on their way there now. So if you'd be good enough to put a statement in writing for us?"

I went to the desk in the morning room and tried to phrase my experience as succinctly as possible. I hadn't quite finished when our telephone jangled. Burnall beat my grandfather to it. He came back with a quizzical look on his face.

"Now do you mind telling me the truth, my lady?"

"What do you mean? I've just told you the truth."

"There was no body in the bookshop."

"But I was there. I touched it. It was a dead person. His skin was cold, and I'm sure it was Mr. Solomon's face."

"My lads had to break down the door and they found nothing suspicious inside."

"Then I was right. Those people must have come for the body after I left."

Burnall was staring at me as if he was

trying to read my mind. "It's a serious offense lying to the police."

"I didn't lie!" I could hear myself shouting and I know that a lady never raises her voice. My governess would have been horrified at me. "Look, I might have died last night. Ask those men who fished me out of the Thames this morning if you want proof that I was there."

His look softened a little. "I don't doubt that you had some kind of frightening experience, and maybe you were locked in the bookshop by mistake, but I think you let your imagination run away with you, didn't you? Maybe you touched a cushion or a pile of rags?"

"A pile of rags that was wearing glasses and had teeth? I felt his face, Chief Inspector, and he was dead. If you'd like to take me there, I'll show you the exact spot where he was lying. If you look carefully enough you'll find traces of blood, I'm certain. But this isn't the important matter today. If these people are planning some kind of dramatic and violent act, you need to have men on the alert and in place."

"And where would you suggest that I place these men?" he asked.

"I have no idea. A first step would be to arrest Edward Fotheringay."

"I have already told my men to bring him in for questioning. If you're sure you can remember no more specifics, then I don't see what else I can do at this moment."

"You don't really believe me, do you?"

"I believe any threat should be taken seriously, but given the vanishing body and the general nature of the danger, I can't judge how much of this is girlish hysteria and how much truth. In fact, if it weren't for Sidney Roberts, I wouldn't be going any further with this. Since he was finished off by an accomplished assassin, I have to accept that there may be something to what you're saying."

He turned back to the door. "I should alert the home secretary, I suppose. If there is some kind of foreign criminal element involved here, then he needs to know. And I suggest you stay put, my lady. If everything you've told me about last night is true, then you're lucky to be alive."

Then he left. My grandfather appeared. "Toffee-nosed geezer, isn't he? Come on, then, up to bed with you. You need a good sleep."

I didn't argue with that. I was beginning to feel sick and hollow inside, as much from fear as from lack of sleep. I went upstairs and curled up under my eiderdown. I must have nodded off immediately because I was awoken by someone shaking me. I started and tried to sit up.

"Sorry to wake you, ducks"—my grandfather's face was peering at me—"but I just remembered you're supposed to be at that garden party."

"Oh, Lord, I'd completely forgotten." I scrambled out of bed. "What time is it?"

"It's almost one and the party starts at two."

"Goodness. I'd better get a move on, then, hadn't I? For once I wish Mildred was here. She'd know what I was supposed to wear."

I flung open my wardrobe and realized that my trunk, containing almost all my clothes, was still up at Dippings. I had nothing to wear. I couldn't go. Then a chilling thought struck me: royal garden party. The king and queen mingling with their subjects on the palace lawn. Could this have been the event those conspirators had planned for?

I rushed downstairs and telephoned Chief Inspector Burnall, only to be told that he was out on a case. The young woman on the switchboard asked if I wanted to be put through to another officer, but I didn't think anyone would take me seriously. Besides, there would be policemen on duty at the palace. I had to go to the garden party myself to alert them. Nothing for it but to use up the last of Binky's money. If the princess came to stay with me again, I'd ask the queen for a contribution. If my suspicion was correct, she'd owe me a little more than a new dress!

I still had the white feather hat I usually wore to weddings, so I put that on—looking rather ridiculous with a simple cotton dress—then I caught a taxi to Harrods. I pointed to the hat. "Something to go with this. Royal garden party. Hurry."

The saleswoman looked startled but she was brilliant. In a few minutes we'd settled on a white silk dress with navy stripes that looked really elegant on me. I put it on, wrote a check, left the cotton dress behind in the changing room and was on my way to Buck House, arriving just a little after two o'clock. I joined the line of people at the side entrance, waiting to be admitted to the grounds. For some of them it was clearly a first visit to royalty and they looked nervous and excited. I heard a man in front of me saying, "If they could see me now, eh, Mother?"

And she replied. "You've done right proud for yourself, Stanley."

The queue inched forward, each person handing in his or her invitation at the gate. When it was my turn I asked, "Can you tell me if someone called Edward Fotheringay was invited today?"

The harried young man shook his head. "Afraid I can't, off the top of my head. We have the master list inside in the palace but if someone presents an invitation we admit them."

"Could you send someone to check for me?"

"I'm afraid we're rather fully occupied at the moment," he replied stiffly.

"Then can you tell me where I would find the person in charge of security?"

The line behind me was murmuring at being held up. The young man looked around, wondering how to get rid of me.

Then he gestured to a uniformed bobby, who came hurrying over. "What seems to be the trouble?" he asked.

I took him aside and told him that we had to find out whether Edward Fotheringay was at the garden party. A matter of national security. I needed to speak to someone in charge. I could tell he wasn't sure whether to believe me or not.

"National security, you say? And your name is, miss?" he asked.

"I am the king's cousin, Lady Georgiana Rannoch," I said, and saw his expression change.

"Very good, m'lady. And you think this young man might try something disruptive?"

"I'm very much afraid he will."

"Follow me, then, your ladyship." He set off at a brisk march, up a flight of steps and into the lower floor of the palace. "If you'll wait here, I'll go and find my superiors."

I waited. Outside in the hallway a grandfather clock was ticking off the minutes with a sonorous tock, tock. At last I couldn't stand it any longer. I stuck my head out the door. Complete silence. No sign of any activity. Had the constable actually believed me or had he dumped me in that room purposely to keep me out of the way? I couldn't wait another second. If Edward was in that crowd, he had to be stopped. The gardens were now overflowing with well-dressed people, top hats and morning coats, flowing silk gowns and Ascot-style hats. I almost got stabbed in the eye by many a protruding feather as I edged my way through the crowd. Some less genteel ladies thought I was trying to gain an advantageous position and blocked me with a threatening elbow.

Waiters were moving through the crowd carrying trays of Pimm's and champagne, canapés and petit fours. I moved into the wake of one of them and let him clear a path for me as my eyes searched left and right for any sign of Edward. But there were any number of dark and elegant young men in top hats, and plenty of bushes and statues to skulk behind. The whole thing was hopeless if that wretched bobby hadn't believed me. Then a voice called my name, and there was Lady Cromer-Strode, waving to me.

"We've been looking for you," she said. "Hanni was afraid you hadn't come."

Hanni was standing beside her, looking sulky in an unbecoming plain gray silk dress.

"Lady Cromer-Strode said I must wear this because I am in mourning for the baroness and my pink frock was not suitable," she said. "It belongs to Fiona. It is too big."

It was. Fiona was a healthy girl. She stood on the other side of her mother, looking resplendent in bright flowery turquoise.

I looked at Hanni, trying to reconcile my suspicions with the person I had entertained for the past week or so. "How are you faring at the Cromer-Strodes', apart from having to wear a dress you don't like? Having a good time?"

Hanni frowned. "It is boring," she said. "Most people went home. Only old people now."

"Darcy and Edward both left?" I asked in a low voice because I didn't want Fiona to hear.

She nodded.

Fiona must have heard her beloved's name. "Edward said he'd be joining us today," she said, "but I haven't seen him yet."

"There was a long line waiting to get in," I said. "He's probably held up outside."

Even as I said it, I realized that the men at the gate would probably not have been instructed to stop Edward from entering. I should go back and warn them. "I'll be back," I said. "Save me a spot."

As I fought my way back toward the gate, a murmur went through the crowd and the Guards band on the terrace struck up the national anthem. The royal couple must have emerged from the palace. An expectant hush fell upon the crowd as they parted to provide a pathway for the king and queen. As everyone was peering forward for that first glimpse of the royal couple, I was the only person hurrying in the wrong direction. I jumped when someone grabbed my arm.

"I didn't know you were coming to this bean feast." It was my mother, looking absolutely ravishing in black and white, a glass of champagne in her hand.

I wasn't usually glad to see her, but today I could have hugged her. "What are you doing here?" I asked.

"Max's idea. His motorcar company wants to go into some kind of partnership with an English company. He thought this would be a good way to meet the owner informally—set things off on the right foot, so to speak. He's probably standing in a corner, doing business even as we speak. I have to say, that man does know how to make money." She glanced at me critically. "Nice dress," she said, "but off the peg. You really should get yourself a good dressmaker."

"Question of money, mother. If you'd like to finance a wardrobe . . ."

"We'll go shopping, darling. . . ."

"Mother," I cut in, "you haven't seen Edward Fotheringay this afternoon, have you?"

She gave me a frosty stare. "Now why should I be looking for Edward Fotheringay?"

"Last time I saw you, I'd say you were rather chummy with him."

"That was a just a mad, impetuous fling," she said. "A sudden yearning for someone nice and solid and British—oh, and young too. Good firm body. But it turned out to be quite wrong for me. The boy has no money and he can't keep his hands off other women. So please don't mention his name again, especially not when Max is around."

"But you haven't seen him today, have you? It's important."

"I haven't been looking for him, darling." She was glancing around, enjoying the admiring and envying stares she was getting. She always did like being the center of attention. I was about to move on when she grabbed my arm again. "I meant to ask you," she said, "who is the pretty little blond girl you brought with you to that party? She's over there now, wearing the most extraordinarily ugly dress."

"That's Princess Hannelore. Didn't I tell you she was staying with me?"

"Princess Hannelore?"

"Of Bavaria, you know."

My mother was staring at Hanni, who was now at the front of the pathway along which the king and queen would be coming. "Unless she has shrunk considerably in the last few weeks, that is definitely not Princess Hannelore." She looked amused at my stunned face. "Hannelore is taller than that, and thinner too, and from what I heard in Germany, she's been quite ill and is currently recuperating on her family's yacht on the Med."

"Then who is this?" I gasped.

"Never seen her before last week," my mother said. "Oh, there's Max now. Yoo-hoo, Max darling!" And she was gone.

Murmurs indicated that the royal couple was approaching. Hanni, or whoever she was, stood there, leaning forward to catch a glimpse with the rest of the crowd. Suspicions raced through my mind. Could Edward have persuaded her to do something for him? Set off a bomb? I studied her carefully. She was not carrying a purse and wore only a small straw hat. Nowhere to conceal a bomb then.

The king and queen had come into view, shaking hands and entering into conversation with those they passed. Still no sign of Edward. Then two things happened at the same moment. I spotted a familiar face. Darcy O'Mara was standing on the opposite side of the reception line. His dark unruly curls had been tamed for the occasion and he looked breathtakingly handsome in a morning suit. Before I could catch his eye I saw Hanni reach into the folds of that voluminous dress and pull out a small pistol.

The king and queen were almost upon them.

"Darcy!" I shouted. "She's got a—"

But I didn't have time to finish the sentence. Darcy rushed forward and threw himself upon Hanni as the gun went off, sounding no louder than a cap pistol. They fell to the ground together. There were screams and shouts, general chaos as policemen and palace servants came running.

"She has a gun!" I screamed. "She was trying to kill Their Majesties!"

"Stupid fools," Hanni spat out at the men who wrestled the gun away from her. "We shall succeed next time."

I waited for Darcy to get up. But he didn't. He was lying on the gravel and a trickle of blood was coming from under his right shoulder.

Chapter 37

"Darcy!" I screamed and fought my way toward him. "He's hurt. Get an ambulance. Do something!"

Hands were already turning him over. His face was ashen white and a big, ugly dark stain decorated his morning coat. "No!" I dropped to the ground beside him.

"He can't be dead. Darcy, please don't die. I'll do anything. Please." I took his hand. It was still warm.

Darcy's eyes fluttered open and focused on me. "Anything?" he whispered, then lapsed into unconsciousness again.

"Out of the way," a voice was saying. "I'm a doctor, let me through." And a portly man in a morning coat knelt beside me, huffing and puffing a little.

He opened Darcy's coat and shirt, took out his own handkerchief and pressed it onto the wound. "You men. Get him into the palace, quickly."

Several men picked up Darcy and the crowd parted for them as they carried him. I glimpsed Her Majesty's shocked face before she turned back to the crowd. "Everything is under control," she said in her clear voice. "We shall proceed with the party as if nothing had happened." And she began to move through the crowd, shaking hands again.

"Edward Fotheringay," I shouted as the police dragged Hanni away. "He must be here somewhere. Don't let him leave."

Then I stumbled up the steps after the procession. They placed Darcy on the floor in a serving area, below the *piano nobile.* The portly doctor had stripped off his coat, rolled up his sleeves and was examining Darcy's body.

I could stand it no longer. "Shouldn't we

have called an ambulance? Shouldn't he be going to hospital instead of your wasting time examining him here?"

He looked up at me, his big, bearded face red with effort. "My dear young lady. I am considered by most to be the premier surgeon in England, although a young pup from St. Thomas's would no doubt dispute that fact. I just need to check whether—ah, good. Yes."

He looked up at the crowd that had now gathered around us. "My car and driver are waiting outside. Be good enough to summon them, my man." This to one of the palace staff who stood nearby, wide-eyed. "And you, bring towels. We need to stop the bleeding."

Then he stood up with some difficulty. "Westminster is closest, I suppose, but Thomas's is bigger and, as an old University College Hospital man, I regret to say probably better in an emergency situation. That's it then. Carry him out to my car. We'll go to Thomas's."

I touched his arm. "Is he going to be all right? Is he going to live?"

He looked down at me and smiled. "He's a lucky devil. The bullet went through his right shoulder, appears to have missed his lung, and came out the other side. So no need to dig around to locate it. All he needs is cleaning and sewing up, and I can do those myself. He's going to be devilishly sore for a while, of course, but unless he insists on throwing himself into the path of bullets on a regular basis, I can safely say that he'll lead a long and happy life."

Tears flooded into my eyes. I turned away and headed back to the gardens because I didn't want the staff to see me crying. Outside in the bright sunlight I was immediately accosted by plainclothes security men, who were now very interested to hear what I had to say. So I had to go through the story, from the arrival of the mock-princess to the episode after the communist rally the night before. They took notes, painfully slowly, and asked me the same questions over and over, while all the time all I wanted to do was be with Darcy.

At last they let me go. I took a taxi to St. Thomas's Hospital across the Thames. In usual infuriating hospital fashion they wouldn't let me see Darcy for what seemed like ages. I sat in that dismal waiting room with its brown linoleum and drab green walls plastered with cheerful notices, ranging from *Coughs and sneezes spread disease* to *You can't catch venereal disease from lavatory seats.*

When I had badgered a passing nurse for the umpteenth time I was finally permitted to see him. He was tucked into white starched sheets and his face looked as pale as the pillow behind him. His eyes were closed and I couldn't detect any breathing. I must have let out a little gasp because his eyes opened, then focused on me and he smiled.

"Hello," I said, feeling suddenly shy. "How are you feeling?"

"Floating, actually. I think they must have given me something. It's rather nice."

"You knew, didn't you?" I said, perching on the edge of his bed. "You knew she was going to do something like that?"

"Suspected it, yes. We were tipped off that they planned to send agents over here by someone within the party in Germany, so I kept a close eye on that young lady."

"That's why you were playing up to her and being so friendly?" Relief flooded through me.

"It wasn't exactly a hard assignment,"

he said. "Now if they'd asked me to shadow the baroness—well, the poor old thing might still be alive, but it would have been a harder job."

I looked at him until he said, "What?"

"Darcy—who are you?"

"You know who I am. The Honorable Darcy O'Mara, heir to the now landless Lord Kilhenny."

"I meant what are you?"

"A wild Irish boy who enjoys the occasional bit of fun and excitement," he said, with the ghost of his usual wicked grin.

"You're not going to tell me any more, are you?"

"They told me not to talk."

"You're infuriating, do you know that?" I said more vehemently than I intended, in the way that one does after a shock. "You scared the daylights out of me. Don't ever do something like that again."

"But if it takes something like this to get you to come willingly to my bed, then it was worth it. And I haven't forgotten your promise."

"What promise?"

"That you'd do anything if I didn't die."

"You just get yourself strong enough

first," I said. I leaned forward and kissed his forehead.

"Oh, believe me, I fully intend to be strong enough." He reached up to touch my face.

"There will be no more of that," said the ward sister firmly. "In fact it's time you went."

Darcy's hand remained touching my cheek.

"Come back soon, won't you?" he whispered. "Don't leave me to the mercies of that dragon."

"I heard that," said the sister.

Rannoch House
Monday, June 27, 1932

Diary,
Eventful day ahead.

Mildred arrived back in London last night and announced her intention to leave me. It seems Lady Cromer- Strode has made her an offer she can't refuse. I tried not to smile when she imparted this sad news to me.

Darcy will be released from hospital later today.

Oh, and the queen has summoned me.

"What an extraordinary thing to have happened, wasn't it, Georgiana?" the queen said. It was several days later and order had been restored to Buckingham Palace. The press had had a field day with headlines about anarchists and assassins in our midst and the outpouring of love for the royal family had been most touching. So Hanni and her misguided friends had achieved quite the opposite of their objective.

"Most extraordinary, ma'am."

"That young woman duped all of us. I still can't imagine how she got away with it."

"She seized the opportunity, ma'am. From what we have been told, they had a communist agent working inside the Bavarian court. They were hoping to create instability in Germany and topple the current German government. When the real Princess Hannelore fell ill suddenly and the king wrote a letter to tell you that she could not accept your kind invitation after all, that letter was intercepted. The royal party departed for their yacht and a long cruise and the communists sent this girl in Hannelore's place. She's an actress, you know, and she has worked bit-parts in Hollywood. She realized that her English would sound American, hence she pretended to be a fan of American films. I must admit she played her part very well. She only slipped up once that I could tell."

"When was that?"

"She said the Jungfrau was in Bavaria. Of course it's in Switzerland. What Bavarian would not know the names of her own mountains?"

"She was really German?"

"Yes, but not Bavarian."

"So the girl was really the ringleader? She seemed so sweet and innocent."

"As I said, she played her part remarkably well. She's older than eighteen, of course, but she looks remarkably young for her age. But she wasn't the ringleader, as you put it. The maid—Irmgardt—she was the agent sent from Russia to oversee the whole thing. She was the one whose voice I heard that night in the bookshop. They caught her at Dover, trying to escape."

"And the baroness—was she part of their plot?"

"Absolutely not. She was a real baroness. She hadn't seen Hannelore for some time so she was easily deceived, but obviously her presence was becoming a threat to them. First they managed to banish her to the Dowager Countess Sophia's, but then, when they were together again, she threatened to telephone the princess's father. Of course that would have upset the whole apple cart. It was the maid Irmgardt who put the drug in her tea to produce a heart attack. Hanni and Edward Fotheringay had a perfect alibi, in a car with me."

"Horrible, utterly horrible." The queen shuddered. "And who did kill that poor young man at the bookshop?"

"Sidney Roberts? Hanni did it herself, of course. She was, after all, a trained assassin. One gathers that the knife had a folding blade, so she was able to hide it quite easily. You're very lucky to be alive, ma'am. She was constantly looking for opportunities to kill you. She kept pestering me to take her to the palace, then to take her to see you at Sandringham."

"Goodness." The queen had to take a sip of tea. "One doesn't expect such threats in the English countryside, does one?"

"Or from the English nobility," I added.

"I'm so glad they finally caught Edward Fotheringay trying to flee the country."

"Of course that boy was only half English, so one understands," the queen said. "He had a Russian mother, didn't he?"

"An aristocrat, which makes it even more strange that he was seduced by communism."

"Young people are so strange," the queen said. "Except you, of course. You've done splendidly, Georgiana. The king and I are most grateful." She paused, looked at me and sighed.

"And all this leaves my son no nearer to making a good match, does it?"

"I'm afraid not, ma'am."

"I worry what will happen to the empire when the king dies, Georgiana, if the boy can't even choose a bride for the good of his country. There are so many suitable girls to choose from—you, for example."

"Oh no, ma'am," I said. "I could never compete with Mrs. Simpson." Besides, I thought but didn't say out loud, my interests lie elsewhere.